ME AGAIN

ME AGAIN

KEITH CRONIN

FIVE STAR
A part of Gale, Cengage Learning

GALE
CENGAGE Learning·

Detroit • New York • San Francisco • New Haven, Conn • Waterville, Maine • London

GALE
CENGAGE Learning™

LIBRARY OF CONGRESS CATALOGING-IN-PUBLICATION DATA

Cronin, Keith.
  Me again / Keith Cronin. — 1st ed.
    p. cm.
  ISBN-13: 978-1-4328-2503-4 (hardcover)
  ISBN-10: 1-4328-2503-8 (hardcover)
    1. Cerebrovascular disease—Patients—Fiction. 2. Identity (Psychology)—Fiction. 3. Self-realization—Fiction. I. Title.
  PS3603.R663M4 2011
  813'.6—dc22   2011016075

First Edition. First Printing: August 2011.
Published in 2011 in conjunction with Tekno Books.

Printed in the United States of America
1 2 3 4 5 6 7 15 14 13 12 11

This book is dedicated to the memory of Dan and Carolyn Cronin, who taught me how to communicate; to Dennis, who continues to teach me how to be strong; to Jennifer, for asking me to be her father; and to Linda, for her steadfast love and support. When it comes to family, I'm well aware that I lucked out.

ACKNOWLEDGMENTS

This novel was never meant to be an inspirational how-to for stroke recovery, something I am in no way qualified to write. But as I was completing the manuscript, I lost my mother to heart disease, and found I had little stomach for using an affliction that touches so many people—some 795,000 Americans each year, and that's just the victims, not their loved ones—as the basis for a story meant merely to entertain.

So I made myself a promise. If this book sold, I'd use it to help others as well. That's why **25% of any money I make from ME AGAIN is being donated to the American Stroke Association,** a division of the American Heart Association that focuses on reducing risk, disability and death from stroke through research, education, fund raising and advocacy.

Stroke is the third leading cause of death, killing more than 137,000 people each year, and it is the leading cause of adult disability. My hope is that my little what-if story can do something to help change that, while still managing to entertain people on airplanes.

As a writer, I owe a tremendous debt to numerous other writers for their support, suggestions and encouragement. Special thanks to Kim Byrne for introducing me to the Five Star imprint, and to Karen Dionne and Chris Graham for building the amazing Backspace online community that has connected me with so many wonderful writers. Sara Gruen, Jon Clinch, Susan Henderson, Marlys Pearson, Mark Bastable, A.S.

Acknowledgments

King, Tish Cohen, Danielle Younge-Ullman, Patricia Wood, Jael McHenry, Jackie Kessler, Lauren Baratz-Logsted, Maggie Dana, Lynn Sinclair, Maureen Ogle, Terri Molina, David Fausel, and Kelly Mustian (who provided the word "pelican" for this novel) are among the many writers whose friendship and support have meant so much to me. My heartfelt gratitude also goes to Catherine Magee Johansen, Dawn Kintigh Trombo, and Steve Argy for reading and critiquing my work over the years, and last but not least to my editor Gordon Aalborg for his literary insight and contagious enthusiasm.

There are two births: the one when light
First strikes the new awakened sense;
The other when two souls unite,
And we must count our life from thence,
When you loved me and I loved you,
Then both of us were born anew.

~ William Cartwright

It seems to be a rule of wisdom never to rely on your
memory alone, scarcely even in acts of pure memory, but
to bring the past for judgment into the thousand-eyed
present, and live ever in a new day.

~ Ralph Waldo Emerson

CHAPTER 1

I was born on a Tuesday morning. It was a difficult birth, because I was thirty-four years old.

I opened my eyes, and saw a long bar of blue-white light. It hung directly over me, making me realize I was lying on my back. Looking into the light made my eyes hurt, so I closed them, welcoming the darkness. But then it seemed particularly important to see that light again, so I reopened my eyes, blinking repeatedly to adjust to the glare.

I became aware of movement. A blurry female figure clad in white entered my view on one side. I lay staring at her, instinctively trying to blink her into focus, but with no success. Suddenly she drew closer, leaning down over me. For a brief moment our eyes met. Then I blinked.

"Jesus," she said. The name sounded familiar.

She disappeared from view, and I realized that I couldn't raise or turn my head to try to locate her. In fact, the only thing I could feel—or move—was my eyes. I had a vague sense that this was not good.

Although she was out of my sight, I could hear her. She was speaking, a rapid stream of words I wasn't quite able to follow. Other voices joined in, overlapping each other in conversation, and the name Jesus came up repeatedly.

I formed my first conscious thought: *I must be Jesus.*

The voices grew louder, and several faces entered my field of vision, looming over me.

"He's awake."

"That's impossible."

"Jesus."

"He heard you—look, he's looking at you!"

"Get a flashlight."

I felt fingers touch my face—I suddenly became aware of *having* a face. A moment before, all I had was eyes. Now I had a forehead, a cheek. I took a breath, discovering a nose, a mouth. My world was growing.

Then a beam of light drilled into one of my eyes, hurting me. I made a sound.

It wasn't a word. For some reason, I couldn't speak. I wanted to—I understood what the faces surrounding me were saying—but I couldn't manage to form any words in response.

I made another sound.

"Jesus."

No, that wasn't the sound I made—that was the response my sound elicited from the blurry woman in white. With her were several other blurry women, some in white, some in pale colors.

"He's tracking the light. See?"

Again the light stabbed at my eyes, making me blink and look away.

"It's too bright for him. Use your finger."

The caustic beam was extinguished, and now a woman in green held a finger in front of my eyes, moving it back and forth over my face. I tried to look past her finger, wanting to establish eye contact, to find some way of communicating with her. But the wagging finger kept distracting me.

I began to feel annoyed.

I've come to believe that annoyance is probably one of the first emotions each of us experiences. Think about it: the medical profession has adopted some pretty abrasive ways to greet the newborn, whether it's spanking their bottoms, clipping their

12

umbilical cords, or wagging fingers in front of their faces. To me it's no wonder babies cry so much—look at the indignities to which they are subjected the moment they emerge. You'd think they could come up with more pleasant ways to welcome a new arrival.

At any rate, it eventually occurred to me that if I made an effort to watch the woman's finger, perhaps she would stop waving the damn thing in my face and simply talk to me. That was what I wanted most of all, for people to stop talking *about* me and start talking *to* me.

With some effort, I forced my eyes to follow the motion of her finger.

"Whoa," the woman said succinctly. I tried to answer, but again only succeeded in emitting a sound—something guttural and raw.

The woman looked at me for a long moment. Then she turned and spoke. "Beth, get Doctor Spence on the phone. Tell him to get his ass up here, stat."

It's hard to explain the effect this woman's last remark had on me. The word "doctor" . . . well, it triggered something. It made me for the first time stop to wonder where I was. With that word came the realization that I was in some sort of medical facility. A hospital, perhaps. This meant I was sick, or that something had happened to me. Something bad.

Dr. Spence would confirm my suspicions.

"Well, look who's awake," a male voice bellowed. A man came into view, holding up one fist over my face. Just as I realized what that fist held, a shaft of light shot into my head. I closed my eyes and groaned, the sound foreign and ugly.

A woman spoke. "The penlight bothers him. But he followed Karen's finger. We all saw it."

This prompted the man to repeat the finger-in-my-face routine. Eager to see this game end, I did my best to track the movement of his finger with my eyes.

"Well, I'll be," the man said. "He's responsive." He began to scribble something on a clipboard.

I decided the time had come to assert myself. Okay, maybe that's stating the case a bit grandiosely. But I wanted somebody to talk to me.

I made my sound—the only sound I seemed capable of making—as loud as I could.

This got their attention.

The man put his clipboard down and stared at me. Leaning in close, the man said, "Mr. Hooper, I'm Doctor Spence. Can you hear me?"

I wanted to say yes. I formed the word in my mind. Then I tried to send that order to my mouth. But I couldn't seem to remember how to make my mouth do what I wanted. So I made my sound again. I kept it short this time, truncating the groan to a brief grunt.

"Jesus," the now familiar female voice said.

Apparently my name was Jesus Hooper. But somehow that didn't seem right.

The man—Dr. Spence—spoke to me again. "Mr. Hooper, I want to make sure I understand you. So I need to make sure you understand me. I know you can't talk right now—there's a reason for that, and I'll explain it to you in a moment. But can you . . . well, can you grunt for me again?"

Now we were getting somewhere. I quickly issued a grunt, drawing gasps and nervous laughter from my audience.

Dr. Spence hastily jotted something on his clipboard. "That's excellent, Mr. Hooper—really excellent! Now, let's see if we can take it a step further. Let's see if you can answer yes or no. How about if we say one grunt means yes, and two means no? Do you understand?"

But I didn't. Those words he had used—*one* and *two*—

plunged me into confusion. The words were familiar, but I couldn't remember what they meant. I *almost* knew, but couldn't quite summon the information. Silent and confused, I stared at the doctor.

He nodded, then said, "Do you understand what one and two are? If you do, then try to grunt for me. If you don't, well, just remain silent."

I did as I was told. The only sound in the room was some softly beeping medical machine.

"Tell you what," Dr. Spence said, "let's try switching things around. I'll ask it a different way. If you understand what one and two are, stay silent. But if you don't understand, please grunt."

My grunt drew more chatter from my onlookers.

"Okay, Mr. Hooper, that's great. Just great. Now we're making some progress. How about we skip all that one and two stuff, and try something a little easier? If I ask you something and the answer is yes, go ahead and grunt. If the answer is no, you stay silent. Do you think you can do that?"

I grunted. I was becoming an old pro at this stuff.

"Excellent. Okay, Mr. Hooper. I'm going to explain a little about what happened to you, and where you are. Would you like that?"

I felt the grunt I emitted was particularly enthusiastic.

"Okay," the doctor said, "let me see how I can sum things up. You had a stroke, Mr. Hooper, and that stroke put you in a coma. You remained in that coma for a little more than six years. Now, because you've been in a coma so long, your body probably can't move—you may not even feel your body right now. That may change, but we'll get to that."

Dr. Spence paused, rubbing his face with his hand. "The even more important thing is that, well, how should I put this? A stroke can do things to your brain. It can change things. It's

15

likely you'll have forgotten some things. Maybe a lot of things. You know, like what one and two mean—things like that. A stroke can produce substantial changes in your brain, so I want you to understand that."

The doctor looked at me, trying to read my expression, which made me realize I couldn't really feel anything beyond my face. I seemed to be all eyes, nose, and mouth, emerging like an island from some murky pool, taking in air and light while the rest of my body drifted unseen below the surface.

The man's voice brought my attention back to him. "Mr. Hooper? That was a lot of information I just dumped on you—I apologize. Let's back up for a second, and see how well I'm getting through." Turning to the others who surrounded my bed, he said, "The rest of you chime in, too, in case I forget anything. But go slow—we don't want to overwhelm him." Once again I was being talked *about*, not *to*. It was something I would learn to get used to.

"First, let's sit him up so we're not all hovering right on top of him." A mechanical whirring slowly changed my view, elevating my upper body into a sitting position. I couldn't feel my body bending, but the ceiling swept out of view, and I found myself facing Dr. Spence and several women in medical pajamas, crowded into a small room that my bed nearly filled.

A lengthy dialog of questions, grunts, and silent pauses then ensued. I'll spare you a complete transcription—it's an awkward read—but here's a summary of some of the highlights:

Did I know what a stroke was, what a coma was, and what aphasia was?

Yes, yes, and no. Aphasia had to be explained to me. According to Dr. Spence it was becoming clear that I was at least partially aphasic—this meant my language abilities had been impaired. Although it appeared that I could understand the words I heard, I wasn't able to form language to reply. It wasn't

16

that I was mute; I could make sounds. But I couldn't arrange these sounds to make sense. Spence told me things could be much worse—that some stroke victims couldn't understand anything people said to them. And he tried to reassure me, telling me that my condition was not necessarily permanent. I would have felt better if he hadn't bothered to use the word *necessarily* to qualify that statement.

Was I in any pain? Could I move any of my limbs?

Nope and nope. The former was a relief, but the latter was deeply unsettling, particularly now that I could see the unmoving shapes of my feet under the blanket that covered them. And my hands, veiny and pale, were completely unfamiliar. I could not will them to move, which made them very hard to look at. Instead I focused on the people talking to me.

Here was a biggie: did I know WHO I was?

They asked me this first as a yes-no, and then got clever by saying several different names, and telling me to grunt if I recognized my own. Sort of an auditory police lineup, but pretty effective.

Upon hearing it, I did recognize my first name, and duly grunted. Turns out I was *Jonathan* Hooper, not Jesus. But this Jesus was familiar, and apparently the guy was a fan of mine—the phrase *Jesus loves me* kept coming to mind.

Did I understand that I had been unconscious for six years?

I remained silent, baffled by the concept of "six years," and worried about the emphasis they seemed to be placing on the question. A quick volley of related questions led my interviewers to determine that my absence of math skills seemingly extended into a lack of understanding of other quantitative measurements, such as years, months, and so on. But I did seem to get the difference between big and small, and was beginning to grasp that I had been asleep a much bigger amount of time than was considered normal or good.

Keith Cronin

Trying to convey to me the actual length of my coma was a challenge for the group surrounding me, who tried explaining that I was now thirty-four, which of course was not helpful. Then one nurse had an inspiration, and ran to get her purse. When she returned with it, she extracted her wallet and shook it, spilling out a lengthy accordion of plastic-encased credit cards and photographs that dangled almost to the floor. Leafing through them, she selected a photo and held it up for me to see.

"This is Megan—my daughter—when she was a newborn, just a couple of days old. This picture was taken around the same time you had your stroke. Do you understand?"

My grunt indicated assent. The tiny infant had the wrinkled misshapen look that can only be found appealing by blood relatives. My aphasia saved me from having to come up an obligatory compliment denoting the beauty of this human-raisin hybrid.

The nurse shuffled through more folds of her extensive collection, saying, "I just got these back from the Fotomat." Finally locating the desired photo, she leaned over me once again, displaying a new image for my perusal.

"This is Megan now," the nurse announced.

No grunt from me. This time I managed a full-on scream.

CHAPTER 2

"There's still no answer," Julie said. "We've been trying all afternoon, and all we get is the damned machine."

I had calmed down a little, and was getting acquainted with the hospital staff. Julie was the lady in white who was always talking about Jesus. Karen wore green, and enjoyed waving her fingers in front of my face. And the big guy in blue with the clipboard was Dr. Spence, who seemed to be in charge. He had ordered his staff to try to get in touch with my parents, to notify them of my awakening. But they weren't answering their phone.

"Give it another hour," Dr. Spence said. "Then if you still can't get through, leave a message. But no details—just tell them to call us immediately."

Julie winced. "Can I at least tell them it's not bad news? They might think he died or something."

Dr. Spence considered this, then nodded. While I was getting very tired of being spoken of in the third person, I suppose it was to the hospital's credit that they thought an answering machine was too informal and undependable a medium by which to transmit such portentous news.

After several more unsuccessful attempts at reaching my parents, Julie finally left a rather generic message for them to call "as soon as possible," going so far as to mention that she had some "really good news."

While they waited for my parents to respond, Dr. Spence and company continued to work on communicating with me. I had a lot of questions, but found them impossible to express via grunting. Still, my caregivers managed to fill in some of the blanks for me—you know, little things like where I was, what had happened to me. And why I couldn't talk, move, or remember much of anything.

From them I learned that the stroke I'd suffered was "sudden and catastrophic" (love those medical terms), which meant one minute I was sitting in a restaurant in Chicago complaining of a headache, and the next I was gone.

My family had done their best, shipping my inert form to various medical institutions, consulting some renowned special-ists. But the prognosis was uniformly discouraging, and as my coma extended into weeks and months, expectations for my recovery had dwindled.

Finally my parents had put me here in the stroke unit of a hospital in St. Louis, which was within driving range of their home in Springfield, Illinois. This was, my caregivers informed me, a facility that specialized in the long-term care of non-responsive patients. Sort of a cold storage for the stubbornly unconscious.

Three nights after Julie left a message for them, my parents called the hospital. Yes, I'm using a number here; when I do, I'm merely parroting numbers and statistics that were described to me, but I'm a reporter unable to substantiate his facts. I as-sume these quantities make sense, and offer them simply to provide context.

Back to my parents—they were thrilled by the news and im-mediately made arrangements to travel down to St. Louis. It turned out they had been off on a vacation, and had neglected to provide their itinerary to the hospital. Lest I paint too nega-tive a picture of my parents' sense of responsibility, I later learned that for the first year or so of my coma, they would call the hospital if they so much as left their house to go out to dinner, always leaving word of where they would be, how to reach them, and when they would be back—just on the off chance that I might suddenly wake up. Over the years they became less diligent, and although they did eventually purchase an answering machine (a big leap for this low-tech couple, who to this day eschew the use of cellular phones), invariably they would return from their outings to find no word of any miraculous recoveries on my part.

While we waited to hear from my parents, my interrogation/ education by the stroke unit staff had continued, and I was regaining enough of my faculties to now be thoroughly freaked out. When I woke up, I had been something not quite human—a grunting, blinking blob. Now as I was becoming more self-aware, I was beginning to realize who and what I was, and that a huge chunk of it—of me—was missing.

Would I recover? Would I be able to move my atrophied limbs? Would I be able to speak again? Nobody knew what to tell me, or even how to talk to me, not knowing how much I was comprehending. Everyone treated me as something alien and, I think, more than a little frightening.

My parents arrived on Saturday morning. It went badly.

Prior to their arrival, the nurses told me repeatedly how excited my parents would be to see me, with an enthusiasm that seemed a bit forced. But I had a problem. Hell, I had a lot of problems, but here was a new one. Based, I guess, on me having remembered my own name, everybody assumed I remembered my own family. I did not.

Let me clarify: I understood what parents were, but couldn't remember my own, try as I might. Unable to alert anybody, I resigned myself to my fate, and tried to approach this awkward little matter as scientifically as I could. My plan was to wait and see if their appearance triggered any memories.

On that much-heralded day, a pleasant looking couple was ushered into my room. Expectant gazes populated the faces of all who crowded into the room for this momentous occasion. My parents—I felt safe in assuming them to be my parents, based on their age and lack of medical attire—shared this expectant look, with an added top note of fear. They leaned over my bed while Dr. Spence made introductions. I stared up at them, trying to find something familiar, opening my metaphorical ears to the possibility of any bells going off. No dice.

The woman—my mother—smiled down at me, but I could see that she was fighting back tears. Her gaze grew more intense, as if she were trying to see *into* me, to drill past the communication barrier she was facing. She hadn't even spoken, yet she radiated so much warmth. And so much pain. Even though I couldn't remember her, the look on her face made me want to somehow ease her mind. I resolved to try.

"Jonathan," she said. "My Jonny."

I responded with what I hoped was a warm, engaging grunt. She began to cry.

"Look, Ellen—he's smiling at you," the man said. This would be my father.

The stroke had done some funny things to my facial muscles, leaving me with one corner of my mouth upturned in a perpetual smirk. I didn't think I was smiling, but it was hard to tell. My face still felt heavy and numb, a sensation not unlike the handiwork of a dentist who didn't believe in scrimping on the Novocain.

"Can you understand me, Jonathan?" my mother asked. I grunted. Although she had obviously been thrown by my first grunt, apparently she had been briefed on my rather limited vocabulary, and was now gamely attempting to communicate.

"Are you in any pain?"

I remained silent. Although highly uncomfortable, and seriously weirded out, I couldn't profess to being in any pain.

"We're going to take care of you, Jonathan." She leaned forward and patted my hand. "Everything is going to be all right."

Even without being able to remember this woman, I could recognize a lie when I heard one.

She went on. "As soon as they tell us you're able to travel, we're going to have you brought back home. Springfield has an excellent stroke facility, what with the university's medical school being right there in town."

Unable to recall a damn thing about Springfield, I continued playing the strong silent type.

"We'll make sure it's a nice place. Because, well, you're probably going to need to stay in rehab for a while—have they told you that?"

I grunted. They had *not* told me that, but it was clear to me that I was a long way from being ready to be reintroduced into polite society.

"They've got to do a lot of tests," she continued. Tests. I didn't like the sound of that.

"And they're going to help you get stronger, Jonathan. Like you were before."

Like you were before. I couldn't remember much about that, but I was pretty sure nothing was going to be quite like it was before.

My father hadn't spoken in a while. I was later to learn that this was consistent with the dynamic of their marriage. He apparently felt that she did enough talking for the both of them.

Flustered by the awkward silence, my mother added, "And of course, when they say you're ready, you can come home to us. We'll have a room set up for you." She hesitated. "It's not *your* old room—we, uh, gave that to Teddy, and he changed things around a lot."

It must have been apparent that I had no idea who Teddy was. She frowned. "You do remember Teddy, don't you? Your brother?"

Shit. Nobody had said anything about a brother. I suddenly found myself having a hard time maintaining my cool while it was becoming more and more apparent to me what a piece of Swiss cheese my brain had become. And that was actually the thought I had—I'm not being clever—I thought to myself "Shit, my brain has turned to Swiss cheese."

And then I thought about the fact that I could remember what Swiss cheese was, but had forgotten an entire brother. What the hell kind of priorities were running what was left of my mental filing cabinet?

But it got worse. Sensing my confusion, my mother asked The Killer Question.

"You do remember *us,* don't you?"

I couldn't bear the pain I saw on her face. So I did the only thing I could do.

I grunted.

The palpable relief that washed over that sweet woman's face made the sin forgivable.

My parents drove back to Illinois the next day, where they began making arrangements for me to be sent to an inpatient rehabilitation center in Springfield, their hometown. Well, it was my hometown, too, but I didn't remember it. I was informed that I had grown up there, but had moved upstate to Chicago after I finished college.

I was in little position to argue with this decision, so when my doctors were satisfied with my roadworthiness, I bade a wordless farewell to my St. Louis caregivers, and was soon installed into my new quarters at the rehab facility in Springfield.

After a lengthy and grunt-filled intake interview, my new keepers went to work on rebuilding me. This would be a complex task, starting with my body. Six years in bed does not do wonders for the physique: I wasn't paralyzed, yet I couldn't move. My muscles were atrophied, my body withered.

I was told that in the type of facility where I'd spent the last six years, the staff would perform perfunctory attempts at physical therapy, to minimize these effects and try to keep their patients from shriveling up entirely. I can only imagine what those therapy sessions were like: I picture some deranged aerobics instructor, clad in spandex and sporting the requisite sweat-absorbing headband, manipulating my unresisting limbs in a sort of full-sized puppet show, all the while chanting, "Work that body! Feel the burn! No pain, no gain!" At least my imagination wasn't damaged by the stroke. On second thought, maybe it was.

My recovery would be made much more difficult by the fact that not just my body needed rehabilitation. My brain was also on the injured list, and the true extent of the damage took a long time to reveal itself.

The brain is tricky—the actual physical lump of stuff in your skull gives precious little outward indication of its state of health, quite unlike the way the rest of your body manifests any injuries it sustains. And the information contained within the brain is not arranged in any way that mere humans have yet figured out. I remembered some things, and had forgotten others, with no discernible rhyme or reason.

In some instances this damage could be repaired—I just had to relearn various skills, ideas, or concepts. A nuisance, to be sure, but I could be taught. I did well with shapes, colors, and names of common objects, although I still have a tendency to say "kangaroo" when I mean "giraffe." Fortunately the relative scarcity of either kangaroos or giraffes in central Illinois prevents me from committing this faux pas with any frequency.

But in other areas, it gradually became clear that even the potential for learning certain concepts had been permanently eliminated. For example, I cannot count. Period. Repeated attempts to jump-start my mathematical neurons have met with nothing but failure and frustration any time I attempt to move beyond the number three. I read a story about a primitive tribe somewhere that has only a few words to express numeric quantities: *one, two,* and *many.* I would fit right in with that tribe, were it not for their affinity for rather drastic body piercing.

Let's see—what else? Although I eventually regained many of my basic motor skills, I cannot for the life of me tie a knot—the architecture of the process eludes me. This limits my choice of footwear somewhat, although they're doing some stylish things these days with Velcro straps.

While dealing with aphasia was a major challenge, it turned out that I got off easy compared to many other stroke victims. First of all, there were far more severe forms of aphasia than what I had suffered, which could include the lack of the ability to understand language at all, the ability to understand individual words but not syntax, and a myriad of other equally unpleasant combinations. What's worse, many who were stricken with aphasia never recovered. So in the long run, I got lucky: I could understand spoken language from the get-go; I just needed to work on being able to join the conversation.

To assist me in attaining that goal, a speech therapist was assigned to me, a perky woman named Patti who seemed to be in a perpetually good mood. Over the months I met several speech therapists, and they were all equally perky—apparently such manic cheerfulness was a prerequisite for the job.

At times I wondered if it were the *only* requirement for the job—despite what I'm sure were very good intentions on Patti's part, I found her approach lacked any discernible structure, and her tone was condescending and smarmy, as if she were speaking at all times to a small child. Worst of all was her habit of referring to me as "we," constantly asking me if *we* were having a nice day, or if *we* would like to try saying that word again, and so on. It annoyed me.

That is to say, we were annoyed.

CHAPTER 3

It was a strange experience, learning to speak at the age of thirty-four. For one thing, I probably put a bit more thought into what I wanted to say than most babies, who tend to choose some variation of "mama" or "dada" as their first word. And babies are of course far too young to remember their first words, which are either memorialized by family members or simply lost to the ages.

Not me. I remember my first word very clearly. It was "pencil."

Several days before I was able to form the word with my mouth, I realized that I could envision words. I could write. Which meant I could read.

That sounds backwards, I guess. You'd think I would realize I could read before I tried to write anything. But I didn't have the opportunity. For one thing, nobody had remembered I was nearsighted—apparently the eyeglasses I had historically worn got lost somewhere in the shuffle between medical facilities over the past six years. As a result, I couldn't read any of the signs on the wall urging me to be quiet and not to smoke (guidelines with which I was already quite compliant). But beyond that, the simple fact of the matter was that nobody had ever offered me anything to read.

No, my caregivers weren't being stupid. They just hadn't thought of a way to determine whether I could read. Think about it: if they held a paper in front of me that said "see Dick run," I couldn't read it back to them. I could only grunt. Nobody thought to hold the same manuscript in front of me and simply ask, "Can you read this?" Plenty of trees. No forest.

Instead they chose to focus on speech therapy with me, teaching me to form the sounds that make up the English language. What about sign language? That requires a cooperative body, which I did not yet have. As a result I wasn't yet able to mime the act of writing, at least not in a way anybody understood. I tried, though. Apparently my earliest attempts made my keepers think I wanted to wash my hands. A bowl, washcloth, and soap were provided forthwith.

So it was to my great relief that one morning while Patti was perkily trying to get me to say my name, I instead managed to croak "pencil." I accompanied this utterance with hand gestures, at the risk of once again making what must be the universal sign for washing hands. But lo and behold, Patti understood. She sprinted off, returning momentarily with a pencil and notepad.

I crammed the pencil into the crook of my left thumb and forefinger and managed to scrawl *I CAN READ (I THINK)*.

Incidentally, I'm rather proud of that. How many other newborns make parenthetic remarks right out of the chute?

This created a new level of hubbub around me, and I was soon surrounded by people clad in medical scrubs, all scrambling to witness this latest development. A new series of interviews/interrogations promptly began, and one of the first things my slowly recovering body experienced was a righteous case of writer's cramp. But my newfound ability to write was such a liberating tool—I was finally able to express things I'd been thinking for days on end, not the least of which was the need for a pair of eyeglasses.

Although writing was difficult, it got easier with practice. My penmanship was very crude, a condition no doubt exacerbated by the fact that I was writing with my left hand. I believe it was my father who first noticed this, and commented that he was pretty sure I was right-handed. He and my mother soon dug up some family photos that supported that claim. But the pencil felt even more foreign in my right hand, so I stuck with the left, and to this day I'm a devout southpaw. As I've observed, the brain is an odd critter.

It is rare that somebody with my level of brain damage is able to learn to speak *and* write, so efforts to develop my speech took a bit of a back seat while the medical staff handed me a stack of legal pads and Number Two pencils and picked my brain, poring over my written responses.

Through this mercifully grunt-free set of Q&A we were able to determine much more clearly just how much of my grey matter was still in working order. I had a lot of questions, too, and was immeasurably relieved to finally have a way to ask them.

But with this quantum leap in my ability to communicate with The Outside World came new difficulties. There was the issue of my parents, and this guy Teddy. It's a lot easier to tell a lie with a grunt than it is to painstakingly write it out. But that's what I had to do. I just saw no reason to crush my family's hopes. Particularly my mother. There was something about her that made me want to *strive*, for lack of a better word. I wanted to make her happy, to make her proud. I wanted to earn the love that she was so obviously willing to give. Swiss cheese or not, I knew love when I saw it.

Love. That was a whole 'nother can of worms (I think I heard my father say that, one of the few phrases I've picked up from this taciturn man). I've already indicated that I had a mother, a father, and a brother. But there was another character in this play, whom I found out about belatedly.

My parents hadn't mentioned her, for reasons that later

became clear to me. So I was unprepared when Geraldine, one of the day-shift nurses, told me I had a visitor named Victoria.

"Who?" I asked. This was one of the handful of words I could currently enunciate with any consistency.

"Victoria," said Geraldine, with a tone that suggested I should know who that was. As she walked out the door, opening it to admit my visitor, she clarified. "Your girlfriend."

I would say that my jaw dropped, but the stroke had rendered such a reaction impossible. Suffice to say that my smirk was stretched to new lengths, and any gift for gab I'd been developing promptly escaped me.

Wordless, I watched as a beautiful woman walked into the room.

She was far more attractive than anybody I'd seen so far in the hospital, looking more like the starlets who populated the soap operas I was slowly becoming addicted to. (Part of my practice regimen for regaining my ability to speak was to watch TV—lots of TV—and try to mimic what I heard. You got Shakespeare; I got *General Hospital.* Oh, and *Gilligan's Island,* from which I've gathered that a three-hour tour can be a very long time.)

Victoria stopped at the side of my bed, hands clasped in front of her, holding a tiny purse molded to look like a seashell. I noticed that she wore her hair just like Tiffany Grange, the actress who portrays Alexis Blake, the conniving heiress who would go to any lengths to manipulate the inhabitants of *Sunset Bay.* I then reflected that maybe I was watching a little too much TV.

Victoria broke the silence. "Hello, Jonathan," she said, her voice husky and solemn.

"Hi," I replied, demonstrating my mastery of the monosyllabic.

She was gorgeous. Her hair was a beautiful mixture of reds,

browns and golds; her eyes a penetrating pale green; her lips pouty and pink. She wore snug-fitting grey pants and a pale, clingy grey sweater, and her body was . . . well . . . remarkable. I had enough brain cells left to determine that this woman was truly a knockout.

And as far as I could tell, I'd never seen her before in my life.

"I'm sorry I haven't called," Victoria said. "I—well—it's been a long . . ."

Her words drew to a halt, so she took the moment to draw up a chair and sit down beside my bed before trying to start the conversation again. "I mean, this was kind of an unexpected surprise."

I was gaining enough command of the language to wonder if there were any other kind of surprise, but I dismissed the thought and looked up at her in silence. She looked as awkward as I felt. Becoming aware of my gaze, she bit her lip timidly.

Eager to get past this moment, I grabbed my handy pad and pencil, and quickly scrawled *HARD FOR ME TO TALK. OK IF I WRITE?*

I showed her the pad. She read it, and then looked at me and nodded eagerly, making sure I could see her gesture. Then she realized it didn't mean *she* couldn't talk, and she stammered, "Oh! I can still—I mean . . ."

She paused, collecting herself, and finally said, "Okay. I'll talk. You write. I'm sure this is hard for you, and—well—it's kind of hard for me, too."

She smiled nervously, revealing an amazing amount of teeth of preternatural whiteness. I nodded encouragingly.

"So," Victoria said, looking at me and changing her expression to one of great concern, "how do you feel?"

OK I GUESS, I wrote. *MY BODY HASN'T CAUGHT UP WITH MY BRAIN YET. AND MY BRAIN HAS SOME PROBLEMS TOO.* I looked at my words, finding them grim and pathetic. I tried to lighten things up, closing with *YOU LOOK GREAT.*

Handing the pad to her, I watched her read. Her face took on an expression of intense concentration, her lips pressed together, her brow somewhat furrowed. I began to notice she seemed capable of registering a variety of readily recognizable emotions, apparently on command, as if to help anyone watching—her audience?—to understand what she was feeling at any given moment. Intense concentration suddenly gave way to beaming delight: she had read the last sentence, and lit up like a Christmas tree.

Again, I actually *thought* that phrase, saying to myself, "She just lit up like a Christmas tree." I could remember what a Christmas tree was, but couldn't remember my own family. Or my girlfriend.

Strokes suck.

CHAPTER 4

Victoria didn't stay long. There were only a couple of key points she had come to communicate to me—it was sort of a good news, bad news thing.

She started with the bad.

"I waited a long time, Jon. A really, really long time. And the doctors all said you weren't going to get any better."

These remarks were punctuated with downturned eyes and the occasionally bitten lower lip. I'd been watching enough TV to recognize acting when I saw it. I mean, it was pretty good acting, I'll admit, but her every gesture seemed so . . . *studied*. Then I wondered why I was focusing on such a thing, and finally decided it was because I just didn't feel any emotional connection to this woman. Yes, she was beautiful, but I didn't know her from Adam. And yes, I did remember Adam. And Eve. Just not Victoria.

"Finally," Victoria said with a rather dramatic toss of her hair, "I had to move on."

At this she leaned forward, placing one hand on mine. Doctor Lance Stone does that on *Surgeons in Love* whenever he's delivering bad news with his trademark heartfelt empathy. *Surgeons* was a favorite with the day-shift nurses at the stroke unit, but I considered the storylines on *General Hospital* to be more compelling.

At any rate, as Victoria clasped my hand and stared into my eyes, she quietly said, "I'm with someone else now, Jon. I'm sorry. But I wanted to be completely honest with you. You deserve that."

I could tell she expected a response, but I was literally speechless. I'd just received a dramatic farewell from a person I'd only just met, so my primary sentiment was one of confusion rather than loss. But I was gaining a larger sense of loss, an awareness that so much of the life I'd had was gone. I just didn't remember enough of it to miss it—at least not yet. And that felt pretty crappy.

This latter realization must have shown on my face—Victoria then added her other hand to the one gripping mine, and leaned in even closer.

"Oh, Jon—I've hurt you. I'm so sorry."

It looked like she was about to cry, and I knew I didn't want that.

I nodded towards the notepad she had trapped under our clasping hands. Realizing she had effectively muted me, she pulled back.

"Oh! Sorry! There must be so much you want to say to me."

Was there? She looked at me imploringly, so I put my pencil to the page. But what to write?

IT'S OK, I finally scrawled. *I UNDERSTAND. LONG TIME, LOTS OF THINGS HAVE CHANGED.*

I showed her the pad, and she nodded enthusiastically, again falling into the habit of remaining silent around somebody who can't talk—I got that a lot in those days.

I continued. *IT'S GOOD THAT YOU MOVED ON. WOULDN'T WANT TO KEEP YOU FROM BEING HAPPY. I'LL BE OK.*

This latest passage relieved her considerably, I could tell. Again she unleashed her dazzling smile.

Encouraged by this, I added, *THE NEW GUY—HOPE HE TREATS YOU WELL.* That looked pretty stupid, but I went ahead and showed it to her. Hey, *you* try to be a witty conversationalist under these conditions.

Victoria continued to smile, although she dialed it down a notch. "Yes," she said. "He's really good to me. He's . . . well, I guess you could say he's a lot like you. Well, a lot like you were. Oh, God, I didn't mean—"

I waved a hand, trying to curtail her embarrassment. I was getting used to the idea that I was not the man I used to be. It seemed everybody I met found some way to make that point painfully clear.

IT'S OK, I wrote again. *REALLY.*

Victoria's smile began to return as she read this. So I concluded with *I'LL BE FINE.*

This was evidently enough to satisfy Victoria. With that bit of unpleasantness out of the way, she abruptly moved on to the good news portion of her visit. She stood, and swiveled her torso back and forth, giving me a variety of angles on her extremely curvaceous body.

"Do you notice anything different about me?" she asked, her voice now taking on a teasing tone. Gone was any remorse or even concern. In its place was a little girl proud of some new acquisition or accomplishment. But what was it? Had she lost weight? Changed her hair?

Floundering, I pointed my pencil towards the top of the pad, where I'd written *YOU LOOK GREAT.* This was a trick I had learned from extensive communication in this manner: every now and then you can recycle a remark.

This time Victoria waved a hand, as if to say *oh, I know that, silly.* Lowering her voice, she said, "I finally got them done." She smiled conspiratorially, then arched her back. My eyes focused on the most conspicuous feature of her anatomy. Both of them.

"You know, like we always talked about. I finally went ahead and did it. They came out great, don't you think?" She offered me several more angles of perspective. Unsure of proper protocol for commenting on the aesthetic qualities of one's ex-girlfriend's breasts, I remained silent, and tried to smile appreciatively.

Victoria's face grew more serious. "It's something I did for myself. You know, part of my moving on. I had to cope with losing you, so I wanted to do something nice for myself and kind of make a fresh start, you know? So I guess you could say they're kind of symbolic."

I was still at a stage where I tired easily, and I was finding the introduction and subsequent removal of a girlfriend a bit overwhelming. The addition of her new-and-improved bosom and the philosophy that accompanied it were enough to push me over the edge. I yawned.

The yawn brought back Serious And Concerned Victoria (yes, I had already begun adding subtitles to her facial expressions—please pardon my cynicism), and she said, "Oh, you're probably tired. This had to be an awful strain on you. I just needed to see you, you know, to get this off my chest." She giggled, realizing how chest-centric our meeting had become.

She patted my hand. "I better get going. But maybe I can, I don't know, visit you again sometime. You know, next time I'm in town. I take the train down here every now and then . . ."

Her voice trailed off, and I assumed she was reconsidering whether additional visits were really such a good idea. Not wanting to prolong this conversation, I faked another yawn and let my eyes droop, a technique I'd picked up for speeding up the endless interviews my doctors put me through.

Victoria took the hint. "I'll go now," she said. "You take care. And Jon, I'm really sorry about everything, but I'm so glad you're back. We really missed you."

I wasn't sure who she meant by *we*. But at that point I wasn't sure about much of anything.

After Victoria left, I looked at my notepad to review my side of the conversation, taking advantage of the instant replay feature inherent to this form of communication. My eyes fixed on one sentence.

I'LL BE FINE.

Yet another thing I wasn't so sure about.

CHAPTER 5

I closed my eyes and started to drift off. I know, you'd think after six years in a coma, I'd have had my fill of sleep, but I still found it necessary to nap frequently. Doctors assured me that as my strength increased, my need for so much sleep would abate.

But like everything else they told me, there was a certain lack of conviction to their words. Some of the best medical minds in the country had determined that I would never awaken from my coma, so I think my return to consciousness had shaken my doctors' professional confidence, leaving them groping for explanations. A *miracle*—that's the word they resorted to most frequently, although some preferred the more scientific-sounding *medical miracle,* perhaps because the term implied that their medical efforts revived me. But they didn't.

They did sustain me; I don't deny that. The comatose are not big participants in life, and require a lot of attention and effort from others in the areas of feeding, hygiene, and waste management, to name a few. For this, I had several hospitals and insurance companies to thank. But as far as me waking up was concerned, nobody had really that figured out, so I tended to consider my doctors' predictions with some degree of skepticism.

At any rate, just as I felt myself falling into that feeling of increased gravity that precedes sleep, I heard a man clear his throat. Startled, I fought through a haze of semi-consciousness and opened my eyes to see a blurry figure standing in the doorway. I reached for my glasses.

"Jonny?" the man said, stepping tentatively closer. As he came into focus I realized I recognized him, which was something I couldn't say about very many people. I recognized him, but I had no memory of him—that was strange. Then I realized how I recognized him. My parents had been showing me photo albums when they visited, in an effort to jog my memory. That's where I had seen this man. That meant this had to be—

"Teddy?" I asked.

The man smiled, then came closer. "Jesus, Jonny—I was afraid you maybe didn't remember me. I mean, Mom and Dad said you'd forgotten a lot of stuff. But I was hoping to God you hadn't forgotten your little brother."

Teddy leaned down, offering me his hand.

"How ya doin', bro?" he asked, crushing my hand in his.

"Hi," I said. Okay, so today wasn't my day for clever conversation.

Teddy let go of my hand and plopped into the chair next to my bed.

"Man, it's good to see you," he said. "I never thought I'd see the day."

I groped for my notepad and went through the familiar litany of asking if I could write rather than talk.

Scanning the note I showed him, he said, "Sure, bro. That's cool. Whatever works for you." Then he scowled at me. "You can hear me okay, right? I mean, you don't need me to write, too, do you?"

I shook my head and tried to smile. I was getting better at smiling—it was something I'd been practicing in the mirror. Smiling seemed to put the people around me more at ease. My condition caused most of them to approach me with a level of exaggerated diplomacy that attempted to ignore all the ways in which I was not quite up to snuff. I think one of the main differences between my kind of brain damage and mental retardation is that at least I was aware of people's discomfort with my plight. But I'm not sure I'd call this an advantage.

I decided to take the lead, and wrote *SO WHAT'S NEW?*

I reflected that literally anything he might say in response would qualify. Sort of like those commercials I've seen for TV reruns, where the network proudly proclaims "It's new to *you*"— that pretty well summed up what every day was like for me.

Teddy read my words, then laughed. "Jesus, where do I begin?" He pulled a heavy gold ring off his pinky and began to fidget with it. It was molded to look like a rough gold nugget.

"Well, for one thing, work is going great. I'm kicking ass and taking names. Bro, you wouldn't believe how good I'm doing. I mean, things got a little weird after all that Enron and World-Com shit. They've really tightened up on things since then, you know, with everybody paying a lot more attention to the books these days. But we came through without a scratch, thank God. The old man just put a couple of guys quietly out to pasture, you know, real low-profile like, and nobody has said boo."

"Boo?" I said. The word made no sense to me. Then again, neither did anything else he'd just said.

Teddy looked at me, picking up on this. "Maybe I should slow down. I mean, did you get any of that?"

Here I'll confess to falling into my old habits from my grunting days: since the answer to his question was no, I remained silent.

"Jonny, did Mom and Dad tell you about my job?"

THEY SAID YOU WORK IN CHICAGO, I wrote.

"Did they tell you where? Or what I was doing?"

I shook my head.

Teddy slipped his ring back on his finger. "Jonny, I'm at Fisk and Tucker. Just like you. Well, like you were. You know, at your old firm."

He seemed nervous about telling me this. I couldn't understand why. Clearly we'd grown up with similar interests and had thus pursued the same profession.

Teddy went on. "Let me tell you, a lot has changed in the last six years, bro." He was watching me intently, looking for some reaction that I didn't know how to provide.

"I mean, I know I was never any good in school. Hell, that's why I quit—which was a dumb-ass move, I finally realized. Shit, I only needed eight credits." Teddy laughed again, shaking his head at whatever he was remembering.

"Anyhoo, a year or so after you got sick, Mom and Dad finally talked me into going back and finishing school. I got the sheepskin, and then started looking for work in Chicago. I mean, Mom and Dad are cool to live with and all, but shit, I was pushing thirty, you know? It was time to get the hell out of Springfield. You know what I'm talking about—hell, you left skid marks out of here when you split town."

This last bit corroborated what my parents had told me. Apparently I'd not been a fan of Springfield, although I couldn't remember why. All I had seen of it so far was this facility, and the only unusual thing I had observed was an inordinate profusion of Lincoln-related items in the hospital gift shop.

"Christ, I thought Mom and Dad had told you about this. About how your buddy hooked me up. You know, Brandon? He was awesome, man. Promised me a job as soon as I passed the CPA exam."

Incidentally, abbreviations and acronyms were still tricky for me. But my parents had told me enough about my old job for me to have remembered this term. And my old job had apparently become my brother's new job.

I guess I haven't mentioned yet that I used to be an accountant. A licensed CPA.

And now I couldn't even count.

As if he had read my mind, Teddy spoke up.

"Mom and Dad say you're having some trouble with numbers and stuff."

He smiled as he said this, an odd smile. I guess he was trying to encourage me.

YEAH, I wrote, *CAN'T REMEMBER HOW NUMBERS WORK. I FORGOT A LOT OF THINGS.*

Like you, for instance, I thought silently.

Teddy nodded thoughtfully as he read my words, still managing to keep that encouraging smile going. Then his face grew concerned.

"Is that going to be permanent? Or will it come back eventually?"

I shrugged, another gesture I'd mastered that had simplified communication for me significantly. When you know as little as I did, a shortcut for saying "I don't know" can come in *very* handy.

"Well," Teddy said, his smile returning, "probably best not to rush things. You just take it easy and keep on getting better."

His smile was beginning to annoy me—it was seeming less sympathetic and more, I don't know, *triumphant.* But I was probably just getting cranky. I should have been happy to hear about how well he was doing, but it had been a taxing day, what with me gaining and losing a girlfriend in a matter of minutes.

That reminded me . . .

VICTORIA WAS HERE, I wrote.

"Really?" Teddy's smile dimmed a little. "Wow—that must have been kinda strange, after all these years."

IT'S OVER, I wrote, then thought of the exact words she had used. *SHE MOVED ON.*

Teddy grimaced in sympathy as he read. Come to think of it, he had probably assumed Victoria would have given up on me— hell, everybody else had—and had been waiting to see how badly I'd take the news.

"Wow," he said again. "That's, uh . . . that's rough, bro."

I shrugged again. Versatile thing, this shrugging.

For the second time today I wrote *LOTS OF THINGS HAVE CHANGED.*

Teddy's smile was returning to its original wattage. "Ain't that the truth," he said. "Things have changed *completely.*" The big gold ring came off his finger and was back in play.

I decided to change the subject. Time for some small talk— talk that didn't focus on yet another aspect of my life that sucked.

HOW LONG ARE YOU IN TOWN?

"Just for the day," Teddy said. "I've got to take the train back home tomorrow. Listen, I'm real sorry it took me 'til now to get down here. Things have just been crazy at work, you know?"

IT'S OK. DOCTORS ARE KEEPING ME BUSY.

"I'll bet they are," Teddy said. "Well, you just keep taking it one step at a time, bro. Slow and steady wins the race, right?"

Well, I had the slow part down. The steady, not so much. And I wasn't yet taking *any* steps at a time. My physical therapy sessions were focused mostly on restoring my ability to flex and move my limbs, but I was far from being able to support my own weight yet.

"Slow and steady," he repeated, apparently running out of things to say.

I couldn't even talk, and I felt the same.

"You just stay focused on what's important, bro," said Teddy. "I mean, you can't be thinking about coming back to work any time soon. You've got bigger fish to fry, what with the fascia and all."

I wrote *YOU MEAN APHASIA?*

"Yeah, whatever it's called. That thing with the talking. So you'll probably have your hands full for a while."

I nodded. Currently my hands were full of a pencil and paper, but I knew what he meant.

Teddy continued to speak. One downside of my current form of communication was that it left a lot of silence, which I've found people feel compelled to fill.

"Probably just as well. I know I told you I'm doing great and all, but there've been some cutbacks at the firm. So I probably wouldn't get my heart set on coming back there anytime soon." Teddy had now taken to repeatedly slipping the ring first on his left pinky, then on his right.

"But me and Brandon, we'll be sure to put in a good word for you with the other firms up there. You know, if you get the whole math thing together and all."

I had a feeling that *the whole math thing* wasn't coming back to me. Ever.

It was strange how I could sense that, but it was like I was walking down a long narrow hallway, lined on both sides with a seeming endless series of doors. Some of them were wide open—those were the memories I hadn't lost. Some doors were slightly ajar—things that had escaped my mind, but easy enough to retrieve by opening the door and walking in. Then there were some closed doors. The parts of my mind that lurked behind them were much harder to access. In some cases I felt I was making some headway. But some of those doors were locked, and I didn't always have a key. That's how it felt with numbers. I could just tell that door was never going to open.

And I could tell that's what Teddy was hoping. But why? I decided to push things a bit, and started writing.

DOCTORS SAY MY RECOVERY IS A MIRACLE. Well, that much was true. But I continued with *SO I BET I'LL BE*

COUNTING IN NO TIME.

Bull's-eye. Teddy's eyes bulged as he read. And the smile he'd adopted when I handed him the pad became tight and forced.

"I bet you will, too, bro," he finally said. "And I'll do everything in my power to help you."

I smiled. He smiled. We were a very cheerful pair.

The silence went on. I was used to it, and assumed that he would crack first. Sure enough, he finally spoke, his face growing serious once again.

"Man, I still can't get over the fact that you could even *have* a stroke when you did. Christ, bro, you were only twenty-eight." Teddy shook his head. "That just blows my mind."

A blown mind was a subject I knew a little something about.

IT'S RARE, I wrote, *BUT NOT UNHEARD OF.*

I looked at my words and realized I was parroting a phrase my doctors had used to describe the likelihood of a young man having a stroke: *rare, but not unheard of.* Those same doctors had repeatedly found it necessary to quote statistics supporting this fact. Perhaps they thought I might take some consolation from hearing the demographics of my fellow stroke victims quantified, forgetting that the numbers they recited made no sense to me. Or maybe they were just trying to convince me that yes, it could happen to somebody my age. I was convinced. Really.

Teddy switched his smile back on. "Well, thank God for miracles," he said. "It's really a . . . a *blessing,* the way you came back. And after we'd almost given up on you."

Almost?

"Anyhoo . . ." Teddy said, looking at his watch. "Jesus, look at the time. I need to get over to Mom and Dad's." He stood and pushed the chair back.

"You know how Mom is when she cooks—she'll give me hell if I show up late for dinner."

I smiled, having no idea how Mom was when she cooked.

"Listen, I promise the next time I come down we'll have lots more time together. It'll be great—just like old times."

He leaned towards me—for a moment I thought he was going to try to hug me. Instead, he clapped a hand on my shoulder.

"I'll catch you later, bro," he said, slipping the massive ring back on its original finger. "It's been *so* good to see you."

"You too," I managed to say.

He walked towards the door, then stopped and turned to face me. "Oh, and don't worry. I mean, I won't tell anybody at the firm about your little problem with numbers. Mum's the word on that."

"Mum?" I repeated. Figures of speech that didn't make literal sense were still hard for me. That was one of those closed doors, but I was working on it, and could feel the lock jiggle when I worked the key.

Teddy said, "Totally mum, trust me."

He made a zipping-his-lips gesture, then turned and walked away, still smiling.

I drifted off to sleep with a lot on my mind. Although today's visitors had provided some clues, I was really starting to wonder what kind of person I used to be.

CHAPTER 6

I first saw Rebecca in Physical Therapy. She was holding herself upright, making her way slowly through that device that looks like the parallel bars they show in Olympic gymnastic competitions. Set about waist-high, the bars allowed her to support herself with her arms while she worked on putting one foot in front of the other.

I watched her, trying to pick up any pointers. I hadn't yet worked my way up to standing or walking; we were still rebuilding my strength and range of motion, a process that usually required me to sit in some elaborate exercise machine that focused on a specific muscle group. At the moment, I was doing something my trainer called preacher curls on a machine devised to develop the biceps, using a pathetically low weight that made me glad I couldn't understand numbers.

The woman's triceps flexed as she held herself up. It was clear she was in the early stages of learning how to walk—she was supporting most of her weight with her arms, awkwardly throwing one leg forward, letting the foot fall where it may, then shifting her weight and repeating the routine with the other leg. The process looked exhausting. Her face glistened with sweat, as did her arms, which were exposed by the tank top she wore. She was in good shape—she certainly wasn't a withered coma victim like me. I wondered if perhaps her legs had been injured in an auto accident.

Her physical therapist stood in front of her, a beefy middle-

aged man with a buzz cut whose eyes kept drifting to a television mounted high on one wall, where a football team in red and white uniforms battled a team dressed in dark blue. The volume was muted, but every now and then I'd hear the man swear under his breath, or emit a hissing "Yesssss!"

The woman—I didn't know her name yet—ignored her trainer, and focused on walking. When she reached one end of the bars, she performed a tricky looking maneuver, placing both hands on one bar, then letting go with one hand and swinging around in an awkward pivot that culminated in her catching the other bar with her free hand, now facing the opposite direction. She pulled it off, but just barely, making me dread the day when I would be expected to execute that move. I hoped my therapist would be paying more attention to me than her guy was.

My physical therapist, a young, cheerful guy named Leon, noticed me watching her.

"That's a fine looking woman, no doubt," he said. "Shame about what happened to her."

"What happened?" I asked. Yes, I had graduated to sentences that contained more than a single syllable.

"Stroke, same as you. Shit, she can't even be thirty years old yet, and she's havin' a stroke, a fine looking woman like that? That's fucked up, man. You know what I'm talkin' about?"

I nodded, acknowledging one of the rare instances where I did know what somebody was talking about.

"Shit," said Leon. "Now I went and lost track of how many reps you've done. And I know *you* sure as hell weren't keeping track."

As Leon had gotten to know me, he often made jokes about the problems I had, and liked to tease me about what he called my "math issues," a topic that arose frequently, given the amount of counting associated with repetitive physical exercise.

But it didn't bother me—he was one of the only people I'd encountered who would talk to me directly about my problems, instead of trying to sugar-coat or ignore them. I sensed no mean-spiritedness in Leon's teasing; if anything, he was trying to get me to "lighten up, motherfucker" (another Leonism) in the face of some pretty oppressive circumstances. I liked Leon, and was thankful he'd been assigned to me.

"Aw, hell," Leon said. "Go ahead and switch to your left arm. Just don't make me lose count. You'll end up with one arm looking like Popeye or somethin'."

Then he shot me a look. "Tell me you do remember who Popeye is."

Slowly, deliberately, I said, "I yam what I yam."

It was possibly my longest sentence to date, and it elicited a howl of laughter from Leon that made me smile.

Leon's outburst made the woman's trainer look away from the TV for a moment, curious as to the cause of the commotion. The woman remained focused on her walking. Her hair was a light brown that faded into blonde, pulled back in a loose ponytail that was now matted with sweat. Her face registered pure determination, with no self-consciousness about her bedraggled appearance. It made her look . . . wonderful.

Her therapist looked at his watch. "Okay, hon," he said, "let's wrap this up. I'll get the chair ready."

The man had to walk past us to get to where he'd stowed her wheelchair. As he did, he held out a fist in front of Leon. I watched as Leon made a fist and gently swung it down on top of the other man's fist.

"Leon," the man said.

"My man Bruce," Leon replied.

The woman's trainer—Bruce—laid his clipboard down on a bench next to me and knelt down to adjust the wheelchair. I craned my neck and managed to make out a name written on

the clipboard: *Rebecca Chase.*

Bruce maneuvered the wheelchair past us and wheeled it into position behind the woman. On cue, she slumped into the chair, and Bruce handed her a towel. Then he turned her wheelchair to face the door, and she looked directly at me for the first time. Her eyes were dark brown, almost black, and seemed to shine more than most people's eyes. But I might have been losing some objectivity.

As Bruce wheeled her past us, the woman spoke to me.

"You're really skinny," she said.

With that, they were gone, leaving me to listen to Leon trying to choke back his laughter.

I worked to form a word. "Rebecca?"

"Yeah," said Leon, regaining his composure. "That's Rebecca. She's a fine looking woman, but that stroke left her kind of . . . *funny.* Talks kinda like a zombie or somethin'."

Leon put a hand on the machine, stopping my arm's motion. "That's enough, Popeye. Let's move on to the leg machines. Here, let me help you."

As Leon lifted me up, an indignity I'd had to get used to in order to get from one machine to the next, he said, "She's right about that, though. You are one skinny motherfucker."

At first my parents visited me every day. They'd often come together, although there were days that I don't think my father said anything more than hello or goodbye to me. But my mother easily carried the conversational load, acting as a sort of oral historian for me, trying to fill in the many blanks in my memory. She brought photo albums, newspaper clippings, anything she could think of to try to get me reacquainted with the world I'd lost.

Mom—it felt odd, calling a stranger *Mom,* but it made her so happy—really made an effort. A thin woman whose brown hair was giving in to grey, her default expression was a kindly, sincere smile, and her mood seemed perpetually cheery without veering into that annoyingly forced enthusiasm affected by some of the hospital staff. No, everything about my mom seemed to radiate genuine benevolence, making my inability to remember her all the more frustrating.

Some days she came to see me by herself, offering some excuse why Dad (she insisted I call him that) hadn't been able to accompany her. He and I had so little to say to each other that I didn't mind his absence. But it got to the point where Mom and I were running out of things to talk about, too. Nothing she showed me or said to me had done anything to rekindle any memories, so essentially we were strangers, struggling to get to know each other. No, that's not quite right, because it implies that she had something to learn about me. She already knew me. But I didn't know either of us.

When Mom finally cut her visitation back to every other day or so, I'll admit I was relieved. Plus, it gave me more free time, and I had plenty to work on. My speech was getting better, although talking was still hard work for me, and I often found it easier simply to write. But what I was really forced to focus on was my physical therapy.

It occurs to me that if my story were being presented as a TV Movie of the Week, at some point we'd cut to a brief montage of me going through the grueling process of months of physical rehabilitation. You know, lots of heart-tugging shots of me enduring repeated pain and failure, peppered with a few small victories, and spliced with close-ups of my sweat-beaded face grimacing in pain (shot from the non-smirking side, of course). And all this would naturally be accompanied by a suitably dramatic and/or triumphant soundtrack, perhaps a song that didn't quite make it into one of the *Rocky* movies.

But I'll spare you. The process was lengthy, grueling, and

extremely unglamorous. While a great fuss was made when I was finally able to take my first tentative steps, I have to say that the first time I wiped my own ass was a triumph every bit as momentous. I hated being helpless.

And I hated physical therapy. Well, except for Rebecca. She was usually there during my sessions with Leon, and when I was strong enough to go to the PT room on my own to practice, I'd often run into her there. She was way ahead of me—she got around the hospital using a walker, while I was still wheelchair-bound. But it was in those practice sessions that I finally had a chance to meet her, something I had been wanting very much to do.

As often seems to be the case for me, the reality didn't live up to the anticipation.

One evening I wheeled into the PT room to find it unoccupied except for Rebecca, who was pumping away on a machine that exercised her legs. I hated that machine—even on its lowest setting I found it excruciating, but she was powering on through, her skin glazed with sweat.

While I didn't want to interrupt her, I felt it would be rude to ignore her, since we were the only two people in the room. So I tentatively rolled over to the leg-press machine and said, "Hi."

I know, I know. I really needed to up my syllable usage.

She looked at me for a moment, then said, "Did you want to use this machine?" She spoke softly, her voice low in pitch and slightly scratchy.

"No," I said. "Well, yes. But not now."

"Okay," she said, and continued pumping away.

I was about to turn my wheelchair and roll away, but I decided to take one last shot. I said the line I'd been practicing. I had it down to where I didn't slur the words at all, if I really concentrated.

"My name is Jonathan. I just wanted to say hi."

She stopped pumping and looked at me again. "You already said hi."

"I know, but—" Shit. This didn't fit with the second line I'd rehearsed.

"I . . . I just wanted . . . to meet you."

"Oh," she said. "Why?"

Christ, were all women this hard to talk to?

"I just . . . you seemed . . . we're both . . ."

Shit. Shit shit shit. I gave up. Between her less-than-warm reception, the weird defensive questions she surprised me with, and the difficulty I had in getting a message from my brain to my mouth in a timely manner, I felt helpless and stupid.

Turning my wheelchair to go, I managed to say, "Sorry, Rebecca."

At this she surprised me further. She smiled. Not a big smile—just a small upturning at the corners of her mouth, accompanied by her eyes becoming somehow brighter. It was a good little smile, simple and real. But it quickly dissolved into a scowl.

"How do you know my name?" she demanded.

Shit.

"Saw it," I said, "on Bruce's clipboard."

Then, for reasons I cannot explain, I announced, "I can read." Immediately I felt like an idiot.

"I can read, too," Rebecca said. "Can you write?"

"Yes," I said, puzzled by the question.

"I'm having trouble with that. It takes me longer than it should."

"That's how . . . talking is for me," I stammered. "Easier for me to write."

"That's weird," she said.

"Weird," I agreed, back to my monosyllabic self.

Rebecca sat up in the machine, leaning closer to me.

"I like how my name sounds when you say it."

She spoke in a near monotone, I was noticing, making it hard to read any emotions that might be behind the words. Not sure how to respond, I said, "Rebecca?"

"Rebecca," she said. "Everybody calls me Becky, and I don't think I like it. But I like it when you say Rebecca."

"Rebecca," I said quickly, eager to please. Again I promptly felt like an idiot, but it was a feeling I was getting used to.

"I wish my husband would call me Rebecca."

Shit. Shit. Shit. Sorry for the language—just recalling my thoughts at the time.

"He calls me Becky, too. Sometimes just Beck. I don't like that."

I didn't like it either.

Rebecca stood up, toweling herself off with one hand while she gripped her walker with the other.

"You can use this now. I need to work on my arms. So my left arm doesn't get . . . what's that thing where one side of your body doesn't get as strong as the other?"

"Neglect," I said, having become quite the expert on stroke terminology. I was facing this problem with my right arm, which wasn't being nearly as cooperative as the left.

"Neglect," she repeated, nodding. She began to push her walker away, then turned to face me.

"You're Jonathan."

"Yes."

"Do people call you things you don't like?"

I thought about this. "My brother calls me bro. I don't think I like that."

"People shouldn't call people things they don't like," Rebecca said, still in that gentle monotone.

Not knowing how else to respond, I nodded. Satisfied, Rebecca scooted her walker towards one of the other weight machines.

"You're still skinny," she said over her shoulder, "but you're getting better."

It was amazing how good that rather dubious compliment made me feel.

I eased myself from my wheelchair into the leg machine Rebecca had occupied. I couldn't even get the thing to move with the weights she had set up, so I reset it to lift the least possible weight, hoping she wouldn't notice. Then I went to work on my legs, while Rebecca began doing left-handed preacher curls. The only sound in the room was our breathing, punctuated by the clank of the weights.

CHAPTER 7

My mother visited me the next day, arriving with a thin photo album tucked under her arm.

"I was straightening up the room you'll be staying in," she said, "and I came across some pictures I didn't think you'd seen yet."

I thanked her without enthusiasm. I'd gone through endless photos already during her visits, but I never saw anything or anybody I remembered. I felt like a crime victim paging through mug shots, but never finding the person who'd done him wrong.

While Mom and I struggled to make small talk, I idly flipped through the pages of the album. Most of the photos were of me as a young boy, often shown playing with Teddy. I detected a recurring theme: in one shot I held a gleaming trophy over my head while Teddy looked on sullenly; in another I had him pinned down in a wrestling maneuver. The next page featured a shot of me holding Teddy in a choke hold, giving the top of his head what I believe my father called "noogies" with the closed knuckles of my free hand.

A grainy black-and-white enlargement that took up most of the adjoining page showed us each wearing boxing gloves, with me taking a swing at the smaller boy while he shielded his head with his arms. I was starting to understand why I sensed such mixed emotions coming from Teddy during his visit—the evidence was starting to suggest that having me for a big brother had come with a distinct downside.

I was nearing the final pages of the album, while my mother was jabbering about some ongoing war between my father and a squirrel who kept raiding the backyard birdfeeder, when her voice suddenly faded away, along with everything else in the room.

All that remained was the photograph in front of me. It showed me as a young boy, on my knees in the grass, playing with a large black dog. The dog stared straight at the camera.

Straight at me.

"Jonny? Are you all right?"

My mother's voice drew me back into the room from wherever I'd just been.

"Oh—sorry, Mom! I just . . . this dog . . ."

"Do you remember Rufus?" my mother asked, her eyes wide. "We only had him for a few years. He—"

Rufus.

Yes. I remembered.

Rufus.

A strange feeling surged in my chest, and I felt my throat tighten. For a moment I thought I was becoming ill, then I re-alized that I was simply *feeling*. Responding for the first time to something from my past that I recognized.

"Rufus," I said aloud, trying the name out. "Rufus!"

I felt simultaneously happy and sad as I stared at that furry black face. It was a happy face. A loving face.

"Tell me about Rufus," I demanded, not looking up. I didn't dare tear my eyes away from my first glimpse of an honest-to-God memory.

My mother laughed. "Rufus," she said, "was a handful. Full of love and sweet as sugar, but utterly impossible to control. He was always getting outside, chasing cats and picking fights with dogs, even if they were twice his size."

She shook her head. "He was a fighter right up to the end."

"Rufus is dead?" I realized immediately how stupid my question was. Even without grasping the math, I knew a dog that had been full-grown when that picture was taken—when I was just a small boy—couldn't still be alive.

My mother nodded. "Cancer. We did everything we could for him, but it got so bad we finally had to put him to sleep." Looking at me uncertainly, she said, "Do you understand what putting something to sleep is?"

"Yeah," I said, "I understand." I could definitely relate to the concept of being put to sleep, although in my case it hadn't been done to me on purpose. Nor, as it turned out, had it been permanent, despite some widely held expectations.

"You were heartbroken. You loved that dog dearly. And the feeling was mutual." She smiled, remembering. "He belonged to all of us, and your poor father got stuck with walking him when it rained and taking him to the vet and such, but there was never any question that Rufus was *your* dog. I swear, that dog stuck to you like glue. We used to call him your shadow."

I stopped talking. I was doing something foreign and new. I was remembering. Not in a very clear way—more at an emotional level. I remembered the love. And I remembered the sense of loss.

I remembered something else. A name. Maddy. No, that was wrong. Maggie?

"Did we have another dog?" I asked. "After Rufus?"

Again my mother shook her head. "No, Rufus was our one and only." She smiled affectionately at the photo. "We couldn't bear to get any more pets after what happened," she concluded, looking away.

I sensed I had raised a sore subject, and regretted it. But my relentlessly cheerful mother quickly turned back to face me, her smile once more in place.

"Let's look through the rest of this album," she said, "and see if there are any more shots of Rufus. He was such a cute dogger-wogger."

She laughed at herself. "Listen to me. It's been twenty-some years, but I'm talking just like I did when Rufus was around. What is it about dogs that makes us fall into baby-talk?"

"Dogger-wogger," I repeated. "Think I remember that. Hey—did we used to call him . . . Rufus the doofus?"

Now we were both laughing. I was glad to see my mother's mood lightening. And I was delighted to have opened another door in my hallway of memories. I flipped the page, looking for more pictures of Rufus.

Looking for more memories.

In the days that passed, I managed to have a number of brief—and, mercifully, less disastrous—conversations with Rebecca since that debacle in the PT room. Still, I was surprised when one day at lunchtime she approached my table in the hospital cafeteria.

"Can I sit here?" she asked. She balanced a tray of food on top of her walker.

I had my mouth full of grilled cheese sandwich, so I grunted and nodded. Yes, those communication skills had really come a long way.

She put her tray on the table and sat down across from me. "I like their grilled cheese, too," she said, looking at my plate.

I managed to swallow, and dabbed hastily at my mouth with a napkin before replying.

"Yeah," I said. "Grilled cheese is good." Unlike my conversational skills, I reflected.

"But I think their mashed potatoes are the instant kind," Rebecca said. "And their fish sticks are nasty."

Being rather partial to the hospital's fish sticks, I remained silent.

"After lunch, can you help me with something?" she said, pausing to taste her tomato soup.

"Sure. What is it?"

Rebecca put down her spoon. "I need a guy's opinion. You're a guy." Again her quiet, level voice made this remark hard to read, but I'll admit to being somewhat pleased to have had my gender noted and acknowledged.

"I could have asked Bruce—you know, my PT coach—but he and I don't talk much. And your coach always looks like he wants to have sex with me."

One thing I had been learning from my brief encounters with Rebecca was that she tended to speak her mind very directly, with little regard for how others might react to her words. From my study of strokes, I had learned that this lack of self-editing was one of the many after-effects a stroke could cause. The thing was, I found her directness rather endearing. And for whatever reason, her quiet, deadpan delivery heightened the effect.

I smiled. "Leon looks at most pretty women that way." My God—had I actually managed to compliment her in a moderately smooth way? Perhaps there was hope for my linguistic neurons after all.

But rather than smiling at me, Rebecca simply looked puzzled. "You think I'm pretty?" she asked, clearly surprised.

"Yes," I said, and then decided to elaborate. Speaking carefully, I said, "I think you're very pretty, Rebecca."

This got a smile—that nice, simple smile. I assumed it was in response to the compliment, but then she said, "I like it a lot when you say my name like that."

Resisting the temptation to begin endlessly repeating her name, I instead managed to say, "How can I help?"

Rebecca's face grew serious again, and she leaned forward.

"I was wondering if you could come by my room after lunch."

It would be both cliché and accurate to say that my heart leapt.

"I've got two new outfits that a friend brought me from home," she said, "and I want to know which one you think looks best."

My heart now mounted a trampoline and began to execute a flawless series of back flips.

"My husband is coming by this afternoon, and I want to surprise him by being all dressed up for him," she concluded.

My heart fell into a kitchen garbage disposal.

"I'd be glad to help," I lied.

Rebecca's room, which was on the next floor up from me, was configured just like mine. A narrow bed lined the left wall. In the right rear corner, a bulky armoire housed a narrow closet, dresser drawers, and a small TV with a built-in video player. Completing the ensemble was a small writing desk along the right wall, adorned with several framed photos.

While Rebecca adjusted the curtains to let more light into the room, I drew my wheelchair up beside the desk to examine the photos. Each showed Rebecca with a tall, athletic man smiling confidently at the camera. I hated him instantly.

But then I noticed how different Rebecca looked in these photos. Her hair was a lighter blonde, and she wore a lot of makeup, though it was expertly applied. And her smile, wide and toothy, had a forced, almost manic zest that matched her husband's. Nothing like the quiet little Mona Lisa smiles she occasionally graced me with. I decided I liked her new smile better.

"That's Big Bob," Rebecca said from behind me. "My husband."

"He looks . . . big," I said, having resumed my normal level of conversational incompetence.

"He says he's six foot five," Rebecca said. "But I think he may only be six three."

I gave a neutral nod, not feeling like getting into my "math issues," as Leon called them.

Pointing to one of the photos, Rebecca said, "That's us at an awards banquet that our church has every year. Bob's very active in the church."

Great, I thought. In addition to being big and great looking, the guy was a saint. Probably had a Nobel Prize gathering dust on his mantle.

"So why do you think he would do that?" Rebecca asked, breaking my self-pitying train of thought.

"Do what?"

"Lie about his height. Why would I care if he was taller?"

For once I pieced out her meaning from context, and was able to speculate. "For some guys, being big is really important, I guess."

"I guess," she agreed. "It sounds like you're getting better at talking."

"Sometimes," I said. Then I added, "Thanks."

Rebecca joined me in staring at the photos. "I look different in those pictures, don't I?"

This was dangerous ground, and I knew it. "Maybe a little," I allowed. "I guess your hair was lighter then."

"Big Bob wants me to bleach my hair. He says it's mousy looking right now."

"I like your hair," I said.

She looked at me dubiously. "But it's two colors. It's blonde on the ends, and brown where it's growing out. I mean, I definitely need to do something about it. But I kind of think I have bigger problems to work on, you know?"

I stuck to my story. "I like your hair," I repeated.

Ignoring me, she pointed at another one of the photos. "It's more than the hair. Look at how much makeup I have on in this one—this was at a wedding reception down in Florida. And look at the neckline on that dress."

Feeling awkward, I looked away.

Rebecca picked up the church banquet photo, examining it closely for a long moment. Then she set it back down and said, "And my smile looks fake."

"Your smile looks like his," I blurted, instantly regretting my candor.

She stared at the photo, and said, "It does, doesn't it? I kind of think Bob brought me these pictures to remind me who I am—who I'm supposed to be."

"What?" A brilliant retort on my part, I'll grant you. But I was confused by the turn this conversation was taking.

"He could have just brought me pictures of himself," Rebecca said. "I mean, it makes sense for a woman to want pictures of her husband when she's away from him. But every picture he brought has me in it, too. And they all show me looking all . . . *perfect* like that. Not like I look now."

"You think you look better in those pictures?" I asked. Okay, I've already acknowledged that this was dangerous ground, but what did I have to lose? She was married, after all; she wasn't somebody who was available to me, despite any furtive hopes I might have harbored. But she was somebody whose well-being I cared about.

"Don't you?" she asked. "Look at me there. Low-cut dress, tons of makeup, perfect hair. And look at me now—in sweats and a ponytail."

I worked hard on a sentence that I felt was important to get right. "In the pictures," I said, "you just look different. Not better. Different."

A trace of a smile emerged, but she caught herself.

"Anyway," she said, turning to open the armoire, "tell me

what you think of these. I bought them both right before my stroke, so Bob's never seen me in either of them."

She supported herself with one hand on her walker, and held a dress up in front of her on a hanger, a price tag dangling from its shoulder. The dress was definitely very eye-catching: it was the deep red of cafeteria ketchup, and seemed . . . well, rather short.

Reading my thoughts, Rebecca frowned. "I think my legs are probably too pale for something so short." She turned to put the dress back in the armoire and said, "How about this other one?"

She pulled out another dress, holding it up for me to see. This was a slightly longer, more billowy affair, made of a black fabric with a light floral pattern. The black emphasized the darkness of her eyes.

"I like that one," I said. "It's not as flashy, but more . . . pretty." Sort of like the Rebecca I was getting to know versus the one in the photos.

"Good, so it's not just me."

While she hung the dress back up, she said, "The red one seems more like something to wear to a nice restaurant or a nightclub. Not to go for a walk in the hospital garden. Oh, and speaking of going for a walk, want to see something?"

With that, she stepped tentatively away from her walker and picked up a cane that I hadn't noticed lying on the bed.

"Look," she said, again with that shy little smile. She began to walk slowly back and forth in the room, using only a cane.

"Rebecca, that's great! I can't believe it!"

"I've been practicing so hard," she said. "Thank God the floors in PT are padded—I went down a lot. But I'm getting there, aren't I?"

Her voice might not have registered her emotions, but her face did: this was the most light I'd ever seen in her eyes.

"Getting there? You *are* there," I said, smiling helplessly. "You're there."

"I can't wait to show Big Bob," she said.

Not wanting to diminish her excitement, I steeled myself and replied. "He'll be amazed," I promised. "You're doing so great. You'll knock him dead."

She plopped down on the bed next to where I sat in my wheelchair. "God, I hope so." Turning to face me, she said, "Thank you for helping me with this."

"Glad to help," I said.

"It really means a lot to me."

I nodded, unsure what to say.

After an awkward silence, she said, "Well, I better start getting ready."

She struggled to her feet, leaning in close to me as she pushed herself off the bed. With only the cane to support her, it took her a moment to get herself upright and stable again. During that moment I took in her smell, fresh and clean. And I felt an ache in my heart, not unlike the feeling of loss I experienced when I learned about Rufus.

"When's your husband coming?" I asked, regaining my composure.

"At three," she said. "So I've still got a couple hours to get ready. I've got one of the nurses coming to help me with my makeup."

She looked at me intently, again with that extra light in her eyes. "Then, when it's time, instead of waiting for Bob to come up to my room, I'm going to go down and meet him in the lobby. Standing on my own two feet, with only this cane to help me. He's going to be so surprised."

Even with that muted, scratchy, vulnerable little voice, I could hear her pride.

"He'll be amazed," I assured her again.

Rebecca's gaze shifted to the clock over the door. Picking up her cue, I said, "I'll get going. Have a great visit, okay?" I began to wheel out of the room.

"I will. And thank you, Jonathan. You helped me a lot."

"You're welcome, Rebecca. Good luck."

At the sound of her name she gave me one last little smile, then closed the door as I wheeled into the hallway.

"Knock him dead," I said quietly, rolling towards the elevator. "Knock him dead."

A voice answered me from my left, in words I didn't quite catch. I stopped and swiveled my wheelchair in front of a door that stood open along the hallway, and saw a familiar face.

"Oh," I said. "Hi, Mr. Samuels."

The old man sat in a wheelchair by the writing desk in his room, which was set up just like mine and Rebecca's. He was facing his open doorway, watching the hallway traffic as it passed by his room.

He smiled feebly with the side of his face that still worked and said, "Cheese rabbit, suitcase?"

I'd first become acquainted with Mr. Samuels down in the PT room, where he could occasionally be found working on very basic physical movements with his therapist. Already old and frail, his body had been ravaged by a severe stroke some time before my arrival at the hospital. Yet he maintained a pleasant disposition, despite aphasia having rendered him incapable of speaking in a way anybody could understand. Leon had said some of the hospital staff privately called him "Sammy Salad," due to the jumbled "word salad" that came out whenever the man attempted to speak. Aware of how difficult even basic communications can be after a stroke, I chose not to adopt that uncharitable moniker, instead always referring to him by his proper name.

I nodded to him. "Sorry if I disturbed you, Mr. Samuels. I

was just talking to myself."

He waved a bony hand dismissively. "Hamster lightbulb," he said simply.

Nodding was the conversational technique I'd found most successful with Mr. Samuels, so I nodded in his direction, then said, "You have a nice day, okay?"

His expression grew puzzled. "Zucchini?" he asked.

Clearly I should have stuck with a simple nod. Opting for a wave and a smile, I set a new course for my wheelchair and proceeded down the hallway.

CHAPTER 8

That night, after giving my dinner some time to digest, I made my way to the PT room. I was determined to get out of the wheelchair and into a walker, at least for short periods. But that meant I had a lot of work to do on my arms and legs.

Approaching the room, I heard the clank of weights, telling me I would not be working out alone. But the pace of the clanking was unusually rapid—somebody was exercising furiously in there.

As usual, the door was open, but I was surprised to see no light emanating from the room. Why would somebody work out in the dark? Then I remembered that there were numerous patients in the facility who had lost their sight—I often heard the tap of their canes in the hallway.

The steady metallic rhythm grew louder as my chair brought me nearer to the doorway. I wheeled into the room and felt along the wall for a light switch. Finding it, I flicked it on, bathing the room in the harsh glow of fluorescent light.

The rapid clanking continued, and my eyes tracked the source.

Sitting on the leg-press machine, pumping away at a frenzied pace, was Rebecca. She still wore her black flowered dress, but it was soaked with sweat and hiked up in an unladylike way to accommodate the machine. Her face was streaked with makeup and sweat. She ignored me, her eyes clenched shut as she chanted a series of numbers punctuated by short, panting breaths. I presumed these to be a tally of the reps she had performed. They sounded like very large numbers.

"Rebecca?" I said. No answer.

I tried again, louder. Still nothing.

Finally I shouted her name. This got her attention—she stopped pumping her legs and looked over at me.

I saw now that more than sweat was streaking her face. She was crying, her eyes wide and red in their sockets.

"What do you want?" she demanded.

"Are you okay?" I asked. It was a stupid question—clearly she wasn't, so I said, "What's wrong?"

"Me," she said between breaths. "My dress. My hair. My cane. Everything."

Wheeling close to her, I tried to speak in a soothing tone. "What do you mean? What happened today?"

"I worked so hard," she said, starting to sob. "I got dressed up. I fixed my hair. Nora helped me with my makeup. And I walked all the way to the lobby, with just a cane."

She shook her head in disbelief. "Eight weeks ago, my left leg was partially goddamn paralyzed, and today I'm walking to meet my loving husband with nothing but a cane. *You* can't even use a walker yet."

I looked down at my legs, wishing I hadn't worn shorts to work out in tonight. My legs looked pathetically weak and pale.

Seeing my reaction, Rebecca put her hand to her mouth. "God, I'm sorry, Jonathan. I know you were in a coma for years—that wasn't fair. And you're working hard, too."

I started to reply, but she cut me off.

"But I've been working *so* hard. And does he notice? Does he appreciate it?"

Before I could answer, she said, "Not even for a second. First he tells me my eye makeup looks funny. Then he says my dress looks like an old schoolmarm. Then—" She paused to blow her nose into a towel. "Then, he says my cane makes me look like a . . . *like an old lady.*" She nearly hissed the words.

Another nose-blowing episode left a conversational gap for which I had nothing intelligent to offer.

"Not a word about the work it took for me to meet him in the lobby. Not a word about me wearing something other than a sweatsuit for the first time in weeks. Nothing about how hard I'm working, or how good I'm doing. All I hear is how I'm not like I used to be."

Now there was a thought I could relate to.

"I'm so sorry," I began. "I'm sure he didn't mean—"

"That I look like an old lady?" she said. "Oh, he meant it. He tried to act like he was just joking around, but he meant it."

"I mean," I said, "I'm sure he didn't mean to hurt your feelings." It was a lame thing to say, but I needed to say *something* positive.

"No, for that, he'd have to actually *care* about my feelings." Rebecca took several deep breaths, trying to control her sobbing.

I said, "He was probably just joking around. Like you said."

Rebecca looked at me, still breathing hard. "Is that supposed to make it okay? I mean, I think there's a name for that kind of thing, where you say something mean, but say it in a way that if somebody complains about it, it makes them look like the one who's being a jerk."

There was a name for that. But like so much other information in my brain, it wasn't making itself accessible.

"And for all I know, he's right," Rebecca continued. "I mean, I know I've changed. I don't talk the way I used to. And I don't always know what's okay to say and what isn't, so I usually end up saying whatever I'm thinking. Even if I'm not supposed to."

She sniffed. "And I know I didn't used to be this way—believe me, Bob keeps reminding me."

With that she broke into sobs once again, horrible spasms of misery that racked her entire body. It was a terrible thing to watch.

"That's one of the things I like about you." I probably shouldn't have said it, but there it was. And it was true.

"What?" she said, looking up, her eyes still streaming.

"You say what you think," I said. "Most people don't." I thought about Teddy, who claimed to be thankful I had come back. About my mother, who promised my life would be just like it was before. People didn't tell you what they thought. They told you what they thought you wanted to hear.

I pulled my chair closer to her. "I like that about you."

"But I say stupid things. Terrible things." She wiped her face with her towel. "I'm always embarrassing Bob with what I say to him, especially when other people are around. And I called you skinny, and gave you crap for not being able to walk."

"I am skinny," I said. "And I can't walk."

"Not yet," she said.

"No, not yet. You're right. I'm working on it. And I'm getting better. You told me that, and I believed you."

"I was telling the truth," she said. She sniffled loudly, and wiped her nose with the towel, now badly streaked with makeup.

"I know," I said. "You always tell the truth—at least from what I've seen." Without wanting to give away too much, I said, "Even when it's not what I want to hear."

I waited until she was looking at me to say, "I think friends should always tell each other the truth. Even when it's not what they want to hear."

With my linguistic skills, the statement took me a long time to make. But she waited and listened, and when I was done she held my gaze for a long time, her sniffles subsiding.

"Am I your friend?" she asked finally.

"I hope so," I said. Trying to lighten the mood, I added, "I don't give fashion advice to just anybody."

I saw a glimmer of a smile, but only for a moment. She looked down at her dress, wrinkled and bunched. "Following your fashion advice got me told I look like a schoolmarm."

"I don't agree," I said. "Do you?"

"I . . . I *like* this dress," she said, her voice beginning to crack again.

"Me too."

"But I don't know if I'm supposed to."

Seeing my puzzled look, she explained, "I've changed. A lot, apparently, based on what Bob says. I don't act like I used to. I don't feel the same about some things in my life as Bob tells me I used to."

Before I could respond she stopped me. "No, listen. I know some of the things I say now are wrong. Not wrong like they're not true, but wrong like . . . well, because I shouldn't say those things. I should keep them to myself."

Again she stopped me from replying, waving a hand while she focused her thoughts.

"So, what if the things I *feel* are wrong, too? I can fix my arms and legs. But how do I fix that?"

Now she looked at me expectantly. How was I supposed to answer?

I opted for honesty.

"I don't know," I said.

Rebecca and I fell into a routine of eating lunch and dinner together in the cafeteria most days. She didn't do breakfast, I learned, but I needed all the fuel I could get to put some meat on my bones, so I never missed a meal. Besides, I had developed a perverse fondness for the amorphous yellow mass the cafeteria claimed was scrambled eggs.

I enjoyed our conversations—they gave me a chance to

practice speaking. But that's disingenuous; I enjoyed them mostly because they were with *her*. Yes, I had a crush on her, I'll admit it. But there was nothing immoral about it, really. I had no notion of trying to win her affections—she was married, and I understood and accepted that fact. But this didn't change how much I liked her.

And I'll admit that probably much of what drew me to her was the empathy we had for each other. We each knew how it felt to be less than what we once were. And we each knew the sting of being constantly reminded of that fact.

"Cheer up," Rebecca said to me at lunch one day. "That's what he's always saying to me. Cheer up."

The "he" she was referring to was Big Bob.

"He keeps telling me how bubbly I used to be. I don't even know what that means. What's bubbly?"

I pondered this, chewing my grilled cheese. "Did you have to do any speech therapy?" I finally asked.

"Just for a day or two," she said, "until they figured out that my bigger problem was writing, not talking. Why?"

"Well, I'm not sure if it's what Big Bob is talking about, but I guess my speech therapist Patti is pretty bubbly."

"Is she the one I see working with people with all those colored blocks and stuff?"

Patti used those blocks when working on shape recognition with her patients. "Yeah, that's her," I said.

Rebecca wrinkled her nose. "That's bubbly? Do you like it when people act like that?"

I wiped my mouth with my napkin. "To be honest," I said, "I can't stand her."

We ate in silence for a while, then Rebecca spoke.

"Did you go to college?"

"University of Illinois," I said. I didn't remember a moment of it, but I had absorbed enough oral history to know this fact.

"What did you study?"

"Accounting"

"But you can't even count," she said.

"I know. It's one of the things I forgot."

"Wow." The look on Rebecca's face showed that it hadn't registered that her words might have stung me. But the funny thing was, they really hadn't. I liked her candor. Hell, I seemed to like most things about her.

"So do you remember anything from college?" she asked.

I shook my head. "I only know I went there because my mother told me."

"Bob talks about college a lot. That's where we met."

"Where did you go to college?"

"SIU." When she saw me struggling with the acronym, she said, "Southern Illinois University. Not here—the Carbondale campus. My grades weren't good enough for U of I, but a party school like SIU wasn't that hard to get into."

"Party school?" I didn't know the term. Did they teach people to throw parties?

"You really don't remember much, do you? SIU is notorious for being a party school. You know, a place where the students party more than they study."

If I weren't already accustomed to feeling like an idiot several times a day, I'd have been embarrassed. Instead, I nodded, and made some brilliant remark like "Oh."

"I was a cheerleader, and Bob played football. He talks about those days a lot."

I tried to picture Rebecca as a cheerleader, and failed.

"It's weird," she said. "I remember being a cheerleader. And I think I enjoyed it. But what I don't remember is why."

"Why?" Monosyllable Boy had returned, it seemed.

"Why I liked it. This is the kind of stuff that I get worried about—the stuff I don't know how to fix. How do you change what you like and don't like? I mean, I'm supposed to like cheerleading, right?" She paused to sip her drink. "And what happens if I like something I'm not supposed to?"

Looking at Rebecca, I knew exactly what *that* felt like.

"I don't know," I said, repeating what seemed to have become my mantra.

"Anyway, Bob talks about those days all the time. I asked him why, and he said he's just trying to remind me of the past, to *help me heal.*" She drew quote marks in the air with her fingers to emphasize the phrase. "It's like he thinks talking about how I used to be will teach me how to be that way again."

Even though I reflexively hated every too-tall fiber in that man's being, I felt I had to offer some defense. "My mother does that," I said. "Shows me old photographs, tells me old stories." I shrugged. "I think she's just trying to help."

"I know Bob is trying to help, too," she said. "But I think sometimes he also likes to focus on how *he* was back then, too. He's always saying *those were the best years of my life, Becky*—you know, things like that."

"Glory days," I said.

"What?"

"I heard a song on the radio about this guy," I said, pausing to sip my iced tea while I formed my next sentence. "The best time he ever had was when he was young, so he spends all his time dwelling on that." I remember liking the sound of the drums in that song—powerful and steady.

"Yeah, well, I think Bob is doing the glory days thing, at least a little. But with him it's both of us he's remembering. It sounds like his favorite times with me were when we were back in college."

"Bruce Springsteen," I blurted.

"What?"

"I just remembered who sang that song," I said, rightfully

proud of having snatched a few more brain cells from the jaws of stroke-induced amnesia.

"Well, duh," Rebecca said, ever the diplomat.

CHAPTER 9

"Why do they call it a stroke?" Rebecca asked me one night at dinner.

I had wondered about that myself. Perhaps to find a more gentle way to talk about it in polite company? After all, *brain attack* does sound rather harsh in comparison, and *cerebrovascular accident* is such a mouthful. And it's certainly not because it's considered a stroke of *luck,* unless you're counting bad luck. Bottom line: a stroke isn't gentle, it's not lucky, and it's not something you expect to experience in your twenties.

Okay, that's what I *thought.* What I *said* was, "I don't know."

Rebecca nodded, as if I'd answered her question. Then she went back to spooling some overcooked pasta around her fork. Monday was spaghetti night in the cafeteria.

"Oh, I meant to tell you," Rebecca said, "I got the last signoff I needed this afternoon, so it's official. Thursday's the big day."

"Big day?"

"I'm leaving, Jonathan," she said quietly. "I get to go home."

My stomach lurched, probably making room for my sinking heart. Her news was made worse by the smile that accompanied it. It was the first time her smile had made me feel bad.

"Wow," I said, with characteristic eloquence. "That's great."

"I know," she said. Her eyes were shining, the way they did when she smiled. "They were thinking I'd have to be here at least two more weeks, but I've worked so hard that I'm way ahead of schedule."

"That's great," I repeated stupidly.

And I was being stupid. I mean, I'd seen the progress she had made. She still used a cane, but barely limped at all. She'd had far less to rebuild than me, so there was no way she'd be here as long as I would. Still, the idea of facing this place without her, with no other real friends . . . well, it was pretty bleak.

Perhaps reading some portion of my thoughts, she said, "It's going to be kind of weird to leave here. I had just gotten used to it, and now I have to go home. I mean, I'm excited to be going home and all, but it's still going to be kind of weird."

"Weird," I agreed.

"I really liked hanging out with you," she said, causing a flutter somewhere deep inside me. "You're easier to talk to than most people."

Yeah, I thought, with me there's never any danger of being interrupted.

"And you understand how, well, weird all this stroke stuff can be."

"Weird," I repeated, nodding. Whatever my final bill was for speech therapy, I wasn't going to pay it.

"Do you think maybe we could email each other?" she asked, leaning forward.

Seeing my confused look, she said, "Do you know what email is? Do you know how to use a computer?"

I shook my head.

"I thought accountants had to know that stuff," she said.

"They probably do."

"Oh, so you probably forgot."

"Probably."

"Wait—maybe not. I mean, email didn't really start getting big until the last few years. Maybe it happened while you were in a coma."

That put email on a long list of things I might have slept through.

"I can show you," she said. "It's not hard."

"But," I began, determined to get back to using full sentences, "I don't have a computer."

"They've got them here, for the patients to use. Haven't you seen the computer room?"

I had walked by it before—yes, I was walking now, for very short periods, and only with the aid of a walker adorned with neon yellow tennis balls on its feet. I had seen other patients using the computers in that room, but I wasn't sure what they were up to.

"I'll show you after dinner," she said. "It's easy, really."

Seeing the dubious look on my face, she said, "If a cheerleader from a party school can do email, I'm sure an accountant can."

"Ex-accountant."

"Well, I guess I'm an ex-cheerleader, too. But it really is easy—you'll see."

Rebecca smiled encouragingly. "Trust me," she said.

And I did.

In the computer room after dinner, it quickly became apparent that Rebecca's definition of *easy* had little to do with my own. Again and again she walked me through the basic tenets of computer usage. In addition to trying to grasp the incoming flood of terms and techniques, I found it fascinating to observe how she delivered that information. If she saw that one approach wasn't making sense to me, she would try another angle, looking for some way to get her point across.

"You're really good at this," I said.

"No, I'm not. I only know how to do basic stuff, like go online, read email, write a letter."

"No, I mean at showing me this stuff. At *teaching*."

"You think I'm a good teacher?" Her face registered her surprise.

"Definitely. You keep looking for new ways to get through to me." I paused to move the clicking thing she called a mouse over to the left side of the keyboard, having given up on trying to control it with my right hand. "And you never get impatient. That really helps."

Rebecca's face went serious. "I don't like it when people get impatient with me. I mean, I'm doing the best I can. And you are, too. I've seen you, and you work hard at stuff. Maybe not as hard as me, but you're not as strong as me." She stopped herself, quickly looking at me to see if she'd hurt my feelings. "Not yet, I mean. But you're a lot stronger than you were."

We'd see how strong I was come Thursday, I thought.

With Rebecca's help, we created a free email account I could access from any computer, and we sent each other a few test messages. She concluded the session by typing up a list of instructions for me to refer to when using the computer, which she printed out for me on a nearby machine.

"Now, don't lose this," she said as she handed it to me. Like I would ever let go of anything she had given me.

"Thanks," I said.

"Thank *you*," she replied, smiling.

"For what?"

"For saying I was a good teacher. Nobody ever said that to me."

"You are," I insisted. "A really great teacher."

Rebecca's smile faded to a wistful look. "I used to think about being a teacher."

"You'd be great at it."

She shook her head. "I don't have the credentials," she said. "I didn't get an education degree. I was thinking of doing that, then I just went with liberal arts. By sophomore year it was

81

pretty obvious that I was going to end up marrying Bob, and I knew he didn't want me to work. He'd want me to stay home and have babies."

"Do you have . . . babies?" I asked. She had never mentioned any kids, so this had never occurred to me.

"No," Rebecca said, shaking her head. "We tried for a long time, and I went through all kinds of tests. They never could find any reason why I couldn't have kids."

"How about Big Bob?"

Another shake of the head. "I could never get him to go through any tests. For all I know, he's the reason we can't have kids, not me. But I'm not supposed to suggest that. Even with my stroke and all, I know *that's* a subject I'm not supposed to discuss."

Not knowing what to say, I focused my gaze on the list she had given me.

Rebecca sighed. "Two people are married to each other, but still there's stuff they're not supposed to talk about. That's pretty weird, don't you think?"

Opting not to reply with "weird" yet another time, I instead said, "I think I'd want to be able to talk to my wife about anything." Riding this wave of verbal momentum, I added, "And I'd want her to feel the same way."

Rebecca nodded. "That's what I want. And I really kind of need that, since I'm not very good at *not* saying what's on my mind."

I was about to reiterate that this was one of the things I liked about her, but she went on.

"I'm going to have to work on that with Bob."

The noble thing to do would have been to wish her luck.

I re-read the list of computer instructions.

Despite any supplications I made to the vague God I occasionally addressed in a silent stream of thought that some might call prayer, Thursday finally arrived. The big day—well, for Rebecca at least.

I was preparing to go up to her room, to check and see if she'd like to have lunch with me, when she appeared in my doorway.

"Hi, Jonathan." Her smile warmed my heart for one brief moment. Then I realized that it reflected her joy about leaving.

"Hello!" I replied, mustering some false enthusiasm for the occasion. "Are we going to have one last lunch?"

Rebecca shook her head. "No, that's what I came down to tell you. Bob's picking me up at eleven, so I won't be around for lunch." Her smile faded a little. "So I wanted to come down and say goodbye."

"Oh." There was so much I wanted to say, and that's what I came up with.

"You look sad," she said.

Crap. I was smiling, but apparently not very convincingly.

"I'm going to miss you," I allowed myself to say.

"I know," she said. "I was worried that you might get lonely when I leave." Not a word about her missing me, I noted. Ouch.

"Well, you are the main person I talk to," I said.

"Likewise. That's why I'm going to miss you so much."

My heart once again mounted the pogo stick that it seemed to enjoy riding whenever Rebecca was around. Up and down, down and up. Oh well, at least my emotions were getting a good workout.

Rebecca looked at me quizzically. "You do know I'll be back in five days, right?"

"Five days?" This didn't tell me much.

"Tuesday," she said. "I'm coming back once a week for physical therapy and a check-up. The rest of the week I'll be going to an outpatient PT center that's closer to my house."

She looked concerned. "You knew that was how it works, right? You just stay here in the hospital until you don't need to be here all the time. But even when you get out, you're not done—you'll still have to go to PT, and they'll have you come back for a long time, so they can check your progress."

I did know that was in store for me, but I didn't realize it was the case for her as well.

"So I'll be here every Tuesday until they say I don't need to anymore."

"That's great," I said.

"Oh, yeah," Rebecca said. "We all know how much fun physical therapy is."

"I meant it was great because maybe you could come and say hi to me," I clarified.

"I know," she said. "And I will. Maybe we can even work it so that we can have lunch."

"That would be great."

Rebecca turned to look at the clock on my wall. "I kind of need to get going. I've still got a little packing to do before Bob gets here."

"Oh. Okay." We stood, awkward in our silence.

Rebecca finally said, "I . . . I'd like to hug you." Her matter-of-fact tone hid the awkwardness her face conveyed.

"I'd like that," I said. I turned to face her as she came around to one side of my walker.

Her arms, strong from weeks of supporting herself on her walker, clutched me in an embrace I won't soon forget. Letting go of my walker, I hugged back as best I could, not wanting the moment to end. But of course it did. I felt her grip loosen, and we pulled back from each other.

"Thank you," she said. "You helped me a lot while I was here. I like you."

Once again her no-frills style of communication went straight to my insides. Feeling a little wobbly, I sank into my wheelchair.

"I like you, too," I said, sounding like a kindergartner. Stopping myself before making any other puerile utterances, I turned away and rolled my chair over to my desk. "I've got something for you," I said, turning to face her.

Rebecca looked flustered. "You didn't get me a present, did you?"

I had wanted to. I'd scoured the hospital gift shop for nearly an hour, but had been unable to find anything appropriate. A Lincoln paperweight just didn't manage to convey what I felt.

"It's not really a present," I said. Handing her a sheet of paper, I said, "It's a poem. I wrote it on the computer, and wanted to give it to you."

"You wrote me a poem?" Her eyes widened as she reached for the page. Then she read it. Given the length of the poem, she spent an awfully long time reading it.

She looked down at me. "It doesn't rhyme."

Not exactly the reaction I was looking for, so I tried to explain.

"It's a haiku," I said. "They're very short poems, and they don't usually rhyme."

I was starting to feel embarrassed, but Rebecca seemed genuinely interested, so I went on.

"They're based on a certain number of syllables in each line. Five, then seven, then five."

Rebecca's eyes narrowed. "But you can't count."

"No," I said, "but I can hear."

I didn't know how to explain it. There's a sound to haiku—a rhythm. Among the books my mother brought me was an anthology of poetry that had a chapter devoted to haiku. I read the whole chapter aloud one day, looking for another way to practice my speech. After a while, I got a feel for the rhythm.

"I wrote this based on how it sounds," I said. "I think I got it right."

"Five, then seven, then five?" she asked.

I had memorized the sound of that phrase too, which enabled me to say, "Yes, that's the combination. Did I do it right?"

She read the poem again, concentrating hard. Then she looked up and said, "Yes." Her voice was very soft. "You did it."

"It's not very good," I said.

"It's perfect," she said, almost whispering.

I smiled, not faking it this time.

Finally Rebecca cleared her throat. "Thank you, Jonathan. This is very special."

We looked at each other a long moment. It was time, and we knew it.

"Goodbye, Rebecca."

She smiled instinctively at the sound of her full name.

"Goodbye, Jonathan." With that she turned and walked out. While I braced for the now familiar plummet of my heart, I heard her voice call softly from the hallway.

"See you Tuesday!"

This got one last bounce out of the cardiovascular pogo stick. The ascent was nice, but I dreaded the fall.

CHAPTER 10

Learning how to use email on a computer had been hard enough for me. Figuring out what to actually *say* in an email was turning out to be damn near impossible.

Dear Rebecca,
How are you? I am fine.

God, what drivel. I used the Backspace key to delete what I'd written, and tried again.

Dear Rebecca,

Did people start emails by saying *Dear such and such?* I wasn't sure. I gathered email was considered a less formal medium than letters written on actual stationery, which I believe Rebecca called *snail mail.*

Hey—
How are things?

No. I just wasn't a "hey" kind of guy. Again I held down the Backspace key, watching the letters disappear like the dots that Ms. Pac-Man ate in that coin-operated game in the vending area.

Rebecca—
Hope you're doing well.

Better, and it used her name, which I figured she would like. Oh, hell with it.

Dear Rebecca,

Yes. That was how I'd start out. I mean, if she didn't like it, I could pretty much depend on her telling me, right?

Dear Rebecca,
It's been pretty quiet since you left. As you can see, I've managed to log into the email program (is that what you call it—a program?), which I offer as proof that you are indeed a good teacher.
I hope you're having a great time. It must be great to be home.

I looked at my words, musing that it must be great to know more adjectives than *great*. Oh well, I could go back and revise this before sending it.

Let's see—what's new here? I'm getting better with my walker—I barely use my chair anymore. Your old trainer has a new patient, a young woman whom he ignores as thoroughly as he did you. And of course, Leon is eyeing her with dishonorable intentions.

I smiled, recalling Leon's leer.

"She's a fine looking woman," he pronounced when his cohort Bruce entered PT with his new charge. "But not as fine as that Rebecca chick used to come in here. Now that was one righteous lady. Even if she was kind of funny in the head."

I decided not to elaborate on Leon's assessments in my email.

I hope I'll get a chance to see you when you come for therapy on

Tuesday. I'll make every effort to make room for you in my busy social calendar.

I looked at my lame attempt at humor. Knowing Rebecca's tendency to take everything very literally, I drummed a staccato rhythm on the Backspace key once again.

If I'm not in my room, you can probably find me either in PT or the cafeteria.

I stared at the screen for a long time.

I miss you.

Was it proper to say that to a married woman? The fact that I had to ask myself that made me conclude it was not. I deleted it, and went for a lighter approach.

It'll be great to see you—it hasn't been the same since you left.

I simply had to buy a thesaurus, and see what entries I could find under *great*. But that was more like it, tone-wise. I didn't want to write anything inappropriate. Hell, for all I knew she shared her email with her husband. I hoped Big Bob wouldn't have a problem with me calling her *Dear Rebecca*.

Suddenly this whole message seemed like a bad idea. Maybe I should wait until I heard from her. Let her set the tone of our correspondence.

If she ever wrote to me, that is. She was back home, with her husband. She was Outside—that's what everybody who was stuck here called the world beyond the hospital.

She had a husband, a house, and friends.

She had a life.

Why the hell would she waste time being a pen-pal with a guy who couldn't count or tie his own shoes?

I deleted the message.

Referring to the cheat sheet Rebecca had printed out for me, I got ready to log off the computer. That's when I noticed there was a new message in my Inbox—and it was from Rebecca!

She had been writing to me at the same time I was writing to her. Knowing this sent an odd thrill up my spine.

I opened the message, which was entitled *its me*.

hi jonathan -

im home and its weird. and i dont really know why. bob is being nice. extra nice really. but thats what makes it weird. i feel like i should be nice to him since hes being so nice to me. but i cant help feeling he wishes i was like i used to be.

im trying to but its so hard. i dont want to disappoint him. but i dont know how to make myself talk different or act different or feel different.

i know i dont write so great so this is extra hard to try to say in email. but youre the only person i know who gets how weird this is. so i hope you dont mind me writing to you.

i think ill be showing up on tuesday around 2. if you dont know what that means ask Leon or somebody. but its after lunch. ill see you then ok?

sorry for the bad writing. like i said thats hard for me and i dont know why. but i hope youll write me back if your not too busy. i miss talking to you about stuff.

bye,
Rebecca

It took me several minutes, but I finally figured out how to print an email. For some reason I wanted to hold this message in my hands. To be able to take it back to my room with me, and re-read it whenever I wanted to.

I know, this was pretty pathetic. I was acting like a lovesick teenager, over a woman who liked me mostly because I knew what it was like to be brain-damaged. Christ, I was becoming a Jerry Springer guest. *Brain-damaged cheerleaders and the coma victims who have crushes on them.*

No, this was not good.

Still, I couldn't wait 'til Tuesday.

"You have a visitor," the voice on the phone said.

A visitor? Today?

Crap. I had been so sure this was Monday, not Tuesday. Although timekeeping was certainly not my forte, I thought I had been doing pretty well at keeping track of what day it was. This was all wrong—I wasn't ready. I was in my most ragged warm-up pants and a T-shirt badly stained from my earliest attempts to feed myself. I'd been saving my nicer clothes—such as they were—for Rebecca's visit tomorrow. Or was it today? Crap.

"Mr. Hooper?" The voice interrupted my self-reproach.

"Oh, I'm sorry," I said. "You can send her up."

"Um, it's a he, Mr. Hooper, not a she."

Who the hell was visiting me, if not Rebecca? My mother had already stopped by that morning, and my father never visited by himself.

"Mr. Hooper?"

"Sorry. Send *him* up, then." A brief glimmer of acuity prompted me to add, "Er, can you tell me his name?"

"Brandon Cox."

"Okay . . . thanks," I replied, then hurried to change my shirt, wondering who the hell Brandon Cox was.

I decided to meet him standing up, so I propped myself up on my walker just inside my open doorway and soon heard the sound of approaching footsteps. In a moment, a man about as tall as I imagined Big Bob to be peered into my room. But this man was big in every way, most notably in the midsection.

"Jon-Jon!" the man bellowed, holding out his right hand. I shifted my weight awkwardly on my walker to free up my right hand to shake his. His grip was warm, strong, and unpleasantly moist.

"Brandon?" I replied, retrieving my hand and finding it was now slippery when I gripped my walker.

"I knew you'd remember me," the man said. "Teddy said you'd forgotten a lot, but I told him *bullshit, he'll remember me.* Christ, look at you. You must have lost forty pounds. Damn, I need to have me a coma!" He patted his gut, sheathed in an expensive-looking suit jacket.

"Uh, you want to come in?" I asked, backing my walker up to make room for him.

"Yeah, let's see how they've got you set up here," the man said, striding past me. "Not bad, not bad. Is this all covered by insurance, or are they soaking you for it?"

"Um, insurance, I guess."

"See, I told them we were being too generous with the benefits. We've cut way back on that with new hires."

"New hires?"

"At old fistfuckers."

Nothing this man was saying made any sense to me.

Seeing my expression, he said, "Hellooooo? Fisk and Tucker. Come on, Jon-Jon—you mean you don't remember us calling it that? Christ, maybe Teddy wasn't kidding."

I was getting better at piecing together conversational clues, in an effort to spend less time looking like a moron to other people. From this brief dialog I was deducing that I had worked with this man and that he knew my brother. Then I remembered the name—the first name, at least. Teddy had mentioned a

Brandon who had helped him get started at my old firm. This must be—

"Yo, Jon-Jon. Anybody home in there?" The man was waving a hand in front of my face, jarring loose a memory of nurses and doctors doing the same when I first woke up.

"Sorry," I said. I pointed to the lone chair in the room. "Please, have a seat."

As the man lowered his bulk into the chair, I seated myself on the edge of my bed and contemplated my guest. Everything about him was big—his head, his hands; even his teeth, bared in a phony-looking smile.

"Long time no see, eh, Jon-Jon?"

"At least six years," I said, feeling pretty confident I wasn't wrong.

"Six years. Jesus. What was that like? I mean, did you dream?"

The question caught me off guard. I dreamed most every night, but could never quite remember what I dreamed. I wondered if I had six years of dreams stored up somewhere in my mind. Probably behind one of the locked doors.

"No," I said. "It was like I was just switched off during that time." That was as apt a way as I'd found to describe what I'd been through.

Brandon frowned. "And now that you're switched back on, I hear there's some stuff you don't remember."

Immediately I suspected Teddy had briefed this man on my "math issues."

"Yeah, I've got some rough patches in my memory," I said, pleased with my own gift for understatement. "But it's all coming back." I was puzzled by my apparent ability to glibly lie to people I instinctively didn't trust. While it might be a handy survival skill, I wondered where it came from. Was lying one of my skills in my previous life? Or was this some new twist, like my left-handedness?

"Man, I'm glad to hear that," Brandon said. "You and I have some history together, Jon-Jon, and I was worried that you might have forgotten it."

He didn't seem to realize that I didn't remember him, so I chose not to clue him in.

"A lot of it is still pretty foggy," I said.

"Yeah, well, six years in a coma—that's gotta throw a wrench into the works." He ran a hand through his thick, dark hair, revealing a ring on his right pinky. What was it with men from Fisk and Tucker all wearing pinky rings?

Brandon leaned forward in his chair. "Listen, Jon-Jon. I need to know if you remember our, uh, *working relationship.*"

I noticed that he was starting to sweat, but it wasn't at all warm in my room. I tried to remember if Teddy had told me anything more about this guy, but came up with nothing. I decided to take a shot at some improvisation.

"Well," I said, "I haven't forgotten who was the boss, if that's what you're wondering." I wasn't sure where I was going with this, but hoped it would prompt him to reveal some more information. And I was again surprised at how easy I found it to lie.

Brandon shifted uncomfortably. "I'm not talking about you working for me," he said, answering that question for me. "I'm talking about the little, uh, *arrangement* we had on the side. Just you and me." He gave me a little wink that made my skin crawl.

Then I got it. My God—did I used to be gay?

Wait a minute. I had a girlfriend, right? I fought to maintain my composure, and opened my mouth, hoping my newfound gift for spontaneous bullshit wouldn't fail me.

"Just to make sure we're on the same page," I said, not sure where that cliché had come from, "why don't you give me *your* take on that *arrangement* we had." My next step was going to be to confess that I didn't remember him at all, but I wanted to get to the bottom of whatever involvement I'd had with this creepy character.

Brandon looked around the room uneasily. "Mind if I close the door?"

Most of us in this wing left our doors open during the day, a habit I'd fallen into. I gestured towards the door. "Go ahead."

With a grunt Brandon heaved himself out of his chair and lumbered over to the door. He went so far as to poke his head outside the doorway, scanning the hallway for would-be eavesdroppers. Then he closed the door and returned to his chair, where he arranged himself at great length before speaking. His forehead was now shiny with sweat.

A single thought pulsed repeatedly through my head: Please don't be my former lover. Please don't be my former lover. Please don't . . .

Again Brandon surveyed the room, focusing primarily on the ceiling. "They don't have any microphones or cameras in here, do they? You know, to monitor your health or whatever?"

"No. I've got a call button by the bed, but that's it."

"Okay, good." Brandon pulled a handkerchief out of his coat pocket and mopped his forehead.

"A lot has changed at the firm," he began, reinforcing what Teddy had told me. "Hell, a lot has changed in the accounting business, what with Enron, WorldCom, and all those other idiots who were dumb enough to get caught."

This was the second time I'd heard these company names. I made a mental note to do some searching on the Internet about them, to see what all the fuss was about.

"But that was all while you were in a coma," he said. "Back when you were at the firm, things were different. We had a lot more freedom, without all the scrutiny. It gave us more, you know, *artistic license* with how we handled our clients."

"Artistic license?" I asked. "In accounting?"

Brandon laughed. "Well, maybe you never thought of it in those terms, but I've got to tell you, you were a real artist with some of the schemes you came up with."

"I never thought of myself as an artist," I said honestly.

"Well, I did. I'd round up the right kind of clients—you know, people who knew how to play our kind of ball—and then you'd work your magic with all the details. I swear, you could make your computer stand up and do tricks, and when it came to SEC regulations, you could smell a loophole a mile away. Man, we pulled some sweet scams, you and me—it was a match made in heaven."

Great. So I wasn't his lover—I was his *accomplice?*

"Things were just starting to get good," Brandon said, "and then you went and had a stroke."

"Sorry about that," I said. "That screwed up a few things for me, too."

Brandon went on, my sarcasm leaving him unfazed. "It sure as hell screwed up *our* operation, that's for sure. Like I said, I was the people person. You were the brains." He laughed bitterly. "And now you've got brain damage—ain't that a kick in the balls?"

Wow—even Leon wasn't that direct with me.

Brandon lowered his voice, finally getting to the point. "So what I need to know is where's the money?"

"The money?"

"The money we scammed, Jon-Jon! We had just gotten things moving when you went all Terri Schiavo on me. I brokered the deals, but you handled the mechanics. So you had all the money."

Brandon glared at me, his voice dropping an octave. "And half of it is mine."

CHAPTER 11

This had gone far enough.

"Brandon," I said, "I have to tell you—I have no idea what you're talking about."

I guess I was expecting him to register some surprise. Instead, his eyes narrowed.

"Well, isn't that convenient?" he said.

"Convenient?"

"This was just what I was worried you might do. Play the coma card."

"Coma card?" I stammered, apparently unable to do anything but repeat his words.

"Yeah. Pretty fucking convenient. You've got the money, you have a coma, and *voila*—you just can't seem to remember where that money is." Brandon shook his head. "I can't believe you'd pull this on me, after all I did for you."

"I'm not pulling anything," I protested. "I don't remember anything about any money."

Aware that I was becoming a bit shrill, I softened my voice. "Brandon, I have major memory loss. *Major.* I barely remember anything. Or anybody."

"Yeah, but you remembered me," he said, his face growing red as he spoke. I realized then that my earlier tactic of trying to conceal my memory loss was backfiring.

"Well, no—not really," I said. "Teddy mentioned you, but other than that, I really don't remember you."

"This is bullshit!" Brandon was out of his chair now. For a moment I thought he was going to hit me, but instead he began pacing back and forth on the small stretch of open floor.

He stopped, pointing at me. "So you expect me to believe you don't remember a fucking thing from our past?"

"It's the truth," I said, offering a lame shrug.

Brandon lowered his voice—and his finger—attempting a calmer approach. "Look, Jon-Jon. I can understand not wanting to admit to anything, particularly with what's been going on in our line of work recently. But this is you and me talking. We've been through a lot together. I'm not asking you to confess your sins to the world."

He edged closer to me. "I'm asking you where you put the fucking money. Before you took your little siesta, we should have racked up around three hundred K, maybe even four hundred. So I figure you owe me at least a hundred and fifty K."

I saw that straight denial was getting me nowhere with the man, and his tone suggested that these were large numbers. So I looked for a way to stall.

"Brandon, I'm sorry. I do have brain damage, and I've suffered a lot of memory loss. But it's coming back, bit by bit."

This seemed to encourage Brandon, who took a slightly more relaxed stance in front of me.

"It's just taking me a while to get my brain back together. I mean, remember, I was 'switched off' for a long time. I need to . . . recharge my batteries."

I saw this was going over fairly well, and once again noted how I seemed able to speak much more eloquently when I was trying to deceive or manipulate somebody. But as I gained more awareness of what sort of man I'd been, this was starting to make sense.

"So, how long until you're fully recharged?" Brandon said.

I gave another one of my trademark shrugs. "Nobody knows. Hell, nobody's even figured out why I'm even awake. They say it's a medical miracle." I know, I was pushing it, but they *did* say that, after all.

Brandon smiled bitterly. "That's great, miracle boy. But how much *do* you remember?"

I pondered this. I didn't think I wanted this man to be aware of the full extent of my problems—it seemed like that could make me more vulnerable, although I wasn't sure just how. So once again, I let the falsehoods fly, marveling at how easily they flowed from my lips.

"I remember the basic stuff," I began. "Who I am, my family, my girlfriend. Well, my ex-girlfriend."

Brandon cringed. "Yeah, I wondered about that—that's gotta be awkward as hell."

"You knew Victoria left me?"

Brandon gave me an odd look and tugged uncomfortably at his collar. "Yeah," he said, "I think maybe Teddy mentioned something about that to me."

"She moved on," I said. "And I really can't blame her. I guess she has some new boyfriend now."

"Yeah, that's what I hear." He was still staring at me. "You seem to be taking it well."

Again I shrugged. "What can I do?"

Brandon stared at me a moment longer, then sank heavily into the chair. "How about work? What do you remember from Fisk and Tucker?"

"That part's really foggy."

His eyes narrowed. "You said that already. How foggy are we talking?"

I tried to lighten things up a bit. "Let's just say O'Hare is still totally fogged in," I said, pulling a phrase out of God knows where. I'd probably heard it on a TV weather report. Slang, cliché, metaphor—all of it was right there, as long as I was lying. But trying to say something halfway intelligent to Rebecca in words that contained more than a syllable was still a major effort. The way my brain worked really worried me.

"But the fog is going to clear up, right?" Brandon said, again leaning forward.

"It's clearing," I said, "slowly but surely." Well, the slowly part was accurate, at least. "But there are still a lot of patches of fog." At this point I reflected that I had probably wrung as much mileage as I could from my fog metaphor.

Brandon said, "Speaking of O'Hare, is all your stuff still up in Chicago?"

"What stuff?"

"The stuff you owned when you lived there. Your car, your clothes, your furniture."

"Oh. My mother said it's all in storage. I haven't seen any of it yet."

"Down here or up there?"

"I don't understand."

"Your stuff—is it down here in Springfield, or up in Chicago?"

"Chicago," I said. A month or so into my coma—back when there was still some hope that I would recover—my parents had decided to pack up and store all my belongings in Chicago, thinking it would make it easier for me to get back to my life up there. So much for that plan.

Brandon's face brightened. "Well, maybe I could look through your stuff when I go back home. You know, to see if there's any sign of where you put the money. Maybe you wrote something down. I mean, you probably stuck the money in a safe deposit box or something, right?"

I didn't know. But what I did know was that there was no way I'd let this guy look through my belongings unsupervised.

"Actually," I said, "the first thing I'm going to do when they let me out of here is go check on my storage space. If you want, I can let you know, and we can go there together." This was not going to happen, at least not on my first trip to the warehouse. But it seemed to placate him.

"Yeah, well, I guess that would be okay," Brandon allowed. "Any idea how soon that will happen?"

I shook my head. "I don't know yet. I'm hoping to get out of here in a few weeks, but it may be a while before I'm ready to make the trip to Chicago."

"But you'll let me know when you do, right?"

"Definitely," I lied. "Make sure you give me your number before you go."

After Brandon left, I closed the door and sat back down on my bed, replaying the conversation. His visit had chipped away more of the stone in which my past life was encased. But the fossil that was being unearthed was beginning to frighten me.

I'd had my suspicions, to be sure. But now I was finding out that not only was I a jerk; I was a thief. A crook. Some kind of embezzler or something. I needed to look up the names and terms Brandon had used, to find out just what sort of trouble I'd been getting myself into. But it didn't look good.

Who else knew about this?

I couldn't ask Teddy—if he had known about it, I didn't want to expose how little I remembered. And if he hadn't, I didn't want to give him any new artillery to use against me.

Maybe Victoria knew, but I couldn't see any graceful way to ask her. *Hi, Vic. Yes, your boobs look great. Hey, listen, back when we were dating, was I by any chance, you know, stealing money?* No, probably not the smoothest approach.

My God—could I be arrested? For a crime I couldn't remember committing? Was there some kind of statute of limitations for this sort of thing? If so, I prayed it was less than six years. I could see the headline now: *Man Wakes from Coma Only to Go to Prison.*

No, this didn't look good.

I went to the PT room, and worked out my frustrations on the leg press machine. I was eager to show Rebecca how much my walking had improved over the last few days. Thinking about her raised my spirits somewhat, and I was feeling better when I finished my workout.

The feeling was short-lived. After a shower, I went to the computer room to find out what this Enron stuff was all about. And of course, to check for email from Rebecca. I struck out on the latter, but found plenty of information on the former. Soon I was even more freaked out.

Apparently during my six-year nap, the accounting world had gone crazy, with accountants, auditors, and corporate executives colluding with each other, playing all sorts of games with other people's money. I couldn't understand the more technical descriptions of their malfeasance, but one thing was clear: some key people in my line of work had let their greed take over, and had violated the trust their profession had historically been afforded.

And they had done it at the expense of people helpless to stop them, burning up their pensions and investments and leaving them with nothing. Some of the worst offenders had been sent to jail, but that didn't really solve their victims' problems, did it? I was appalled, unable to imagine what kind of person could do something like that.

Then I looked in the mirror, and saw the answer.

CHAPTER 12

It was Tuesday, and I felt like crap. I hadn't slept well, troubled by recurring dreams of police officers raiding my room and leading me off handcuffed to my walker. It figures that the first time I actually had dreams I could remember, they were nightmares.

At breakfast I nibbled half-heartedly at my *I Can't Believe They're Not Eggs* and doubled up on my coffee dosage. Then I put in a hard morning of physical therapy under the watchful eye—and colorful commentary—of Leon. Still, even after a shower and a hot lunch (Tuesday was Sloppy Joe day), the man who faced me in the mirror looked haggard and guilty.

I sat down on my bed, killing time by idly flipping through one of the photo albums my mother had brought. By now the faces in the photos were familiar to me, but the people behind them remained a mystery.

"Anybody home?" a low-pitched female voice said.

Startled, I opened my eyes and realized I was lying on my bed. I sat up awkwardly, adjusting my glasses and looking around for the source of that voice. Rebecca stood in the doorway.

"Sorry if I kept you waiting," she said.

I shook my head and blinked, still groggy. "No, I'm sorry," I said, "I must have dozed off. I didn't get much sleep last night."

Rebecca walked into the room, her cane tapping on the linoleum floor. "Yeah, you look pretty tired."

103

Great. I wait for days to see her, and when she finally shows up, I look like death warmed over. Then again, in many respects I really *was* death warmed over.

"How are you?" I asked, trying to at least rise to my usual level of conversational ineptitude.

"I'm good," she said. "Bruce wasn't here, so instead I did my PT with Lucinda. Have you ever worked with her before?"

"No, I've only worked with Leon. Is it just me, or does Lucinda look like she could bench-press Leon?"

Rebecca smiled. "I think you're right," she said, "but she was actually really good to work with. I may try to set my schedule so I get her every week, instead of Bruce."

"That will give Bruce more time to watch sports on TV," I said.

"So it's win-win," she said. "Listen to me—I'm sounding like Big Bob. He's always talking saying things like *win-win, big picture, think outside the box.* You know, stuff like that."

"Outside the box?" I asked.

"That's probably one you slept through," Rebecca said. "Every year there are more buzzwords and clichés."

Realizing she was still standing over me, I said, "Please—have a seat." I gestured towards my chair.

"Actually, I'm dying for a soda. Want to go down to the cafeteria?"

"Sure," I said, although I'd been hoping to have a more private visit with her. Forcing a smile, I said, "It will give me a chance to show off my formidable skills with a walker."

Rebecca stepped back, making room for me. "As Lucinda says, *show me what you've got.*"

Armed respectively with cane and walker, Rebecca and I made our way down to the cafeteria. Midway between meals, it was virtually empty, affording us more privacy than I'd expected. We seated ourselves across from each other at a table in the far corner of the room, she with a diet cola, and I with a light brown flavorless drink that a chrome-plated dispenser claimed was iced tea.

Rebecca had seemed fairly cheerful when she showed up, but now was looking more serious, so I tried to set a light tone.

"So, it must be great to finally be home," I offered.

She took a moment to respond, considering her words. "I guess so. I mean, I'm glad to not be in a hospital anymore. And I'm feeling a lot better. But it's still pretty weird."

"You said that in your email," I said. "Do you mean it's weird to not be here anymore?" I know for me the concept of leaving here was a very strange one—it was the only home I had known.

"No, that's not it," she said. "I was definitely ready to get out of here. But what's weird is, well, going home." She hesitated. "Home to Bob. To my life."

I wasn't sure how to answer, so I didn't.

"I don't know how to explain it," she said. "I mean, he's really working hard to be nice to me. Maybe he's working too hard—I don't know. He keeps on bringing friends around and dragging me all over town, to all the places we used to go. It's like he wants to remind me of who I used to be."

"Well, in my case," I said, "I need a lot of reminding."

"That's just it," she said. "In your case, that's true. You've forgotten a bunch of stuff, so you need people to remind you."

She leaned forward, her voice simultaneously more soft and more serious. "That's what Big Bob doesn't seem to get. He keeps trying to remind me of stuff, but I haven't forgotten anything, not like you have. I remember him. I remember all our friends, all the people from church."

She paused again, choosing her words. "What I don't remember is . . . is why I felt the way I did about some of them."

While I tried to process this bombshell, she went on.

"I mean, maybe it's because I've talked so much about you

and how you lost so much of your memory. Maybe that's why Bob thinks I've lost mine, too."

"You talk about me to Big Bob?" I asked, unable to contain my surprise.

"Well, yeah—of course," she said. "You're my friend, and one of the people who helped me the most while I was here. Plus, the stuff that happened to you is pretty weird, so it's interesting to talk about."

Once again her lack of diplomatic filters had come shining through, but again, I wasn't offended. Her candor continued to refresh me. And perhaps some not terribly noble part of me was simply glad to learn she had been thinking about me.

"But it's different for you than for me," she said. "I know I've changed, but it was my personality that changed—my feelings. But I didn't lose my memory. For you, it's the opposite. You did lose your memory, but you didn't change as a person."

"I kind of hope I did," I said.

"What do you mean?"

"I'm starting to get the impression that I wasn't a very nice guy. You know, before my stroke."

"Why would you think that?"

I decided not to get into it right now.

"Never mind," I said, "let's talk about you. You keep talking like you're not as good a person as you used to be. But you're smart, you're logical, you work really hard, and you help people—at least, you helped me."

This was one of my lengthier remarks, but I was getting more and more control of my speech these days. The trick was to talk very slowly. That gave me time to think and also to concentrate on not slurring my words. When I was either too tired or in too much of a hurry, my L's still got pretty mushy.

I went on. "I mean, sure, sometimes you're not the most diplomatic person. But is that really such a big deal? Is that all this boils down to?"

Now Rebecca shook her head. "I wish that was all it was. You've only seen this side of me."

"I like this side of you," I said before I could stop myself.

She didn't smile, but her face softened perceptibly.

"Thank you, Jonathan. I like you, too. And I appreciate that. And no, it's not like I got meaner, or stupider—although sometimes I say stupid things. It's just that I don't act the way I used to."

"Bubbly?" I said.

"Yes. I was bubbly. I was really outgoing. I'd wear all these really stylish clothes. And I put a lot of time into my appearance. I'm talking a *lot* of time."

I wanted to tell her how beautiful I thought she was, even right now. Even with her hair pulled back in a messy ponytail. Even in her t-shirt and sweatpants. But I didn't want to focus on her looks. Instead, I said, "Well, is it that you were such a different person, or that you just had a different, I don't know, *style?*"

She thought about this. "Maybe a part of it is style," she said. "But I get the impression my style was one of the main things people liked about me."

I knew there was possibly some truth in that. Already I had absorbed enough—on TV and around the hospital—to realize that many men seemed to care only for a woman's beauty, not her personality. I found myself susceptible to both.

"I like your style just fine," I said. Appropriateness be damned—this woman needed to hear it from somebody if she wasn't hearing it at home.

"Thanks," she said. "But it's more than how I look. It's how I *feel* about things, too. That's probably the biggest change in me. And I bet it's what's making me act different."

Rebecca looked across the room, towards the kitchen. "Do

you like orange sherbet?" she asked abruptly.

"Pardon?"

"The orange sherbet they serve here—have you ever had it?"

"Yeah, I guess so," I said. "Want me to see if they have any in the freezer?"

"No," she said, shaking her head. "I'm trying to explain something. Did you like that sherbet?"

"No, not particularly."

"Me neither." She leaned forward, her voice growing more insistent. "Now imagine everybody telling you that you used to just *love* that orange sherbet. And that it's really important that you start loving it again."

I tried to imagine this, still baffled by the path this conversation was taking.

"That's what my life is like right now. I don't like orange sherbet, but I used to. And now everybody wants me to like it again, and tells me that if I don't, I'm just not the person I used to be. And not the kind of person they want to be with."

Again I marveled at her ability to explain concepts. She really would have been a great teacher.

"That's what I wanted to tell you when I emailed, but I couldn't find the words."

"You just found them," I said. "I understand."

"Great," she said, easing back in her seat. "But what am I supposed to do about it?"

I had no answer.

Rebecca said, "For now, I'm going with what seems to be the most popular approach."

"What's that?"

"Keep trying the orange sherbet, and hope I start liking it."

She gave me a hard look. "How much luck do you think I'm going to have with that?"

Before I could reply, a voice called out, interrupting.

"There you are—I was looking all over the wing for you!"

We turned to see Lucinda striding towards our table. She was an attractive woman, given the fact that she looked like she could play linebacker for the Bears.

"Hi, Lucinda," Rebecca said, smiling. "Do you know Jonathan?"

Lucinda eyed me coolly. "You work with Leon, right?"

I nodded, glad she wasn't offering to shake my hand. I'd be worried about ever being able to use that hand again.

"Don't you be paying no attention to Leon," she said. "Boy has a dirty mind." With that she turned to Rebecca. "Honey, your ride is here."

Rebecca glanced at her watch and grimaced. "Wow, I really lost track of time. Thanks, Lucinda—I'll be right out."

Lucinda swiveled and walked away, her gait both appealing and frightening to observe. She was a lot of woman.

Rebecca shrugged apologetically. "I've got to go," she said, standing up. "Big Bob is here."

"Oh, okay," I said, not wanting the conversation to end.

As if reading my thoughts, Rebecca said, "We'll talk more about this next week." She looked again at her watch. "Big Bob goes nuts if he has to wait."

Giving me one last smile, she said, "It was nice getting to talk to you. Want to do this again next Tuesday?"

"Okay," I repeated stupidly.

"Okay," she said, and turned to make her way between the tables towards the exit. She called softly over her shoulder, "Don't forget to email me." Then she was gone, leaving only the rhythmic echo of her cane tapping down the hallway that would take her back to Big Bob.

I took a final sip of my iced tea, pushed back my chair, and pulled myself up on my walker. Then I began the long, lonely walk to my room.

Rounding a bend in the hallway on the way to the elevators, I encountered Mr. Samuels, being wheeled towards me by a burly orderly whom I didn't recognize. The old man's eyes brightened at the sight of me, and he laboriously lifted one shaky hand off his armrest in an abbreviated wave.

"Hi, Mr. Samuels," I said.

"Ah, banjo poodle," he replied agreeably. Then with a knowing nod he added, "Salami."

On a whim, I said, "On rye, with provolone?"

Even with his partially frozen face, the change in his expression was clear. His eyes narrowed, then he shook his head in disdain and muttered "pelican," in exactly the tone one might use when calling somebody an *idiot*.

The orderly shot me a look that suggested he shared Mr. Samuels's opinion, then wheeled his elderly charge past me. I made the rest of the trip back to my room in silence.

CHAPTER 13

Rebecca emailed me several times during the week that followed. One night we actually had something like a real-time conversation, both being logged onto our computers at the same time, one of us emailing the other then waiting several minutes for the other to respond. But we weren't really talking about much of anything—she continued to be frustrated by her inability to put her thoughts into writing.

I on the other hand was much more comfortable expressing myself in writing, but that skill ended up backfiring on me. After one of my more eloquent messages to her, she wrote back:

see this is why I feel so stupid. you just said a bunch of stuff i totally agree with and said it really well but i cant come up with anything better than saying 'me too' when i try to agree with you. even though the stuff you said is really really true. some teacher i would be. i cant even write.

Cursing myself, I wrote a heartfelt (but very simply worded) apology, and suggested maybe she might prefer to talk on the phone, something I'm surprised hadn't occurred to either of us. I gave her the phone number for my hospital room, logged off the computer, and went back to my room, waiting for the phone to ring.

She didn't call. And I received no more emails from her that week.

Again and again I drafted email entreaties to her, only to

delete them, wary of either being inappropriate, or worse, driving away the only person I considered a friend.

It was a long week, even for a man who couldn't count the days.

When Tuesday finally arrived, I dressed for the occasion in my finest warm-up pants and T-shirt, reflecting that a shopping trip was definitely in order as soon as I got Outside.

Shortly after lunch, my phone rang.

"Hi, it's me," said Rebecca when I answered. "I changed my time so that I could get Lucinda again. We just finished, and I need to cool off. Want to meet me in the cafeteria?"

"Sure," I said. "I'll be right down."

Rebecca was seated at the table where we'd sat during her last visit, with a styrofoam cup in her hand and another placed across the table from her. She gave a small smile when she saw me.

"Hi, Jonathan," she said as I approached. "I went ahead and got our drinks. You like the iced tea, right?"

Although I'd sworn off the vile brown stuff after our last meeting, I smiled and said, "That's fine—thanks."

I stationed my walker next to the table and eased into a chair across from her.

"You're walking better," she said.

"Thanks. How did your PT go?"

"Really really good," Rebecca said. "Lucinda thinks I'm ready to lose the cane."

"Really? That's terrific."

"Want to see?" Rebecca said, rising from the table but leaving her cane leaning against the table's edge. She proceeded to walk down the aisle along the table, with no additional support. Although she still had a slight limp, there was a distinctly feminine sway to her walk that I'd never seen before, which tugged at me in a primal and not altogether honorable way.

Turning around, she spread her hands proudly. "Well? What do you think?"

"You look . . . great," was all I could manage. This won me a smile, which, compounded with the walk I had just witnessed, threatened to reduce me to a quivering mass of . . . I don't know, something that quivers. Christ, this woman—this *married* woman—rendered me speechless. Not good.

"Thanks," she said, sitting back down. "It feels so good to just *walk*, you know?"

"I can only imagine," I said honestly.

She frowned. "Did I do it again—did I say something stupid? Was I not supposed to talk about my walking since you can't walk yet?"

"No, no—it's fine," I protested. "You don't ever need to worry about what you say around me. Not ever."

Rebecca sank back in her chair. "God, do you know how nice that is?" she said with a sigh. "When I'm with Big Bob, I always have to be *so* careful what I say. And no matter how hard I try, I always seem to say something stupid."

"I'm sure that's not true."

"Tell Big Bob that," she said.

I suddenly wanted to tell Big Bob that and much more. Perhaps with a baseball bat.

Instead, I said, "Listen, I'm sorry about that email I sent you. I never heard back from you, so I feel like *I'm* the one who must have said something stupid."

Rebecca leaned forward. "No, that's not it at all. That was really sweet when you apologized, even though you had nothing to apologize for. You write really well. I only wish I could, too."

"But I never heard from you."

"Yeah, Big Bob came in and asked what I was doing. I told him I was writing to you, and he said *Why are you wasting time talking to Coma Boy? You should be hanging around people whose brains actually work.* Then we got into a whole big thing."

"Coma Boy?" I asked.

She must have read my face. "God, Jonathan, I'm sorry. I shouldn't have said that to you. He just really made me mad when he said that stuff." She paused. "You know *I* don't call you that, don't you? I mean, even after my stroke I know not to be a complete jerk."

This got a grudging laugh out of me.

"Anyway," she said, "he knows more about computers than me, and I started thinking he might just try to go in and read my emails, so that made me not want to write any more. I mean, it's not like we're writing about stuff I want to hide from him— you're just my friend, and he knows it. But I still don't like the idea of somebody snooping through what I write, so I stopped."

I sat silently, taking it in. Trying not to blush from the humili-ation of his assessment of me, and stinging from being called just a friend. That was stupid, I know. I *was* just a friend—that's all I could ever be. So why did it hurt so much to be called that?

"A whole big thing?" I repeated. "You mean you argued about it?"

"Bigtime," she said. "It went on for hours. I was trying to make him understand how much it helps to have somebody to talk to who has gone through something similar. Somebody who *gets* me, you know?"

She shook her head. "He just kept saying that if I wanted to get healthy—to *get right in the head,* as he likes to call it—I need to hang around healthy people."

"Not people like Coma Boy," I said bitterly.

"Jonathan, I'm really sorry I said that."

"You didn't," I said. "He did."

Rebecca shrugged. "He can be kind of a jerk sometimes."

When I didn't respond, she flushed and said, "Look at me—

I'm doing it again. I shouldn't talk that way about my husband. God, Jonathan, do you have any idea how hard it is to always be worried about saying the wrong thing?"

I smiled feebly. "Actually, I think I do. In your case, you may not know certain unspoken diplomatic rules. In mine, I just don't know much about anything or anybody."

"Boy, we're a pair, aren't we?" Rebecca said.

God, I wish we were, I thought.

Trying to steer the conversation back on course, I said, "So, Project Orange Sherbet is hitting some speed bumps."

"Yeah," she said, smiling grimly at the reference. "And that isn't even the worst of it."

"How do you mean?"

Rebecca's face grew more serious. "Things got really messed up when we started having sex," she said, looking directly at me.

I willed myself not to react. Yes, this was jarring and unexpected, but I'd just finished telling her how she never needed to worry about what she said to me. I mean, wasn't that what true friendship was about?

"What happened?" I asked as calmly as I could.

"We started having sex," she said simply. "I mean, he's my husband, and we sleep in the same bed, and my body is healthy enough for it. And he's waited for weeks now, so it seemed like it was what I was supposed to do."

It was the most loveless description of two partners coupling that I'd ever heard. Not sure how to proceed, I said, "And there were problems?"

"It felt so weird," she said. "I mean, physically it felt okay. Everything still works, and all. But as far as what I felt for him—that was all weird."

She stared at me. "And he could tell," she said. "I wasn't responding to him like I used to, and that made him upset. The first time, we ended up just stopping."

"How about the next time?" I asked, the question piercing me like a sword.

"The next time was better," she said. "At least for him."

"Not for you?" I was unable to avoid asking. This conversation was awful to endure, but seemed to provide a necessary release for her. And I wanted desperately to live up to the reality of being her friend, despite her inclination for bluntness. I'd said repeatedly that her honesty was one of the things I liked about her; it was time for me to walk the walk. Even if I needed a walker.

"No, it was still just as weird for me. I just think I hid it. And I think he was too busy enjoying himself to notice. Afterwards he was all sweet and reassuring, saying stuff like *That's more like it, baby—see? We've still got it.*" She had a way of changing her voice when she quoted Big Bob that made me hate the man even more, something I'd thought was impossible.

I remained silent, at a loss for words.

Rebecca wasn't finished. "But the last time was the worst." A tear broke free and began to work its way down her cheek.

"What happened?" I said, putting my hands under the table to hide my clenched fists.

"Things were going okay," she said. "I was still feeling weird, but I was trying to be, you know, enthusiastic. And he seemed to be enjoying it."

She stopped, looking down.

"But then he wanted me to do something. Something I didn't want to do."

Rebecca looked back up, her eyes locking with mine. "He said he wanted to put it in my ass. But I didn't want him to."

"Did you tell him?" I said, aware that my head seem to have suddenly become pressurized. I prayed I wasn't about to have another stroke.

"Of course I did," she said.

"Did he . . . did he force you?"

"No, he wouldn't do that," she said, shaking her head. A second tear began tracking downward. "It's not like he raped me or anything."

I felt my muscles loosen a bit.

"But what he did was almost as bad."

Trying to remain calm, I whispered, "What did he do?"

Rebecca shuddered. "He started talking to me. Pleading with me. Telling me how I always used to love that."

Rebecca leaned forward, her hands on the table. "Jonathan, he was lying to me. He was telling me things that weren't true. Things I never did. It's like he honestly believes I don't remember how I used to be."

She choked back a quick sob, and sniffled violently. "Jonathan, I lost my personality, not my memory. He tried to lie to me—to take advantage of my brain damage—to get me to do something I never wanted to do."

At this point my poker face must have failed me, because she drew back, her face stricken with horror.

"Oh, God. Oh, God. I can't talk to you about this, can I? I can't talk about this to anybody!" She buried her face in her hands, sobbing.

"No, no," I said, reaching across the table to touch her arm. "You *can* talk to me. About this. About *anything.*"

Rebecca lowered her hands, revealing eyes already bloodshot.

"But I've upset you—I can see it on your face."

"You didn't upset me," I insisted. "*He* did. I want to strangle the bastard."

I immediately regretted my words. Now it was my turn to be horrified. "God, Rebecca, I'm sorry. I have no right to talk that way." I stopped before I said anything worse.

Then I realized she had placed her hand on mine.

"It's okay, Jonathan. I wanted to strangle him, too. I mean, it's one thing to have some problems communicating. It's something else to lie to somebody to get sex."

"So what happened?" I asked, dreading the answer.

"I threw him out of bed," she said, with a simplicity that made me want to hug her. "I told him what I just told you—that just because my personality may be messed up, it doesn't mean that my memory is."

"What did he say?"

"I think he was embarrassed to get busted like that. He took his pillow and went off to the couch in the living room. And the next day he was all apologetic and bought me flowers."

Trying to be supportive and hating it, I said, "So is everything back to normal?"

Rebecca gave me a look that was hard to read. It wasn't a smile, but it wasn't a frown. "He's still on the couch," she said, with a look that let me know this portion of the conversation was over.

I was keenly aware of her hand still being on mine.

"Jonathan," she said, "If you're really my friend, will you do me a favor?"

"Of course," I said, finding my voice choked.

Her eyes remained locked on mine, unwavering. "Don't ever lie to me. Not ever."

"I won't," I said, and I meant it. "I promise."

Our conversation lightened up after that, but all too soon it was time for her to go.

"I'll walk you back to your room," she said. "I want to practice without the cane."

"Sounds like a plan," I said. We arranged her cane on top of my walker and headed up to my room. She moved faster than me, but I didn't mind: watching her walk was a newfound pleasure.

Once we got to my room, I lifted the cane off my walker, handing it to Rebecca. She gripped it absently, her eyes on the open photo album on my desk.

"I've seen this guy before," she said.

Surprised, I moved beside her to take a look. She was pointing at a picture of Teddy.

"Are you sure about that?" I said. "He lives up in Chicago. That's my brother."

"Is he the one who calls you bro?"

I smiled at the sharpness of her memory. "That's the one."

Rebecca furrowed her brow. "I haven't been to Chicago in a few years." Then she pointed a finger at the photo. "Wait a minute—he's been here, hasn't he?"

"You're right," I said. "Shortly after I got here, he came and visited me once. It was before I met you."

"That's it," she agreed. "I remember seeing him in the lobby one time when I was down there saying goodbye to Big Bob. He was with his girlfriend—I remember she was really pretty."

Now I frowned. "You may have the wrong guy—Teddy came to see me by himself."

Rebecca continued to stare at the photo. "No, it's him. I remember his girlfriend stayed behind in the lobby while he went off somewhere. Bob kept staring at her."

"That's possible," I said. "It was his first time visiting me, so maybe he didn't want to overwhelm me. I'd only been awake for a few days back then."

Come to think of it, Teddy had never visited me since then. But I couldn't really complain about that fact.

"Well, that's one thing about me that hasn't changed," Rebecca said. "I never forget a face."

"Wish I could say that," I said, following the remark with a smile so that Rebecca wouldn't worry about possibly offending me. She got enough of that at home.

"I've got to go," Rebecca said, looking at her watch. "But I'll see you next week, okay?"

"Sounds good," I said. "Oh, I forgot to tell you—my big day is coming up soon, too."

Rebecca's face brightened. "Really? You're getting out of here? When?"

"If I keep up my progress, it should be in the next week or so," I said. "Then I'll move into my parents' house for a while at least, until I figure out what I'm going to do next."

"That's great news, Jonathan. Will you still be coming here for PT?"

"Oh, yeah," I said. "Probably more than you are—they're saying it may be three or four times a week. And if I'm not mistaken, that means a lot, right?"

Rebecca smiled. "Yes, it's a lot. But finally you'll get to go home, after all these years. God, you must be so excited."

It occurred to me that Rebecca had no idea how little I knew about the home to which I'd be returning. I needed to figure out how much I should tell her. Then I thought of the promise I'd just made.

"Yeah, it's pretty exciting," I said, "and more than a little scary."

"Why is it scary?" she asked, her face growing more serious.

This time I smiled. "That," I said, "is something for us to discuss next week."

Her smile returned, and she reached out her hand to clasp mine for a brief moment.

"Okay, we'll talk about it next week." Her smile faded, and she said, "And Jonathan? Thanks for listening to me. You helped me a lot, really."

"I want to help," I said lamely.

"I know," she said, "and you do. Thanks."

She gave my hand a quick squeeze and was gone, walking out the door holding her cane conspicuously high above the ground.

CHAPTER 14

Sure enough, later that week Leon and his cohorts gave me a clean bill of health—well, clean enough that I no longer needed to live in the hospital's stroke wing. I was to be dismissed the following Wednesday, although I'd be returning for PT several times a week.

My mother was thrilled, and my father's congratulatory remarks seemed genuine. I had grown fond of them, particularly my mother, but I must confess I was nervous at the idea of living with these people. I worried about keeping up the ruse that I remembered them, so I was spending a lot of time with the photo albums my mother brought me—I wanted to seem as familiar with them as possible.

I wasn't sure if Rebecca was checking her email, but I went ahead and wrote her a simple message, letting her know I'd be there when she arrived on Tuesday, but was checking out of the hospital the next day.

It's a good thing I can't count—that saved me the embarrassment of admitting how often I checked for a response from her. A day went by, then another. Finally on Sunday night I got this:

hi jonathan -
thats so great that youre getting out. im so proud of you! ill see you on tuesday and you can tell me all about it. maybe we can arrange our pt schedules so we still run into each other.
not much is different here but im ok. ill call your room when im

done with pt and we can meet in the cafe ok?
see you tues!

bye,

Rebecca

I pictured her smiling as she wrote that, and was smiling myself when I went to bed that night.

On Tuesday I got to the cafeteria at the same time she did, allowing me to select a beverage other than the dreaded iced tea.

Rebecca looked amazing. She was walking without a cane, with just the slightest limp. Her hair was pulled back in a tight ponytail, revealing just how pretty her unmade-up face was. She wore a matching blue warm-up suit that I hadn't seen before that managed to be simultaneously practical and very flattering.

I had to comment. "You look great," I said as we were getting seated at what had become our usual table. "Really great."

"Thanks," she said. "I had to get something to wear instead of those grungy sweatpants, so I got this."

"It looks great," I said. Yes, I was still waiting on that thesaurus. Believe me, it was on my shopping list.

"I had a bunch of workout clothes at home," Rebecca said, "but it was all this skin-tight spandex stuff that made me look like a stripper or something. I used to work out like that, but now I'm too self-conscious. I just don't feel like everybody in the PT room needs to get a look at my body like that—does that make sense?"

"I think you should wear whatever makes you comfortable," I said. "But I think that looks terrific on you. And I like your hair."

Rebecca cast me a dubious look. "At least it's finally long enough that I can get it all pulled back in a ponytail. But Big Bob still wants me to dye it blonde."

"I like it fine," I said resolutely.

"Well, I think it should be all one color or the other," she said, "but it hasn't been my top priority." Rebecca smiled shyly. "Want to know what *has* been my top priority?"

"Absolutely."

Rebecca dug in her purse, then pulled out a set of keys and dropped them on the table between us.

"Check it out," she said, holding her head proudly.

I looked at the keys, not sure what I was supposed to be seeing.

"I drove myself here," she announced. "I passed all the little things they check you for, and my vision and depth perception is good enough, and so is my eye-to-hand coordination. It feels *so* good to be more independent."

"That's excellent, Rebecca," I said. "You're doing so well— I'm glad to see it."

"Well, so are you, apparently. You're still getting out tomorrow, aren't you?"

I nodded. "That's what they tell me. My parents are picking me up in the morning, but I'll be coming back Friday for PT."

We discussed our respective therapy schedules and agreed to try to arrange for them to coincide when possible. Then Rebecca got up and refilled our drinks—a task much easier for her, operating without a cane or walker.

"You're walking great," I said when she returned, figuring that was a much safer remark than *God, I love to watch you walk.*

"Thanks. How about you? Have you tried walking with a cane?"

"A few times, in PT," I said. "I kept falling."

Rebecca frowned and started to apologize, but I cut her off. "It's okay—my legs were pretty badly atrophied, so it's going to be a while before I'm moving around like you are. But I'm still doing well enough that they're letting me out of here. My parents' house is only one story, so I should be able to get around in it okay."

"That's good," she said. "Just keep working at it. You can do it—I know you can."

You hear a lot of cheerleading talk like that in a place like this, and frankly it can get annoying after a while. But she was so genuine in her encouragement that I simply drew from her remarks what I should: inspiration.

My father arrived the next morning, by himself for a change.

"Where's Mom?" I asked.

He shrugged. "Oh, she's fussing around, getting your room arranged just so."

"She doesn't need to fuss over me—I'm sure it will be fine." Then I added, "Just like always," trying to sound familiar with what I'd be walking into.

I had been studying photo albums, trying to get a sense of how the house was laid out, but I was worried that I wouldn't be convincing. The one thing working in my favor was the fact that I'd be staying in a room that hadn't been mine, so I wouldn't be expected to be intimately familiar with it. At least that was my hope.

"Is this all you've got?" my father asked, looking down at the cardboard box and duffle bag on my bed. The box held the books I'd been reading, thanks to my mother's frequent trips to the library. And the bag held my meager collection of clothes.

"That's it," I said. "I like to travel light."

My father looked at me uncertainly, taking a moment to realize I was trying to make a joke. Then he smiled uneasily and said, "Alrighty, then. Let's get going."

With the bag slung over one shoulder, he hefted the box and walked out of the room. I followed close behind, feeling self-conscious about this older man carrying all my things. But it's hard to carry much when you use a walker. And I'd gotten used to needing help with the most rudimentary tasks, although I'd never learned to be truly comfortable with such helplessness.

I had done all the paperwork earlier that morning, so my actual departure from the hospital was free of red tape or drama. I hadn't bothered with big farewells to the staff, since I'd be returning several times a week.

My father seemed to sense the too-easy nature of our exit. He paused in the front lobby and turned to me, mumbling, "Um, do I need to sign something or tip anybody or anything?"

I smiled. "No, Dad—it's fine."

"How about a wheelchair? When I was in for my appendix, they said I had to be escorted out of the hospital in a wheelchair."

"I think we're fine," I said. Actually, they had asked me to call for a wheelchair when I was ready to leave, but we were almost to the door, and nobody was stopping us. "Let's go," I said.

A set of sliding glass doors sensed our presence and opened in front of us with a hiss. Together we stepped out into the sunlight, facing a semicircular driveway set into the side of a hill that sloped gently down to the street, across from which was a large parking lot. Dad—I needed to get used to calling him that—set my things on the sidewalk, and said, "Wait here—I'll go get the car."

Soon he pulled up in a bubble-shaped silver-grey sedan. He got out, popped open the trunk and went about loading my things into the back of the car. Meanwhile I made my way towards the passenger side of the car. Suddenly I found Dad by my side.

"Um, do you need help getting in? How does this work, I mean, with the walker and all?"

I'd had so little contact with him, this sudden burst of solicitousness was simultaneously surprising and disconcerting.

"It's okay," I said, reaching for the rear door. I opened it, leaned one hand on the roof of the car, and wrestled the walker into the back seat. Then I closed the door, one hand still on the roof, and shuffled forward to open the passenger door. I was pretty pleased with myself for improvising this maneuver so successfully.

Then I fell on my ass when I tried to get into the car.

"Jonny! Jesus, are you okay?" My father was on his knees, looking every bit as uncomfortable as I felt.

"Yeah, I'm fine," I said. "I guess I need a little help getting in." He tried to pick me up but I waved him away. "It's okay," I said, "I've had a lot of practice getting up." I flashed him my version of a smile. "That's 'cause I've had a lot of practice falling down."

Dad laughed uneasily, and once I'd managed to prop myself upright, he helped me slide into the car seat, then closed my door for me.

I sat in the front seat fuming in humiliation, while he came around the car and got in.

As he fired up the engine, I muttered, "Nice car," just to have something to say.

He grunted as he swung the car out of the curving driveway. "It's okay, I guess. Your mother wanted an SUV, but I managed to talk her out of it. I mean, am I the only one who realizes that an SUV is just an over-glorified station wagon, with some big tires and a rugged-sounding name? Sports utility, my ass."

"I hear you," I said. This was a phrase I'd picked up from Leon, which I found was coming in handy. On the surface, it seemed to imply agreement. But at its most literal, it simply acknowledged that somebody had said something, without indicating agreement or dissent—or even comprehension. Yes, for a man like me, it was a *very* useful retort.

We drove in silence for a few blocks, then Dad asked, "Any

of this look familiar?"

"Not really," I admitted. I had been staring out the window, soaking in the scenery, and finding myself struck by how green everything was. Other than some experimental walks on the hospital grounds, I'd had very little exposure to life beyond the confines of the hospital walls. It was curiously exciting to be whizzing up a street, watching cars and houses and buildings and trees whipping by, and realizing they were real, tangible things, not just images on my television.

"I'm not surprised," he said. "Most of this area is new, and hell, you haven't really lived here since you went away to school. That's something like fifteen, sixteen years ago." His eyes darted briefly towards me. "That's a long time."

"Yeah," I said. "That much I got."

This got a small smile out of him, and he seemed to relax a bit more.

Dad pointed out a few landmarks as we drove, but I didn't really retain anything he told me. I was too worried about how to handle myself when we finally got to the house. And frankly I was too caught up watching the scenery around me. It really was a pretty town—I wondered why I'd hated it so much.

He turned the car off the busy main street we'd been traveling, taking us into a residential area. Sensing that we might be close to home, I stared intently at my surroundings, looking for something familiar. No luck.

He slowed, then turned the car into the driveway of a pleasant looking single-story house, painted a pale beige with light brown trim. I recognized it from my photo-album studies.

I was home.

Dad helped me without asking, bustling around the car while I was opening my door, pulling my walker out of the back seat and setting it in front of me.

"Thanks," I said. I heaved myself upright without further assistance and said, "Let's go."

Dad hitched the duffle bag up on his shoulder, grabbed my box of books, and led the way.

A white plastic banner was draped across the front door, adorned with brightly colored letters that spelled: WELCOME HOME JOHNNY.

"Your mother had that made," Dad said. "We only realized they spelled Jonny wrong when I went to hang it up this morning. She got all upset about it, but I told her it was no big deal. You're probably best off telling her you didn't notice."

I nodded my assent. Was this where my concern for diplomacy had come from? And with it, my ability to lie?

Dad shifted the cardboard box to one arm to open the front door for me.

"Come on in, Jonny," he said. "Welcome home."

I followed him into a small foyer that opened to larger rooms on either side.

"Jonny!" cried my mother, walking towards me with open arms.

"Hi, Mom," I said distractedly. I was already scanning my surroundings, looking for landmarks. To my left was a dining area—I'd seen it in photos. To my right was a living room, where I saw nothing I recognized.

"It's so good to have you home," my mother said, hugging me awkwardly over my walker, a maneuver that I thought might cause my second fall of the day. But I somehow managed to stay upright, hugging her with one arm while supporting myself with the other.

Dad, still laden with my belongings, said, "I'm going to put Jonny's stuff in his room."

He disappeared down a hallway, and in a moment my mother hurried off to the kitchen, to get me a drink I'd just told her I didn't need. I took advantage of the moment to look around some more. One wall was nearly covered with family photos, mostly me and Teddy, although a few showed some older people I didn't remember. And there was one shot of my parents together, which must have been taken shortly after they married. Their hair was darker and thicker, and I realized for the first time that my mother had been pretty.

"Is everything the way you remember it?" my mother asked, appearing behind me with a glass of iced tea.

I took a sip to gather my thoughts. Mercifully it was much better than the toxic brown stuff they served at the hospital.

"Mostly," I said. I decided to lay some groundwork for the errors I'd inevitably make. "But I have to admit, some of it isn't quite so familiar. It's funny what I can and can't remember."

"It will all come back," she said. "You'll see." I wasn't sure whether she was trying to boost my confidence, or her own.

"I hope so." I sipped my tea, supporting myself with one arm on my walker.

"Why don't you sit down?"

"No, that's okay." Seeing my father return, I said, "Actually, I'd love to see the rest of the house."

My parents then led me on a tour of what my father called *the Hooper Castle,* revealing a pleasant and spacious house that made me realize just how small my room in the hospital had been. In the kitchen, Mom opened a door that she said led to the basement, but I stopped and pointed at my walker.

"I can't do stairs yet," I said.

Without skipping a beat, my mother closed the door and turned. "Just as well," she said. "It's a mess down there."

"Hey," said my father, "*I* know where everything is down there."

"That makes one of us," she said, leading me off in another direction.

Stopping in front of a doorway, she said, "This was your

room, but like I told you, Teddy moved into it later, because it was bigger. I thought about moving you in there, but he still comes down to visit from time to time, and he's really finicky about his things."

"That's fine," I said, surveying the room, which didn't look at all familiar. A large bed took up most of the floor space, and a desk cluttered with computer gear dominated the far corner.

"Teddy leaves his computer here?" I asked.

"Oh, that's his old one," Mom said. "It's slow and obsolete—it must be at least four years old."

I assumed four years must be an awfully long time—I couldn't imagine a computer wearing out.

"Your mother had me take down his posters after he moved out," my father said, "so that took away my only reason for coming into this room."

Mom gave his arm a good-natured slap. "We don't need half-naked women on our walls, George." Turning to me, she said, "Besides, Jonny probably doesn't even know what Baywatch is."

Enjoying a rare moment of clued-in-ness, I smiled conspiratorially at my father. "Who did he have on the wall?" I asked. "Pamela or Yasmine?"

This got a chuckle out of my father, and an indignant scowl from my mother.

"Jonathan!" she barked. "Don't tell me that with everything you've forgotten, you remember . . . *that show?*"

I shook my head, smiling. "No, Mom—it's just one of the shows that was on a lot at the hospital. I watched a lot of TV when I was training myself to speak."

Mom was not amused. "Well, you could have watched PBS," she said, refusing to crack a smile.

"Teddy liked Pamela," my father said, still smiling, "but I was always more of a Yasmine guy. How about you?"

"Yeah, I guess I'd have to go with Yasmine," I agreed.

"How nice for both of you," my mother said, turning to leave. "Now let me show you where the bath towels are. Then I'll show you where you'll be staying."

The tour continued with no further mention of pneumatic young actresses. And in fulfillment of my own dwindling expectations, I didn't see a single thing that triggered any memories. But I felt I'd broken the ice a bit with my father, making the prospect of living under the same roof with him a little less uncomfortable.

I was just getting settled in my new room when my mother appeared in my doorway, knocking on the open door to get my attention.

"I almost forgot," she said, holding out a pale yellow envelope. "This came for you in the mail."

I thanked her and took the envelope, expecting it to be from either a medical provider or an insurance company. But my name and address were handwritten in a crude script, and there was no return address. Curious, I tore it open.

Inside was a greeting card showing a sad-looking puppy with an icepack on its head and a thermometer in its mouth. The card's cheerful red lettering urged me to GET WELL SOON.

"Oh, how cute," Mom said. "Who's it from?"

I opened the card to find out. Inside, the same red font offered me BEST WISHES FOR A FULL AND SPEEDY RECOVERY.

The words FULL and SPEEDY had been underlined by hand, in a dark blue ink that matched the barely legible signature:

- Brandon

CHAPTER 15

"What time should I pick you up?"

My father had opened the back door of the car and was leaning in to pull out my walker.

"I'm not sure, exactly." That much was true—I didn't know if Leon would have a new regimen for me now that I was doing outpatient PT, or just the same old workout. But that wasn't why I was hedging.

"Should I just wait for you?" Dad asked, starting to work on unfolding my walker.

"No!"

My father's bemused look told me I'd answered a little too vehemently.

"I don't want to leave you hanging," I said, trying to recover. "It's just that I'm hoping to spend a little time afterward with a . . . a friend of mine. Would it be okay if I just call you when I'm done?"

Dad looked at me, the beginning of a smile on his face. "Would this friend by any chance be a lady friend?"

"No. I mean, yes. But not like that. She's a lady, yes. But she's just a friend. She's married."

"Too bad," my father said, still smiling.

I started to reply but realized I had nothing to say, because I agreed with him. It was too bad.

I opened my door while Dad set the walker down on the pavement.

"Need a hand?" he asked, standing poised to help.

"No, thanks. I can get out." With that I grabbed the walker and pulled myself out of the car. "I have to get used to doing it myself."

"Fair enough. Just don't be afraid to ask for help when you need it. Sometimes asking for help is harder than the actual thing we need help with."

I looked at him for a moment. He was a heavyset man, slightly taller than me, with a thinning head of grey hair that suggested my own hairline's prospects were less than encouraging. But now and then he surprised me with some quiet insights that let me know that behind his blithe exterior there might be a man of considerable substance. It just wasn't a side he showed very often.

"What you just said—it's very true," I said. "I mean, because of what happened to me, I've had to get used to asking for help. But it never gets any easier."

"It never will," my father said. "But that's okay. That's one of the burdens of being a man." Closing my car door after I had shuffled clear of it, he said, "Me, I'll take that burden any day over having a menstrual cycle."

Like I said, he was not without some insight.

Leon beat me up. Not literally, but the routine he put me through left me weak-kneed and sweaty.

"You need me to get you a wheelchair?" he asked at the end of our session.

"No way," I managed to gasp, my eyes on Rebecca, who was finishing up with Lucinda across the room.

Leon followed my gaze. "She's a fine looking woman. Looking even finer recently, you want my honest opinion."

"I hadn't noticed," I lied.

"Bullshit. Now get out of here so I can get ready for my next victim. And if that arm is sore tonight, put some ice on it, but only thirty minutes."

Seeing my face, he said, "Ah, shit. Let's see—that's, like, one episode of a sitcom. You know, *Friends* or *Seinfeld* or some shit. You got it?"

"Got it," I said. "Thanks."

"No problem. See you Thursday."

I walked towards the door, half hoping Rebecca would call out my name. Then I realized that wasn't her way—she wasn't a yell-across-the-room kind of person. So I stopped and turned, to see if she was looking my way. She wasn't. Then I decided to stop acting like a small child and walked over to her. By the time I got there, she was sitting on a bench, packing her gym bag. Lucinda watched my approach, glaring at me with the disdain she seemed to have for all things male.

"Hi, Rebecca," I said.

She looked up and blessed me with one of her shy little smiles. "Hi, Jonathan—I was hoping we'd get to talk. Do you have time to go get an iced tea in the cafeteria?"

Remembering my promise to never lie to her, I said, "Actually, I think I'd rather have a Diet Coke—isn't that what you usually get?"

"Okay, Diet Coke, then," she said. "What time is your ride coming?"

"I told my dad I'd just call him when I was ready. I mentioned that I might stay and visit for a while."

Rebecca's face grew serious while she made an adjustment to whatever device was holding her hair in a ponytail. "So how does the phone thing work?"

"The phone thing?"

"You can't count," she said, "but you can remember your phone number. How does that work?"

"Oh," I said, finally understanding. "Apparently I'm pretty

good at remembering *sequences*—groups of words, letters; even groups of numbers. They found that out when they were testing me. You know, to assess my brain damage."

"God, I hated all those tests," she said, grimacing at the memory. "But now that you mention it, those I.Q. tests did seem to have a lot of questions where they gave you a series of numbers and then asked you to repeat them from memory."

I nodded. "I actually did really well on those."

"But how can you do that if you don't know what they mean?"

I thought for a moment, and then said, "Grok, snert, flidge, woogle."

Rebecca looked up at me, with much the same expression one might see worn by somebody encountering Mr. Samuels for the first time. "Um . . . pardon?"

"You heard me. Grok, snert, flidge, woogle. Now say that back to me."

I became aware that I was looming over her, so I parked my walker and sat down on an adjacent bench while she thought this over.

Rebecca spoke slowly and deliberately, a determined look on her face. "Grok . . . snert . . . floodge—no, *flidge*. Oh, and woogle." Looking rather pleased with herself, she began zipping up her gym bag.

"See?" I said. "You did just fine with those words. And I assume you don't know what they mean?"

She shook her head. "I think *grok* actually means something. But I get your point."

Encouraged by what looked like the trace of a smile, I said, "My dad had an interesting observation. He pointed out that the way I remember phone numbers isn't really any different than how everybody else does it."

"How do you mean?"

"He said that even people who *can* count aren't actually

thinking about what their phone numbers mean."

The way Rebecca was scrunching up her face told me I still wasn't making any sense to her.

"Think about it," I said. "Do you know what your phone number adds up to?"

Her eyes widened. "I have absolutely no idea."

I nodded. "From what my dad tells me, neither does anybody else. They just remember the sequence."

"I never even thought of that."

"Yeah," I said, "it turns out that the way I do 'the phone thing' is one of the few areas in which I'm actually pretty normal." I leaned closer, adopting a hushed tone. "But don't tell anybody—it could ruin my mystique."

This got a smile. And I realized I was smiling, too.

The moment ended, and Rebecca stood up, slinging her gym bag over her shoulder. "Anyway," she said, "I drove myself here, and Big Bob's at work, so I don't have to hurry home, either. In fact, if you want, I could drive you home."

I'm not sure why, but the idea made me a little uncomfortable. But I couldn't think of any polite way to protest, so I got up awkwardly and mumbled, "If it's not too far out of your way . . ."

"You're out by the mall, aren't you?"

I nodded.

She waved a hand. "That's not far at all. Come on, I need to drink something cold after what Lucinda just put me through."

"Yeah, Leon was pretty brutal with me. I can barely hang on to my walker."

Rebecca looked concerned. "I could get you a wheelchair."

I wasn't about to start going backwards like that. "No, I'll manage." Together we walked to the cafeteria, cheerfully arguing over whose workout had been more cruel and inhuman.

CHAPTER 16

Seated at our usual cafeteria table, Rebecca downed half of her soda in one draft.

Suddenly self-conscious, she said, "Sorry—I was really thirsty." Her face and neck were shiny with a light glaze of sweat, and her skin, still flushed from her efforts, seemed to glow against the pale blue of her warm-up suit. No makeup, hair slick and pulled back, to me she was nothing less than stunning.

Opting for understatement, I said, "You look good."

"Thanks," she said, "you too. You've put on some weight, it looks like."

"Probably because my mother is cooking for me," I said. "Beats hospital food, hands-down."

"I bet. So how's living at home?"

I considered the question. "It's not bad, really. I was all worried about not remembering what it was like, but since I don't remember what much of *anything* is like, it didn't turn out to be a big deal."

"So nothing at home reminds you of anything you've forgotten?"

I shook my head. "Not really. But it's nice—we all get along, and they're really good about helping me. You know, driving me around and stuff."

"When are you going to be able to drive?"

This was embarrassing. "Probably never," I said, my eyes downcast.

"But why not? You've been working really hard, and you can see okay, can't you? I mean, to read road signs and all?"

I looked up at her. "It's what's on those signs that's the problem."

She stared at me for a moment, and then grimaced. "Oh, crap. You mean like speed limits. Highway names. Distances."

I shrugged. "Numbers. Can't live with 'em. Can't live without 'em."

Rebecca looked mortified. "Jonathan, I'm sorry. I wasn't thinking. I—"

"It's not a problem," I said. "You didn't say anything wrong. It just turns out that numbers are a big part of how we live. Well, of how the rest of the world lives. Me, not so much."

"I'm sorry, Jonathan," Rebecca said again.

"Don't worry about it," I said, eager for this portion of the conversation to conclude. "How about you? How are you doing? How are . . . well, how are things with you and Big Bob?" I was bound and determined to do this friendship thing right, even if it forced me to ask questions for which I didn't want to hear the answers.

Rebecca took another sip of her soda, then put her cup down. "Still pretty weird," she said. "But in a different way."

Scared to death of what that remark might mean, I forged ahead nonetheless. "Want to talk about it?"

Rebecca opened her mouth to speak, then stopped herself. Finally she said, "See, this is where being me is really a pain. I *do* want to talk about it, and there's all kinds of stuff I want to say. But I'm not sure if it's stuff I'm supposed to talk about." She gave me a very serious look. "Or whether it's okay to talk about it . . . well, with *you.*"

"I'm your friend," I stated simply.

"I know," she said, "and I'm so glad. But that still won't stop me from saying something stupid. Or something that's better kept to myself."

"Have you talked to any of your other friends about this?"

She scowled. "That's what's so hard. I've got other . . . friends, but I don't really feel comfortable with them anymore, you know? And most of them are people we know from church. So I definitely couldn't tell *them* about what I've been going through with Bob."

"Well," I said, thinking aloud, "You're really my *only* friend. I don't remember anybody else, and the people I've met—outside of my parents, that is—I don't really trust." I stared into her eyes. "But I do trust you."

"I trust you, too. I mean, that stuff I told you about Bob and me—the sex stuff—I haven't talked about that to anybody. Even me, who blurts out everything at the worst possible time—even I know I just couldn't do that. But I felt I could with you."

"So talk to me," I said.

Rebecca sighed. Then she surprised me by asking, "Are you religious?"

I pondered this. "Not really," I finally said. "I've got sort of a vague sense of there being a God, I guess. But I know Mom said I used to hate going to church. How about you?"

"I don't know that I'd call myself religious. I mean, I was raised Catholic, but my family never went to church much."

She paused to sip her drink, then continued.

"Bob's gotten really active with the church since we got married, so I always go with him on Sundays. The people there are nice, and I like some of the music. But I don't think I get as much out of it as he does."

Rebecca frowned. "Now he's started going to church every day."

"Every day? I didn't even know they had church every day. I

thought it was just on Sundays."

"I guess it's different when you're Catholic. They say mass every day at the church we go to, at six-thirty in the morning. So he's been getting up early every morning and going."

"When did that start?"

"The day after I threw him out of bed."

I hated to ask, but I did. "Is he . . . still . . ."

"Sleeping on the couch," she said. "Actually, that's not right. A couple days ago, he started sleeping in the guest room. He actually moved some of his stuff in there. I guess he knows I'm not letting him back in my bed any time soon."

"Are you worried that he'll try to . . . do things you don't want to do?"

"No, it's not that. He's not going to force me to do anything—he's not like that. I just can't get into the same bed with him, not after he lied to me like that. I'm . . . well, I'm not really sure how you get past something like that."

While a part of me was overjoyed with this news, the pain on her face was palpable. So I tried to empathize. "That's got to be awkward. How's he taking it?"

"That's what's so weird. I figured he'd keep pleading with me, you know, trying to soften me up. But instead, he's gotten all religious about it."

"I don't understand. Is he praying for you two to patch things up?"

Rebecca sighed. "No. That's what I thought at first. He's always been very religious, so I figured he started going to church so much because he felt guilty about what he did. I thought maybe he was going to confession or something. But it's not like that."

Rebecca paused, her lips pursed as she looked for a way to explain. Finally, she said, "It's like he's given up on me. I'm not the person he married—he came right out and said that to me.

That person was taken away from him, and in her place, he got stuck with me."

"Now, wait a—"

"No, let me finish, Jonathan. Please." Rebecca's eyes pierced me, and I was silent.

"All this time, Bob had been fighting that. Trying to get me to come around, to be my old self. Now he's accepted the fact that it's not going to happen."

Rebecca's eyes began to well up with tears. "So now he's praying to understand why the woman he loved was taken from him."

"But you're still here," I protested. "You—"

"There's more," Rebecca said. "Bob told me he took his vows *in sickness and in health*. And the way he looks at it: I'm sick, and it's his responsibility to take care of me. So now I've become some . . . cross that he's got to bear."

"My God," I said involuntarily.

"I'm not sure whose God it is," Rebecca said bitterly. "But he's throwing himself into this like I'm some sort of trial for him to endure that will somehow make him more righteous, or holy, or whatever. Do you have any idea what it's like to feel like you're nothing but a burden?"

Rebecca began to sob quietly. I reached instinctively for a nearby napkin dispenser and pulled out a few thin paper napkins to offer her.

"Thanks," she said, then blew her nose loudly. "God, how did things get so messed up?"

"I don't know," I said honestly. "But I think I do know how you feel."

Our conversation dwindled after that, and we finished our drinks in silence. I hated not being able to help, but I couldn't think of anything to say or do.

Finally, Rebecca broke the silence. "Well, I guess we should get going." She fumbled in her gym bag, and extracted a set of keys. "Ready to hit the road?"

"You're sure it's not too much trouble?"

"It's no trouble," she said. "It's not like there's anything I need to hurry home to." She gave me a half-hearted smile, then stood up. I clambered to my feet and followed her out of the cafeteria.

When we got to the hospital entrance, Rebecca turned back towards me and said, "I got a crummy parking place—it's pretty far away. Why don't you wait here, and I'll pull the car around to pick you up."

"Okay," I said, embarrassed by my inability to keep up with her. "Sounds like a plan."

I waited next to the sloping semicircular drive, trying to come up with some more cheerful topics for us to discuss in the car together. Then a shadow fell over me as a huge SUV pulled up, blocking my view of the parking lot.

A window slid down. "Hop on in," came Rebecca's voice from high above me.

The passenger door swung open, and I looked up, wondering how in the hell I was going to get into this behemoth.

"Hang on to the door, and pass me your walker," Rebecca said, holding out her hand. I managed to fold it up and pass it to her without taking a dive. I felt my face flushing again, dreading the humiliation of needing her to give me a boost into her car.

But Rebecca the Teacher was on duty—she called out to me over the thrum of the engine. "Grab that handle, and pull yourself up."

I looked up and saw a handle mounted high inside the frame of the door. Thinking this just might work, I swung my arm up and caught the handle in my hand. Sure enough, I was able to pull myself up and into the seat pretty smoothly, if I say so myself. I made a mental note to thank Leon for pushing me on those preacher curls.

Feeling pretty smug, I reached over to close the door, and promptly found myself falling back out of the car. I grabbed madly for the handle I'd used to pull myself in and somehow managed to catch myself before I tumbled to the pavement. I pulled the door closed with a satisfying thunk and then, crisis averted, sank back into my seat and turned to face Rebecca. To my infinite relief she was busy adjusting her side mirror, and had missed my brief acrobatic act. I exhaled with a sigh and began to wrestle my way into my seatbelt.

Then Rebecca turned to me with an expectant smile and asked me the killer question.

"Okay, where to?"

It was then that I realized I didn't have the slightest idea how to get home. Or even what my address was.

Rebecca had a cell phone, and my parents were home, so I then got to endure the humiliation of listening to her chat with first my mother, then my father. She jotted down some directions on the back of a takeout menu she pulled from her glove compartment, and soon we were on our way to my house.

I'd never felt more helpless or stupid in my life.

I'm afraid I wasn't much of a conversationalist on the way home. I tried to bury my humiliation by focusing on the names I saw on the street signs we passed, determined to memorize the route home.

"It's not a big deal, Jonathan," Rebecca said, reading my thoughts. "I mean, I do the same thing when I'm a passenger—I never pay attention to where the person who's driving is going."

"But I bet you know your address," I said, still sulking.

"Don't be so hard on yourself," she said. "Things are hard enough for you already. Besides, you've made a lot of progress."

I realized I was ruining what could have been a pleasant conversation, so I tried to perk up.

"You're right, I know. I just get frustrated some times when stuff that should be, I don't know, *basic* . . . well, it just eludes me."

"You mean like knowing what's okay to say and what isn't?" Touché.

"Yeah," I said. "Like that. At least you know how I feel."

"That's why I like you," Rebecca said. "You know how I feel, too."

We arrived at my house to an unusual sight: both of my parents were out in the front yard, my mother with a garden hose and my father with some sort of gas-powered hedge clipper. I had lived with these two people long enough to know that they were *not* great outdoorsmen or gardeners, preferring to pay local youths to tend to their yard. They were just manufacturing an opportunity to see Rebecca. Apparently I had been wrong to assume no further embarrassment could befall me today.

Rebecca pulled into the driveway, and I considered my options. If I were an able-bodied young man, I'd have opened my door and sprung from the car, leaning in for a quick thank-you before slamming the door and trotting into the house, calling a breezy *hello* to my parents as I passed.

But no. I was a walker-wielding stroke victim, not at all sure of how to dismount from the towering heights of this wheeled leviathan without ending up sprawled on the pavement, while the object of my unrequited affections looked on in benevolent pity.

Surrendering to the situation, I smiled sheepishly at Rebecca. "So," I said, "would you like to meet my parents?"

My parents greeted Rebecca with much fuss and ceremony, then turned to the task of safely extricating my walker and me from the battleship-sized car. A few moments later we were all seated around our dining-room table, while Mom fetched a tray of iced tea and finger sandwiches she just happened to have prepared. Living in her house and seeing her outside of the confines of my hospital room, I had become much more aware of my mother's quick, birdlike movements. She was constantly darting back and forth, always ready to solve any problem with the appropriate food or beverage.

"It's just so nice to meet one of Jonny's friends," my mother said, pouring tea from a pretty glass pitcher I hadn't seen before.

"Thank you," said Rebecca when her glass was filled. "Jonathan has been a really good friend to me while I was recovering. We met when we were in physical therapy."

"Jonny!" my mother said accusingly. "You never mentioned this delightful young lady to me."

Finding no rocks available for crawling under, I tried to join the conversation. "I mentioned her to Dad, I think."

"That's right," Dad said. "You did." Mercifully he didn't bother to add that the first time I had done so was little more than an hour ago.

Mom said, "Why were you hospitalized, dear? Were you in an accident?"

Rebecca looked surprised. "No, I was in the same wing of the hospital as Jonathan. I had a stroke, too. And now I have brain damage."

If you ever want to grind a conversation to a halt, I suggest you try the phrase "I have brain damage." It will silence the most chipper hostess in the world, I can assure you.

Trying to rescue Rebecca, I said, "Rebecca came back from being paralyzed—she had to learn to walk all over again. And now she doesn't even need a cane."

"Really?" my father said, eager to brighten the conversation. "That's terrific—you must have worked very hard."

"I did," Rebecca said. "I'm still working on it. But Jonathan's

146

doing really well, too. He talks so much better now than when I met him. And he's a really good writer. My writing stinks. And I say stupid things to people."

"Stupid things?" my mother repeated, a puzzled look on her face.

God bless my dad. He stood up and said, "Say, Rebecca, would you like to see some pictures of Jonny when he was just a little boy?"

Rebecca got up and followed my father to the wall of photos. With my eyes I shot daggers, javelins, and garden shears at my mother, silently entreating her not to press Rebecca for more details regarding her affliction. Whether or not she picked up the signal, in a moment her hostess instincts took over, and she joined my father in talking Rebecca through the various photos on the wall.

"You were really cute when you were little," Rebecca said, stopping in front of an old black-and-white shot. I tried not to infer that this meant I was no longer cute.

"And there's your brother," Rebecca said, looking at another photo. "Teddy, right?"

"That's him," I agreed.

"Everybody looks so nice in this one," Rebecca said, pointing to a group shot. "You're all so dressed up."

Mom beamed. "That was our thirtieth wedding anniversary. It was so nice to have everybody together for that party."

Rebecca peered at the photo, then turned to me. "See, I told you your brother's girlfriend was pretty. Look at her—she looks like a movie star or something."

I was sure I had looked at the picture before, having studied all of the photos in the house, but couldn't recall any that showed Teddy with a woman.

"Really?" I said. "Let me see." I got up and eased my walker towards the wall of photographs. As I drew closer I began to realize how utterly silent my parents had become. Puzzled, I looked first at my father, then at my mother. Neither would meet my gaze.

"She really is beautiful," Rebecca said, still staring at the photo. "Big Bob couldn't take his eyes off her when she and Teddy came to the hospital."

I turned my attention to the photo Rebecca was studying. Sure enough, there was a stunning young woman in the photo, standing between Teddy and me.

Victoria.

CHAPTER 17

"Who's ready for more iced tea?" my mother asked, her voice growing shrill.

Dad said, "I, uh, need to go check on a . . . a thing. Down in the basement. There's this thing, and I need to check on it. In the basement." Turning, he muttered, "I'll be right back," and disappeared into the kitchen. A moment later the basement door slammed.

My mother busied herself refilling all the glasses on the dining room table.

"It's okay, Mom," I said, "I think we've had enough tea. Thanks."

Mom put down the pitcher, still avoiding my eyes.

"Well, then," she said, "I'll just leave you two to visit with each other."

Offering her hand to my mother, Rebecca said, "It was really nice to meet you."

Mom gave Rebecca's hand a quick shake and mumbled something about hoping to see her again soon. Then she bustled off to some other part of the house, leaving Rebecca and me standing in front of the wall of photos.

"She's really nice," Rebecca said. "They both are. It's nice to see how well you all get along. My parents drive me crazy— that's one thing that hasn't changed since my stroke."

Looking at Victoria's smiling face in the photo from my parents' anniversary, I said, "Well, the key is to have an honest, open line of communication."

Rebecca surprised me by touching me on the arm. I turned to see her face furrowed with concern.

"Did I just say something stupid again?" she asked. "Your voice sounded really weird just then. I don't think I've ever heard you use that tone. Jonathan, whatever I just said, I'm sorry."

"No, no," I said. "I'm sorry. You didn't say anything to upset me. It's just . . ."

She continued to stare at me. "Jonathan?"

I had promised to be totally honest with her. Now I was finding how hard that could be—or at least how embarrassing.

I forced a weak smile. "Tell you what," I said. "Let's sit down in the living room, and I'll tell you what just happened here. That is, if you don't need to go yet."

Rebecca shrugged. "No, I've got time."

She picked up our tea glasses and followed me as I shuffled to the living room, where we situated ourselves on a pair of couches that faced each other.

"It's kind of funny, really," I began . . .

"Oh. My. God." Rebecca's eyes were wider than I'd ever seen them.

"Yeah," I said, pausing to sip my tea. "Small world, isn't it?"

"So that day I saw her, she was . . ."

"Coming there to break up with me."

"But she didn't tell you she was with Teddy?"

"Not a word. Somehow it didn't come up."

"How about Teddy? What did he say?"

"He just kept telling me how great everything was going," I said. "And how much things had changed for him. I guess he wasn't kidding."

"I just can't believe your own brother could do that to you."

Thinking about what I'd been learning about my relationship with Teddy, I said, "I can. And in his defense, nobody thought I was going to wake up." I thought about Victoria's explanation. "I guess you've got to expect people to eventually move on with their lives, you know?"

"I guess," Rebecca said. "Still, it seems like they could have picked other people to move on with."

"I don't know—Victoria seemed pretty happy."

Rebecca studied me. "You don't sound very upset when you talk about her."

I spoke very quietly. "That's because I don't remember her."

"Not at all?"

I shook my head. "Not at all. When she walked into my hospital room, I had no idea who she was. So that makes it hard for me to get too upset about losing her—I don't remember ever *having* her."

Rebecca frowned, still looking at me intently. "Then what is it?"

"What is what?"

"What are you so upset about? It's not Victoria—I can see that. But you're upset about *something*."

I thought about this. "It's the lies," I said finally. "Nobody would tell me the truth about this. They all tried to hide it from me—even my own parents."

Rebecca nodded. "It's like what you said to me a while ago. About how people tell you what they think you want to hear."

"Instead of what's really going on," I said. "Look, I know they do it to try to spare my feelings, but look how it can turn out." I gestured towards the photo. "I mean, did they think I would never find out?"

"Oh, God," Rebecca said. "I bet they're furious with me for saying anything."

"No, I think they're mostly just embarrassed. You didn't do

anything wrong." Now I reached out and touched her arm. "I'm serious. I know you worry about saying the wrong thing, but that is *not* what happened here. Believe me."

She looked skeptical, but her face was softening. "Okay," she said. "Still I feel like it got me off on the wrong foot with them."

"That's their fault, not yours. But I am curious to see how they try to explain this to me."

"And I bet your next conversation with your brother is going to be interesting."

"Interesting," I said. "That's a good word. Covers a lot of possibilities."

We talked a little longer, then Rebecca said she needed to go. I walked her outside and watched her climb up into the massive machine. She started the engine, then rolled down her window.

Seeing the quizzical look on her face, I said, "Did you forget something?"

"No, I just thought about the main thing I remembered about Victoria, you know, from that time I saw her at the hospital. And that picture of her confirmed it."

"What's that?" I came closer so I could hear her voice over the purring engine.

Putting the car in gear and beginning to back out of the driveway, Rebecca announced, "Her boobs looked fake."

Back inside the house, my parents were waiting for me, each wearing sheepish expressions.

My father began. "Listen, Jonathan. We didn't—"

"No, let me," said my mother. "We just . . ." Her voice tapered off, and she looked helplessly at my father.

"Well?" I said.

Finally my father spoke up. "We just never found the right time to tell you."

"That's just it," Mom said. "When you first woke up, it

seemed like too much to hit you with."

Dad said, "Then as time went on, it reached a point where it seemed like it was too *late* to tell you."

"Plus, you were doing so well," Mom said. "You were making such progress, we didn't want to bring you down." She was clearly flustered. "I mean, this whole thing was all so unexpected."

"Yes," I said, "that's been made abundantly clear to me."

"And Teddy and Victoria seemed so happy together," she said, a remark that set my father to squirming where he stood.

"Well, they do, George. It took Teddy a long time to find his, well, his place in life."

I said, "Looks like the place he found was mine."

It turned out I could stop a conversation every bit as effectively as Rebecca could. We stood there, the three of us silent and unmoving.

Finally my father cleared his throat, breaking the silence. "So, are you and Teddy going to . . . well, are you going to be okay?"

I shrugged. "Were we ever?"

This got one corner of my Dad's mouth to rise, a hint of a sardonic smile.

"To be honest," he said, "I think maybe Teddy's a better match for a woman like Victoria." My mother shot him a look, but he went on, propelled by the momentum of his own candor.

"I don't mean any offense by this, Jonathan, but you've changed a bit since your stroke. And I don't just mean your memory. You act a little . . . *different* now."

"And not in a bad way," my mother hastily added.

"No," Dad said, "not at all in a bad way. But enough that I'd think maybe you and Victoria might not be as . . . compatible as you might have once been."

My mother started to reply, but I held up a hand, and she stopped herself.

"No, it's okay," I said. "I have changed. And I'll concede that Victoria may not be my type—if I even have a type, that is."

"That Rebecca woman was certainly nice," my mother said.

"She's married." My father and I spoke in strident unison.

"Oh," said my mother, holding a hand up to her mouth. "Never mind."

"Look," I said, "I understand why you did what you did. I just need you to not do that anymore."

My gaze moved back and forth between them. At least they were looking me in the eye now.

"I just need to know that there are no more surprises waiting for me. Can you promise me that?"

My parents still looked uneasy. Mom said, "By surprises, you mean . . ."

"Stuff that happened during my coma."

They both seemed to relax a little.

"I think you're all caught up now," Dad said. "The thing with Teddy and Victoria was the one thing we hadn't figured out how to broach."

"I'm serious, Dad," I said. "I don't want to find out later that you had a sex change while I was in a coma. Or that Mom ran off with the mailman. No more surprises."

To my relief, this tactic seemed to lighten their moods.

"Don't worry," my dad said. "No more surprises." He started to walk away, but stopped and said, "Oh, but Jonathan?"

"Yes?"

"It wasn't the mailman. It was the cable guy."

"George!" My mother chased after him as he hurried out of the room. From the laughter I heard, I suspect she caught him.

CHAPTER 18

"Jonathan! Come out here and see who's come to visit!" My mother's singsong voice tore my attention away from the novel I was reading.

"Just a minute," I called, marking my place in the book, a Robert Ludlum thriller about a spy with amnesia. I was on a novels-about-amnesia kick, a self-indulgence that in retrospect seems a little silly. I guess I was looking for people with whom I had something in common, even if they were fictional.

I stood up and checked my appearance in the mirror, dreading the encounter that awaited me. Over the last several weeks my mother had been inviting a steady stream of guests to our house, in an effort to reacquaint me with my life and possibly rekindle some memories. But so far Operation Rekindle was a bust—I had not remembered anybody to whom she introduced me.

Sighing, I flashed a smirk-concealing smile at my reflection in the mirror, then headed down the hallway. I was walking with a cane now, but carried the book with me as a prop. This was an affectation I had recently adopted to hide the way my right arm was never fully extended, a trick I picked up from watching a tape of Bob Dole in an old presidential debate. He carried a pencil in his hand to divert attention from his paralyzed arm. Of course, the damage to Dole's arm came from a war injury; mine came from lying in bed for six years.

My mother stood with her back to me in the foyer, helping a

grey-haired woman off with her coat. As the woman shrugged out of her coat, she turned towards my mother, offering me my first glimpse at her face.

I froze. The book fell out of my hand.

"Mrs. Marigold!"

It was my own voice, but I was unaware of having spoken.

My mother spun around. "Why, Jonny!" she cried with delight. "You remembered!"

But I wasn't looking at her. I was looking into the sparkling eyes of the small but heavyset woman who was walking towards me.

I was looking at the first truly familiar face I had seen. Ever.

"Mrs. Marigold," I said again.

The woman chuckled. "I always loved that name," she said, stopping a few feet away from me. "Now look at how you've grown up."

A wave of memories suddenly surged through my mind, a sensation so powerful it was physically tangible. I staggered back a step, suddenly unsteady on my feet.

I knew her. I remembered her.

And I loved her.

"Mrs. Marigold," I said again, stupidly.

"Isn't that just the cutest thing?" my mother said. "We always got such a kick out of that name. Now let's all sit down and have some coffee. Oh, and Jonny, can you pick up that book?"

My mother shooed us towards the couches in the living room, then bustled off to get the coffee, leaving me and the woman staring across the room at each other.

"You remember me," the woman said, smiling. "I was hoping you would."

I nodded, momentarily speechless. Information was flooding into my brain, and I was trying to process it as best I could.

"You're Mrs. . . . Mrs. Margolis," I finally managed. "But I never called you that. I called you . . ."

"Mrs. Marigold," she said. "You used to get your words confused. You were always in such a hurry to say whatever was on your mind, sometimes the words came out all jumbled."

I couldn't help but smile. "I still have problems with that."

She laughed. "Strokes will do that to a fella."

I heard the clank of china in the kitchen, and was thankful for a moment alone with this woman.

"I remember you," I said.

"I know." She smiled again.

"I don't remember anybody else."

Her eyes narrowed. "Not *anybody* else?" she asked, nodding her head towards the kitchen.

"Nobody," I said. I wasn't sure why I felt comfortable divulging that to this woman, but somehow I sensed I could confide in her.

The woman raised her eyebrows. "Well, that's awkward, isn't it?"

Her understatement made me laugh.

"Yeah," I said, "just a bit."

"It's so good to see you two just chatting away," said my mother, emerging from the kitchen with a tray laden with the paraphernalia of caffeine. Soon we were sipping coffee from delicate porcelain cups and trying to get a conversation started.

It was harder than you would think. On one hand, I was dying to talk with the one person on the planet I felt I knew. But on the other, I was extremely conscious of my mother's feelings. At times I suspected she had figured out that I didn't remember her, so I didn't want to make too big a fuss over Mrs. Margolis in front of her. But it was difficult to contain my excitement over finally finding a link to my past.

My mother got things started. "My goodness, Claudia—how many years do you suppose it's been since you saw Jonny?"

The older woman stirred her coffee, performing some mental calculations. "It must be at least twenty years," she said finally. "How long have you been in this house?"

"Let me think," my mother said. "I guess it will be twenty-five years this Christmas. Goodness, it doesn't seem that long."

Of course, all those numbers didn't mean much to me. But it was clear they were talking about a long time.

Remembering my predicament, my mother tried to offer me some context. "You would have been about nine or ten when we moved to this house, Jonny. That's about the same age as Ryan, that nice blonde-haired boy across the street."

I was barely listening. I was caught up in the foreign feeling of *remembering*.

"You lived . . ." I said to our guest, "next door. In a yellow house. A big yellow house."

She laughed. "Well, it hasn't been yellow in about fifteen years, not since I bought that aluminum siding for the house. But yes, I lived next door. I still live there."

"I remember . . . a tree," I said, as the image of a huge tree materialized in my mind.

"You said it was the best climbing tree in the whole neighborhood," she said, smiling. "You virtually lived in that tree. I used to say you were part monkey."

I closed my eyes, trying to get the images that were rushing by me to slow down. I became aware that I had a headache.

"A big yellow house," I said again, to nobody in particular.

"Jonny, are you all right?" my mother asked. "You look a bit pale."

I opened my eyes. "Sorry. Just having some childhood memories, I guess. But I am a little tired." I wasn't, actually. But I was overwhelmed, and was falling back on one of my defensive tricks. It seemed I still put a lot of energy into self-protection, which was odd considering how completely I relied on others. But it was a strong inclination on my part—instinct, perhaps. Or an old habit from my previous life?

Mrs. Margolis wasn't saying anything. She sat sipping her coffee, looking at me appraisingly over the rim of her cup.

Ever the gracious hostess, my mother redirected her attention to her guest.

"Claudia, I want to apologize for how little we've managed to see each other over the years. You know, since . . . well, since we moved away and all."

"Where do you live?" I asked Mrs. Margolis. "Is it far from here?"

"Not that far," she said. I think I saw my mother squirm at that. "It's about a ten or fifteen minute drive."

I looked at my mother, who didn't miss a beat. "That's about as long as it takes us to get to that seafood place you like, Jonny."

Mrs. Margolis frowned.

"I can't really understand numbers," I explained. "You know, from the stroke."

"He can't understand them *yet*," my mother added quickly. "But he's been doing so well in therapy. It's only a matter of time before he'll be good as new."

I cringed, wondering if she was trying to delude Mrs. Margolis or simply herself.

Something in Mrs. Margolis's expression told me she was thinking the same. "Strokes are funny," she said. "Howard went colorblind after his. And he couldn't tie a knot—that frustrated the bejeezus out of him, him being a sailor and all."

"Howard?" I said. The name was familiar, but I couldn't picture a face.

"Howard was my husband," she said. "He died when you were just a baby, so I doubt you'd remember him."

"You . . . talked about him," I said.

"I still do," she said, with a sad smile.

159

"I can't do knots, either," I volunteered.

"Can you sing?" she asked.

Sing? I could honestly say that was something I had not tried to do since my awakening. "I . . . don't know," I said.

"Howard used to have a lovely singing voice," Mrs. Margolis said, her eyes getting a little misty. "But after the stroke he was tone-deaf."

Fully aware of how arbitrary the damage caused by a stroke can be, I simply nodded.

"Who wants more coffee?" my mother asked with perhaps a little too much enthusiasm. The woman liked keeping things upbeat—it was one of her defining characteristics.

My headache was getting worse. And Mrs. Margolis kept looking at me in a way I found unsettling. Not in a bad or threatening way, but with a familiarity that I hadn't seen expressed by anybody else I had met, as if she knew me better than my own family.

I stood up, finding my legs still a bit shaky.

"I'm sorry," I said, "but I'm not feeling very well. So I think I'm going to go lie down for a bit. But I was wondering . . ."

Mrs. Margolis looked at me expectantly. "Yes?"

"Would it be okay . . . I mean, would you like . . ." I stopped to regroup. "What I mean is, do you think I could come by and visit you sometime?"

Mrs. Margolis beamed. "Jonny, nothing would make me happier. Please come by any time."

"Are you near a bus stop?" I asked. "I can't drive."

"There's one at the end of my block," she said. "The West Governor line."

"Jonny's been doing a great job of getting around town," my mother said. "He's so independent."

Yeah, I thought, that's why I'm thirty-four and live with my parents.

CHAPTER 19

I had a big day planned. After my late-morning physical therapy appointment, I was going to visit Mrs. Margolis. Dad had helped me figure out an elaborate series of bus transfers that would get me first to the hospital, then to her house, then home again. Although I had been using the bus system to get around, this was my most ambitious itinerary to date. Dad kept protesting while he helped me chart my course, offering repeatedly to be my driver for the day. But I was determined to carve out more autonomy in my life, and the city's mass transit system seemed as good a place as any to start.

Rebecca was supposed to meet me after physical therapy. She was down to having her PT check-up every other week, and would soon probably stop coming to the hospital at all. While I was glad she was getting better, I was seeing less and less of her and felt she was fading out of my life.

The prospect saddened me. I had no social life to speak of, other than interacting with my own parents. And of course today's visit with my old neighbor. There was a local support group for stroke victims, and I attended one of their functions. But it only depressed me—I was surrounded by people who were for the most part both older than me and much worse off in terms of the damage done by their strokes. Rebecca didn't attend, nor did any other young, attractive women. I concluded that the stroke victim demographic was probably not the best singles scene for a guy like me. But what was? Amnesiacs

Anonymous?

My bus brought me within walking distance of the hospital, and I used the walk to warm myself up for the torture Leon had in store for me. I was halfway through my session with him when Rebecca walked into the PT room.

I almost didn't recognize her. Her hair was cut very short and was a rich brown, all the blond having been excised by a hairdresser's shears. The boyish cut framed her face in a way that actually emphasized her beauty—an effect I've noticed on some particularly beautiful women. Sometimes the absence of ornament makes true beauty all the more striking.

From the length of my description, I imagine it's clear that I was stunned.

So was Leon. He let out a slow *"Damn,"* stretching the word into several emphatic syllables. We watched, frozen, as she walked across the room to greet the towering Lucinda. Then Rebecca turned and gave us a shy wave, her gentle smile weakening my knees even more than Leon's leg-press routine.

Leon and I waved back, idiotic grins pasted on our faces. Then she turned away and began her workout with Lucinda, who shot us a paint-peeling scowl that jolted us back to reality.

I resumed my exercise, while Leon made a show of marking something on his clipboard.

Under his breath, he said, "Is it just me, or is that Rebecca chick taking her fineness up to a whole new level?"

"It's not just you," I managed to grunt between reps.

"I mean, normally I don't go for short hair on a girl, you know what I'm sayin'? But on that Rebecca chick—*damn . . .*" This time he stretched the word even longer.

Attempting to be suave, I said, "I'll admit, she is not without a certain appeal."

Leon gave me a look that would have done Lucinda proud.

"When did you start talkin' like some home decorating channel fag?"

After my workout, I waited for Rebecca at our usual table in the cafeteria, where I passed the time studying my map for the journey I'd planned.

"Going somewhere?"

I looked up across the table to see Rebecca, who had entered the cafeteria without me noticing. She leaned over, peering at the map.

For a moment I was speechless. Up close, she was even more stunning.

"Oh—hi!" I finally stammered. "I'm just, well, I'm going to visit a lady who used to be our next-door neighbor when I was a kid."

Rebecca sat down across from me and eagerly took the diet cola I'd gotten for her. "Thanks, Jonathan." After a long sip she nodded towards the map and said, "Is this that lady you told me about, with a name like a flower? Magnolia?"

"Marigold," I said. "Mrs. Marigold. At least, that's what I called her when I was a kid. Her real name is Margolis."

"That's really cute." She took another sip of her drink, giving me another moment to just look at her.

"Your hair looks . . . amazing," I managed to say.

"Does it?" Rebecca scrunched up her face. "It's so short."

"But it's so . . . flattering," I said, struggling to find the word. "Seriously, it really shows off how pretty you are."

I suddenly felt stupid and inappropriate, gushing like that.

"Wow—thank you," she said. "I hadn't planned on this, that's for sure."

"What—you mean your hairdresser wasn't supposed to cut so much off?"

"I hadn't planned to cut *any* off, at first." Rebecca ran an exploratory hand through her hair, as if reaffirming the radical decrease in its quantity.

"What do you mean?"

Rebecca took another swallow of soda, then said, "I had originally planned to dye it blonde again. You know, like Big Bob was always asking me to do."

I tried not to scowl at the mention of his name.

Rebecca went on. "He's been a lot nicer recently, and I wanted to do something that showed I was, you know, making an effort, too. So I went to my salon, to have Jamie—that's the girl who does my hair—to have her lighten my hair again."

"What happened?"

Again Rebecca grimaced. "This is embarrassing."

"Go ahead," I said. "This is me. You can't be embarrassed around me."

Rebecca raised an eyebrow. "That's what you think. Have you forgotten my little visit with your parents?"

Actually, I had given that surprisingly little thought, further indication of how unconnected I'd felt with Victoria. But the funny thing was that I hadn't heard a word from Teddy. He seemed to be following in the Hooper family tradition of avoiding problems, with the hope that they will eventually just go away.

"That was no big deal," I said. "So go on—what happened?"

"Well, I got to the salon, and was sitting in the chair with that big apron thingie they drape on you, and suddenly the smells started getting to me."

"The smells?"

Rebecca leaned forward. "Have you ever been in a women's hair salon, Jonathan? Where they do permanents, and dyeing, and stuff?"

"Um, no. My dad took me to his barbershop a while back, when I started getting too shaggy. And I honestly don't remember what I used to do about my hair before my coma.

They kept it trimmed short while I was unconscious."

"Wow, I never thought of that. I guess if they didn't cut your hair for six years, you'd look like a wild man."

"Or a rock star," I offered.

She smiled, no doubt sharing my vision.

"Anyway," she said, "some of the stuff they use on women's hair smells really nasty—these weird chemical odors. I sat down and started smelling them, and it just kind of . . . freaked me out. I don't know why, because I've had my hair treated tons of times. But I started feeling all anxious and weird, and even thought I might throw up."

"Any idea what caused that?"

"I don't know, but it *really* freaked me out. I nearly sprinted out of there. But it didn't end there."

"What happened?"

"I got home, and I was still all worked up. I started looking at old pictures of myself, at all the blond hair I had, and started thinking *I don't want to have to look like that.*"

Rebecca's voice had been growing uncharacteristically strident, and I guess she realized it. She stopped, took a breath, and continued in a lower voice.

"Jonathan, it was weird. But I just didn't want to have to be blonde to please somebody. So I grabbed a pair of scissors, and started hacking all my blonde hair off."

"Wait a minute," I said. "You cut your own hair? And it came out looking like that?"

"God, no," she said with a grimace. "It came out looking awful. Like I was an escaped mental patient or something."

"So what did you do?"

"Well, I put a baseball hat on—that was the first thing." Rebecca rolled her eyes at the memory. "Then I went out and found a barbershop. Not a beauty salon where I'd smell all those smells. Just a regular barbershop with regular guys who just cut hair. I got some old guy who looked like an ex-Marine, and he did . . . *this.*" Rebecca pointed at her hair.

"I love it," I blurted. But to my surprise, she smiled.

"I kind of do, too," she said. "It's just so different—I'm not used to it."

"It really does look good. Really good." Hey, at least I was using words other than *great* for a change.

I had to ask. "So what does Big Bob think?"

Her smile went away, and I mentally kicked myself for asking.

"I'm pretty sure he hates it," she said. "His only comment was, *Well, it'll grow back, right?*"

"What a guy," I said before I could stop myself.

"He's not a bad guy," she said. "He's just really . . . what's the word . . . *fixated* on me looking a certain way."

I didn't want to slam him, but I had to at least say, "Well, he's missing out if he doesn't see how great you look."

Again the smile—but just for a moment. "Thanks, Jonathan." Turning her attention to the map spread in front of me, she said, "So, where does your friend live?"

I showed her where I was heading, and she said, "Oh that's not far. Would you like me to drive you?"

At least this time I had directions. Plus it would be a little more time I could spend with her. After a moment, I said, "That would be great."

We chatted easily in the car on the way to Mrs. Margolis's, our conversation interrupted occasionally as Rebecca paused to refer to the directions I had written down.

After one such lull, Rebecca surprised me by saying, "I promise not to say anything stupid."

She glanced over at me, and I smiled. "I'm not worried about that," I said.

"Then what are you worried about?"

"What do you mean?"

"You seem a little weird when you talk about her. Do you not want me to meet her?"

"No, no—it's not like that at all. I'm totally fine with you meeting her—she's a sweet old lady. She's just . . ."

"She's just what?"

I swiveled in my seat. "Rebecca, we said we'd always be honest with each other, right?"

"Of course," she said, her expression showing she took my concerns seriously.

"Well, other than this lady, nobody else knows this—and I mean nobody. So I need you not to tell anybody."

"Tell anybody what?"

I cleared my throat. "Rebecca, Mrs. Marigold—I mean, Mrs. Margolis—is the *only* person I remember at all from my previous life."

This elicited a sidelong glance from Rebecca. "Wow. Really?"

"Really," I said. "The only one."

Rebecca pondered this as she drove. "Why do you think that is? I mean, you didn't remember your own brother. Or that girl with the fake boobs."

I couldn't help but smile. "No, it's different with Mrs. Margolis. I remembered her. And I remembered liking her. Loving her, really. That's something I haven't felt for anybody from my past. Well, except for Rufus."

"Rufus?"

"He was a dog I had when I was little. I ran across a photo of him one day, and it was like somebody punched me in the stomach—suddenly I remembered this dog that I had loved."

We had come to a stoplight, and Rebecca was looking at me very intently now. "Do you think it could be something where you only remember people you love?"

I considered this. "But what about my parents? I would think I loved them." Allowing myself a smile, I added, "I mean, I can see not remembering Teddy—what little I've seen of him hasn't been too lovable. But my parents are really great."

I paused. "And I would *assume* that I loved Victoria—apparently I was with her for a long time."

Rebecca stepped on the accelerator as the light changed to green. "I can think of a pair of things you might have loved about her."

I laughed. "If you're implying what I think you are, that was something she did during my coma."

"How did you figure that out?" Rebecca asked. "From looking at pictures?"

"Actually, she told me herself. That day she came to visit."

The traffic was fairly heavy on this street, so Rebecca kept her eyes on the road, but that didn't stop her from shaking her head. "So while she's breaking up with you, she finds a way to talk about her boob job?"

"It was a pretty surreal conversation," I allowed.

"Must have been." She checked her mirror, then changed lanes. "But you *do* think you loved her?"

"I don't know," I said, sinking back into my seat. "I guess so. We were together a long time, apparently."

"And you don't remember her at all?"

"Not at all," I said, mentally playing back the only encounter with the woman that I could remember. "You want to know something funny? Well, not funny, but kind of strange?"

"Sure."

"I don't know—it's probably not proper for me to say this . . ." I began.

Rebecca laughed, a rare occurrence. "You're worried about saying the right thing? Have you forgotten who you're talking to?"

"Good point," I said, smiling. "It's weird to say this, but from what little I saw of Victoria . . ." Again I tapered off.

"What?" Rebecca's voice was gently insistent. "Go ahead and say whatever it is."

I sighed. "From what I saw of Victoria, I just, well, I just didn't like her very much. I wasn't attracted to her."

Rebecca raised her eyebrows. "Not attracted to *her?* Jonathan, she's one of the most beautiful women I've ever seen, other than in the movies or something."

"Oh yeah, she's really great *looking,*" I said, "that much is obvious. It's like you said—she looks like a movie star."

Rebecca went on. "And I thought all men liked big boobs."

"I don't know," I said. "She has a great figure, if maybe a bit extreme. But that's not what I'm talking about."

"What, then?"

I tried to assemble my thoughts, recalling my meeting with Victoria. "It was weird. Even during the short conversation we had—and this is *before* she broke up with me—I was noticing that she seemed kind of fake."

"Well, she wasn't exactly candid with you about Teddy."

"No, that's not what I mean. It wasn't that I thought she was lying. It was like what she said—even the expressions on her face—were all just things she thought she should do."

I was having a hard time explaining, and Rebecca's furrowed brow told me I hadn't made my point clear. I tried again.

"It was like she was . . . *acting.* Trying to be some kind of perfect woman or something, but basing it all on really shallow, clichéd stuff."

I shook my head, frustrated by how hard it was for me to articulate this. "Does that make any sense?"

Rebecca nodded. "She sounds like trophy wife material," she said.

Then a look of horror washed over her face, and she turned

to look at me. "Oh, God—I shouldn't have said that, should I?"

I waved a hand. "No, it's fine. And you may be right. I guess I used to make a lot of money, and the photos I've seen make it look like we went out a lot, to all kinds of flashy clubs and events. And she was always right there, smiling for the camera."

I noticed Rebecca was still frowning. "What's wrong?" I asked.

Now Rebecca shook her head, no longer looking at me. "It's just . . . well, here I am, sitting here criticizing this woman I don't even know, even going so far as to call her a trophy wife . . ."

When she didn't continue, I said, "So?"

Rebecca's gaze was cold and level, focused solely on the road in front of her. "So it sounds like exactly what *I* used to be. And what Big Bob wishes I still was."

CHAPTER 20

"I think this is the street," Rebecca said. "What was the house number again?"

As I reached for the map, she turned towards me and said, "Um, can you read the house number?"

I smiled. "Yes—I can *read* numbers fine. They're like . . . like letters in words that I can't understand."

"Oh," she said, nodding. "I wasn't sure how that worked."

I looked at my map and announced, "We're looking for three two five. It's a big yellow house."

Rebecca slowed the car down and strained to read numbers on the sides of houses. Finally she said, "There's three twenty-five, but it's not a yellow house. Are we maybe on the wrong street?"

"No, that's my fault," I said. "I forgot that Mrs. Margolis told me the house wasn't yellow anymore."

Rebecca stopped the car in front of a large grey house. "So, is this it?"

I looked at it for a long moment. It fit the configuration of the house I remembered, but the pale grey siding was throwing me off. I squinted at the house, and the effect was that of looking at a black-and-white photo. Suddenly I felt that strange inner tingling—that all-too-rare sensation that I had learned to associate with *remembering.*

"This is it," I proclaimed.

Rebecca parked the car across the street, and we got out and surveyed the house, neither of us making any move to approach it.

"Are you okay?" she asked.

"Yeah—I'm just trying to see what I can recognize."

I stood taking in its details, comparing it against my own mental picture to see what was new, what was the same.

"Which one was yours?" Rebecca asked.

"My what?" I asked, puzzled.

"Your house. Didn't you say this lady was your next-door neighbor?" Rebecca pointed to the houses on either side. "So, which one is it?"

Whether brain damage or simple stupidity was to blame, I stood there slack-jawed. In all my preparation for this trip, I'd never once thought about the fact that I'd be seeing my old house. I had focused entirely on my meeting with Mrs. Margolis—my one true link to a past I couldn't otherwise access. But I'd never taken the next logical step.

"I don't know," I said stupidly. "Believe it or not, I never even thought that far."

Rebecca was gracious enough not to reply, and I turned my gaze to the house on the right. It seemed to be the mirror image of Mrs. Margolis's house, with all its features reversed. Its driveway was on the left, while Mrs. Margolis's was on the right. Its front door was on the right, as opposed to the left-side door on the house that faced us.

But that was the extent of its similarity; while the grey house in front of us was tidy and well-kept, the one on the right was dilapidated, its shabby white paint peeling, its yard overgrown. An ancient rust-riddled van was parked in the driveway, its side emblazoned with stick-on letters urging us to "Call the Happy Housepainter! No job too large or too small!" Apparently the house the van was parked next to was the exception.

Looking at it, I felt . . . *something*. A name came into my mind: Ronny Something. Bark. Park. No, Clark. Ronny Clark.

"That's not my house," I said quietly. "I think a kid I knew named Ronny Clark lived there. But I'm not sure."

I turned my attention to the house on the left, and nearly fell over.

"What is it?" Rebecca asked, as she saw me lurch backward, groping for the car. I needed something to support me. She hurried over to me while I stabilized myself, leaning heavily against the side of her car. I was aware of her studying me with concern, but my eyes remained locked on the house on the left.

It was nothing much to look at. A white, low-slung house that I think some call a bungalow. It was neither as well-kept as Mrs. Margolis's, nor as run-down as the house on the right. But something about it was making me feel . . . *awful.*

"What is it?" Rebecca repeated. "Are you okay?" Following my stare, she pointed. "Is that your old house? Did you just remember something?"

I became aware that I'd been holding my breath, and exhaled, a long sigh that burned my throat. My legs felt rubbery, and something hot and unpleasant was twisting inside my stomach.

"I don't know," I said, my voice choked.

"You don't look good," Rebecca said. "You look like you just saw something terrible."

"I feel terrible," I said. "But I don't know why. I'm not remembering that house, at least not like I remember this one." I shifted my gaze to Mrs. Margolis's house and instantly felt much better. I shook my head at the weirdness of the situation.

"I don't know what's going on, Rebecca. But looking at that house makes me feel . . . well, it makes me feel really bad. But not for any reason I can identify."

"How about this house?" Rebecca said, pointing to Mrs. Margolis's.

"No, I feel okay looking at it," I said. "This is really weird."

"Why don't we go see your old friend?" Rebecca said. She reached for my arm. "Do you need a hand?"

As always when she touched me, I was extremely conscious of the physical contact.

"No, I'm okay," I said. "Thanks."

On wobbly legs I made my way towards the big grey house, doing my best not to let the smaller house on the left into my peripheral vision.

Mrs. Margolis's house had a raised front porch, which meant I had to navigate several steps. Reading my thoughts, Rebecca said, "Here—give me your cane."

I did so, and she took me by the arm, her grip firm and confident. With my free hand I gripped the banister, and together we worked our way up the stairs.

"Thanks," I said when we reached the surface of the porch. "That was my first time doing stairs."

"It gets easier," Rebecca said. "You'll see."

"I hope you're right."

"Hey, look at me," she said, a request I was all too glad to fulfill.

"I know," I said. "You've been an inspiration to me."

Rebecca gave me a dubious smile. "Seriously?"

I nodded. "Yes. Seriously."

Together we walked towards the front door, and I pressed the doorbell.

Deep inside the house, I heard the bell, a dong-*ding*-dong melody that was instantly familiar to me.

"Isn't that the NBC theme, or jingle, or whatever it's called?" Rebecca asked.

"I don't know," I said, "but I remember hearing it." Suddenly I knew I had pressed that doorbell many, many times. And the memory made me happy.

"This is really cool," Rebecca said quietly.

"What?"

"This whole thing," she said gesturing towards the house, then turning to face me. "Seeing how happy you look. You don't smile much usually."

This caught me by surprise. "I don't?"

She shook her head. "No, you don't. But it's okay—it's not like you're grumpy or anything. You just probably have a lot on your mind."

"In my case," I said, "I think the bigger problem is that there isn't a lot *in* my mind."

We waited at the door, and I made a mental note to myself: Smile more.

CHAPTER 21

"What a delightful young lady," Mrs. Margolis said, after Rebecca excused herself to use the bathroom.

"I agree," I said, between bites of some truly amazing coffee cake that Mrs. Margolis had put out for us.

She nodded knowingly. "Yes, there is definitely some chemistry between you."

I choked on my cake. "But . . . but . . ." I sputtered, "she's married!"

Mrs. Margolis's face turned thoughtful. "Well, that sort of thing can complicate matters."

"That sort of thing?"

She patted my hand, "All I know is, whenever somebody comes into your life, there's a reason. Even if you don't see it at first."

"Well," I allowed, "she *is* a really good friend."

"But you want more than that," Mrs. Margolis said, her smile returning.

"No," I protested. "I don't want to do anything . . . *wrong.*"

Another pat on the hand. "Oh, I know that," she said. "I'm not saying you want to do something wrong. I'm saying you wish things were different."

"Boy, do I." I'm not sure why I felt comfortable being this candid with her, but I did.

"Well, Jonny, in case you haven't noticed, things *can* change. Look at you—you've gone through some very big changes."

"True," I said. "I just . . ."

I stopped myself. I just *what?* Wished Rebecca wasn't married? Wished my brain worked better? What good was wishing?

"Be patient," Mrs. Margolis said. "Good things are happening for you."

This elicited a bitter laugh from me. "Yeah," I said, "really good things. Let's see: a six-year coma, nearly total memory loss, and oh yes, let's not forget a career and a girlfriend, both down the drain. Yeah, life's going great."

Mrs. Margolis kept smiling, but her gaze grew more intent.

"Well, you did wake up. And from what I hear, that wasn't supposed to happen."

Okay, she had me there.

"What wasn't supposed to happen?" Rebecca asked, returning to the cozy living room where we sat.

I smiled sheepishly. "Me waking up."

"Of course you were supposed to," Rebecca said. "Everything happens for a reason."

"Do you believe that?" I asked. I wasn't being argumentative; I was genuinely curious.

"Based on some of the stuff I'm going through," Rebecca said, "I kind of have to."

"More coffee cake?" asked Mrs. Margolis.

"Actually," I said, "I'd love to see that tree you had in the back yard. Is it still there?"

"Oh, it's still there," Mrs. Margolis said. "I had to have it trimmed pretty severely after that awful ice storm we had, but it's a very resilient tree. But I do hope you're not planning to climb it."

I smiled. "No, I'm not quite ready for any tree-climbing just yet."

"Glad to hear it."

The three of us made our way through her kitchen out to the

back porch, which overlooked a beautifully manicured yard lined with flowerbeds guarded by concrete statues of angels, saints, and one stern-looking garden gnome. And at the center of it all stood a majestic maple tree. And I suddenly *knew* it was a maple tree, not because I knew anything about trees, but because I remember being told as a boy that this was a maple tree.

To confirm, I said, "Maple, right?"

Mrs. Margolis nodded. "The leaves are a nuisance during the fall—I have to pay a boy who lives up the street a fortune to rake my yard. But I couldn't bear to cut it down."

We stood looking at the tree, while memories and feelings washed over me in weird, thrilling waves.

"You were like a little monkey, climbing around in that tree," Mrs. Margolis said, smiling at the memory. "You were such a cute little fella."

"He was, wasn't he?" Rebecca said. "I saw some really cute old pictures of him at his parents' house."

On one hand I was flattered by all this attention. But I couldn't help noticing everybody was complimenting me in the past tense.

"Oh, I've got some great old photos of him in one of my albums," Mrs. Margolis said. She paused, her smile flickering and then disappearing for a moment. Then she was all smiles again, saying, "But we'll look at them some other time."

We adjourned to the living room, where Mrs. Margolis directed me to a curio cabinet containing a huge variety of ceramic figurines.

"You used to love looking at all my paddy-whacks," she said.

"Paddy-whacks?" Rebecca asked.

It came to me then—a surge of memory almost physical in its intensity.

"I called them that," I said hesitantly, like a newscaster relaying a story to his audience a moment after it is beamed into his earphones. "Mrs. Marigold—er, Mrs. Margolis told me they were called knick-knacks, and that would always make me think of that song. You know, *knick-knack, paddy-whack, give a dog a bone?* So I called them paddy-whacks."

Rebecca smiled. "You really *were* a cute kid, weren't you?"

Past tense again. Oh, well.

"And now he's a very handsome young man," Mrs. Margolis said, giving me a none-too-subtle conspiratorial wink.

Embarrassed, I said, "Oh yeah. Chicks dig guys with canes."

Mrs. Margolis turned away distractedly. "Howard carried a cane," she said. "You know, because of the shrapnel. From the war."

I felt like an idiot.

"Looks don't matter," Rebecca said. "I mean, Jonathan's really skinny, his mouth is kind of funny, and his right arm doesn't look quite right."

God, this was getting brutal. And I thought she'd missed the whole right arm thing.

"But he's still the nicest guy I know," Rebecca concluded. "That's what's important."

I'll admit, this got a smile out of my funny-looking mouth.

Self-conscious, I turned my attention back to Mrs. Margolis's curios. My gaze fell on a small figurine of a fat smiling man, sitting shirtless and cross-legged, his round belly exposed. It was a deep rich red, made of some sort of glazed clay, and very shiny. Instinctively I picked it up—it nestled in my hand, no larger than a golf ball.

"Buddha belly," I said, not sure where the words came from.

Mrs. Margolis laughed. "*That's* what you called him—I was trying to remember!"

Perplexed, Rebecca leaned close to see the object I held in my hand. I was conscious once again of her wonderful smell, clean and fresh, not cloying like the perfumes so many women wore.

"You always loved my little Buddhas," Mrs. Margolis said. "I had a set of three, but I finally gave you one."

Seeing Rebecca's puzzled look, she said, "I guess I told Jonny that it was good luck to rub his belly. And in classic Jonathan style he came up with a name for the little fella: Buddha belly."

Rebecca said, "Where's the third one?"

"The third what? asked Mrs. Margolis. "Oh, the third Buddha." She frowned. "It got lost, I'm afraid."

"That's too bad," Rebecca said. She reached for the figure, so I handed it to her. She held it in one hand, and rubbed its belly with the index finger of her other hand.

"So this is supposed to bring me luck?" she said.

Mrs. Margolis smiled. "Wait and see," she said. "It just might."

I was still staring at the smiling Buddha. "I think I still have mine," I said. "I seem to remember it. Sitting out somewhere where I could see it every day, like maybe on my dresser or something. But it's not at my parent's house. I don't remember much of anything there."

"Maybe you had it in Chicago," Rebecca said.

I shrugged. "Maybe. In that case, I should find out soon. I'm planning a trip up there, to sort out all the stuff I have in storage."

Rebecca frowned. "How would you get there? Would your parents take you?"

"They offered," I said, "but I told them no, thanks."

"But why not?" Rebecca asked.

Mrs. Margolis looked at me evenly, not saying a word.

"It's a long story," I said, hoping they wouldn't press me. Frankly I was afraid of what I might find in my storage space, worrying that there might be things there that would incriminate me. It just wasn't a risk I wanted to take in front of my parents. They were just too nice to be forced to confront the fact that their son might be a criminal.

"You're not planning to go up there alone, are you?" Mrs. Margolis asked.

"I've been getting around here all right," I said, a little more defensively than I'd intended.

"Jonathan," Rebecca said, "this is Springfield. It's nothing like Chicago." Scowling, she said, "Do you even remember Chicago?"

Crap.

I sighed. "Not really. But I know they've got trains from here that take you straight there, and after that I can take a cab wherever I'm going, right?"

It was Mrs. Margolis's turn to speak. "Jonny, unless you've miraculously remembered how to add and subtract, how on earth are you going to pay the cabby? Just hand him a bunch of bills and ask him to give back the part you don't owe him?"

It occurred to me that perhaps my plan was not yet fully fleshed out.

Instead of poking another hole in my scheme, Mrs. Margolis surprised me by saying, "Why don't we all go up? You know, make a nice day trip out of it. It's only three and a half hours by train, and they run all day."

"That might be fun," Rebecca said. "I've been wanting to go up there to do some shopping. I hate all my clothes, and our mall isn't exactly the greatest."

Now Rebecca and Mrs. Margolis were on a roll, carrying on the conversation quite well without me.

"We could go up first thing in the morning," Mrs. Margolis said. "I think the early train is around six-thirty or seven. How's that sound?"

"That would get us there around ten or so. We could get

Jonathan to his warehouse, then the two of us could go shopping."

"Maybe catch a matinee of one of the big shows. I still haven't seen *Sweeney Todd*, have you?"

"No, but I used to like going to plays."

"Round up Jonathan after the show, maybe grab a quick bite to eat, then take a seven o'clock train, and we're home in time for Leno."

"That sounds good."

"Perfect. When shall we go?"

Their discussion concluded, the two turned to me for input.

"Whenever," I said. "My calendar is open."

CHAPTER 22

"I'd forgotten how much I like riding on trains," Rebecca said, speaking up to be heard over the noise of the rails.

Mrs. Margolis nodded. "It's not elegant, like it used to be. But there's still something very nice about it, I agree."

It *was* nice. The motion of the train was different than riding in a car, simultaneously more powerful and more relaxing. And the scenery was better, too, since the train tracks weren't forced to follow along traffic-laden city streets. It was—to my memory at least—my first glimpse of just how wide open the farmlands of Illinois really were.

"Pretty, isn't it?" Mrs. Margolis said, noting the attention I was paying to the scenery rushing by my window.

"It is," I said. "I didn't realize how beautiful Illinois was."

Rebecca looked at me, her face growing serious. "You don't really know anything beyond the hospital and Springfield, do you?"

"Only what I've seen on TV," I said.

"That's not the same. TV isn't real. It's just weird to think that essentially you're a guy in his thirties who's never even left town."

Mrs. Margolis frowned, getting a glimpse of how blunt Rebecca's comments could sometimes be. I was about to reply when my attention was diverted.

"Over there!" I said, pointing to my left. "Are those cows?"

Mrs. Margolis and Rebecca looked out the window, then

back at me.

"Yes, dear," Mrs. Margolis said. "Those are cows. Herefords, I believe."

"You've never seen cows before?" Rebecca asked. She was starting to laugh, then stopped herself.

"Oh God," she said, "I'm doing it again. I mean, when *would* you have seen cows? There aren't exactly a lot of them roaming around the hospital."

"It's okay," I said. "I just—"

"No, it's not okay," Rebecca said. "I was rude just now, and even I know it. It's hard to grasp just how little of the world you've seen."

"I know what cows are," I said. "I've seen them on TV, and in speech therapy I had to learn and pronounce lots of animals' names. I just never saw one in the flesh before. At least, not that I can remember."

Rebecca looked at me a long time. Then she said, "It's really kind of neat, seeing how new everything is for you. The world must seem so full of surprises."

"That's one way to put it," I said. "And it's true—I've already had plenty of surprises. I just don't know how *neat* it is."

"It's all in how you look at things," Mrs. Margolis said.

I wanted to believe her.

Scanning the countryside through her window, Rebecca said, "Have you seen any horses yet?"

"Just Mr. Ed on TV," I said. Deciding to have some fun, I added, "It must be really interesting to talk with a horse. It's funny that out of all the mammals, they're the only ones who learned how to talk."

Mrs. Margolis stifled a smile, while Rebecca's face drew tight with concern.

"Jonathan," she said, "um, you do realize that horses can't really—"

Unable to maintain a straight face any longer, I let a laugh escape.

Rebecca looked at me sternly, then relented with a grudging smile. "Okay, you had me there for a minute, I'll admit."

Mrs. Margolis said, "I think it's wonderful that you didn't lose your sense of humor, Jonny."

I'd never thought about that before, being more focused on the seemingly more crucial things that I'd lost, such as my memory of all the people in my life, how to count, and so on. And was I really hanging on to my sense of humor, or was this perhaps a new development? Nothing I'd learned about my past suggested that I had ever been a barrel of laughs to be around.

A tall young man with tattooed arms and gaping earlobes stretched wide by some painful-looking earrings escorted us to my storage space. He left us facing a bright orange garage door, one of many that lined the outer enclosure of the facility. I fumbled in my pocket for the key my mother had given me, eyeing the massive padlock that secured the base of the door.

"Wow, how much stuff do you have?" asked Rebecca. "I was expecting a small closet. This is more like a two-car garage."

"Well, I do have a car," I said. "Mom had it put in storage along with my furniture."

"What kind of car?"

I stopped and thought. "I have no idea," I finally said. I had never thought to ask. Since I'd probably never be able to drive again, it hadn't been a pressing concern.

I inserted the key and fussed with the lock until it reluctantly clicked open. It took me a few more moments to figure out the door's latching mechanism—I'm afraid the stroke hadn't done much for my mechanical abilities. Finally I managed to raise the door over our heads.

To my left, Rebecca felt around and found a light switch.

Now a bare bulb cast a yellowish glow over the contents of the room.

Everything in front of us was black. A black desk. Black dresser. Black coffee tables stacked one on top of the other. Along one wall, Rebecca pulled off a dusty sheet to reveal a massive black leather couch.

The other dominant color—is it a color, or a material?—was chrome. If it wasn't black, it was chrome. Or it was black and chrome.

"Not a big fan of earth tones, I see," said Mrs. Margolis, making her way deeper into the storage bay around peninsulas of furniture and boxes.

Rebecca shook her head. "It does sort of scream *swinging bachelor pad*, doesn't it?" Running a finger along the couch she said, "This is really nice leather, though. It must have cost a fortune."

While they each had immediately stepped inside the bay, I remained standing in the doorway, surveying the objects in front of me.

Mrs. Margolis said, "Jonny, are you all right?"

I waved a hand distractedly. "I'm fine. I'm just taking it all in, seeing if I remember anything."

Rebecca poked her head out from behind a mountain of cardboard boxes. "Well?"

"So far nothing's ringing a bell," I said.

"Maybe you should come on inside and take a look."

Reluctantly I complied. I tried to identify why I was so hesitant. I realized that I felt like I was somehow trespassing, going through some stranger's belongings. Even though that stranger was me.

"It looks like they just brought all your stuff here just like it was in your apartment," Rebecca said. She had pulled open a dresser drawer, and held up a pair of socks. "They didn't even empty your drawers."

Mrs. Margolis said, "Take a look in that desk—maybe they left it the same way."

They—whoever they were—had indeed left my desk drawers intact. I opened the left top drawer to find a plastic caddy holding paperclips, postage stamps, and miscellaneous office supplies, including some computer devices that I believe they called *floppy discs*. A shallow center drawer yielded numerous pens, some receipts, a large metal Zippo lighter, a few cigars in tubes with Spanish labels, and an open pack of Marlboros.

"You smoke?" Rebecca asked, leaning over my shoulder.

"I guess I used to," I said. The idea didn't appeal to me at all; I found cigarette smoke very annoying now, and cigar smoke made me gag.

"You don't seem like a smoker," Rebecca said.

"I know what you mean," I said, "but I also know I've changed a lot."

"Well, you had very nice taste in clothing," Mrs. Margolis said, from somewhere in the back of the bay. "Or at least, some very *expensive* tastes."

Rebecca and I followed her voice to a corner of the bay where a lead pipe had been crudely suspended from the ceiling with some sort of wire. On the pipe hung a large assortment of suits, shirts, and pants.

"Hugo Boss, Armani, Brooks Brothers," Mrs. Margolis said, thumbing through the garments, inspecting their labels. "You were clearly a man concerned with your appearance."

I was now a man clad entirely in garments from Target and The Gap. Of course, I was also now a man whose mother did all his clothes shopping. I probably needed to change that, I reflected.

"Try one of them on," Rebecca said, pointing to the suits. I pulled a jacket off a hanger, and brushed the dust off its shoulders. I slipped it on, only to find myself positively swimming in the thing.

"Wow, that thing is huge on you," Rebecca said. "You must have lost a lot of weight."

"Definitely," I said. "I'm thinking of patenting the new Hooper-rific Coma Diet. Just give us six years, and we'll take off those unwanted pounds."

"That might be funny if it weren't so creepy," Rebecca said.

"Maybe a tailor could take these in," Mrs. Margolis said, hanging the jacket back up on the pipe.

"I don't know if I'm really an Armani kind of guy," I said.

"I want to see what you used to drive," Rebecca said, walking over to the left side of the bay, where a dark blue tarp completely covered the unmistakable shape of a car. Other than the couch and a matching leather chair, it was the only thing that had been covered up; the rest of my belongings had all been left exposed to six years of dust.

Together Rebecca and I peeled back the tarp, revealing a low-slung black sports car, all muscular bulges and aerodynamic curves.

"Oh, isn't that a nice-looking car," Mrs. Margolis said.

"My God," Rebecca gasped. "It's a Lamborghini."

She looked at me. "These things cost a fortune. I mean, a serious fortune." Narrowing her eyes the way she did when she was appraising something—or somebody—she said, "You must have been a *really* good accountant."

My stomach lurched. Or a really crooked one, I thought.

Rebecca wasn't letting it go. "So your mother never told you that you had a two-hundred-thousand-dollar car sitting here in storage?"

I assumed that was a large number. A very large number, based on Rebecca's tone. "I guess she didn't know," I said. "She just said I had a nice black car."

"That's kind of an understatement," Rebecca said. "And you don't remember it?"

"Nope."

"That's so weird," Rebecca said.

"Welcome to my world," I said.

"Have you found anything you do remember?" Mrs. Margolis asked.

"Not yet. But there's still a lot of stuff here for me to go through."

Eager to table the car discussion, I threaded my way around stacks of boxes to investigate the large dresser Rebecca had opened. In the top drawer I found a leather jewelry box. Inside was a Rolex watch, some expensive-looking cufflinks, and a bulky gold ring in which a large ruby bulged ostentatiously. I sighed, instinctively knowing which finger it would fit. Sure enough, while it was slightly loose on both my right and left pinky fingers—no doubt the result of my weight loss—it was too small for any of my other fingers. I slipped it on my right pinky and modeled it for Rebecca, the weight of the thing feeling like a doorknob hanging from my hand.

"That's a big ring," Rebecca said, raising an eyebrow. "Really big."

"Yeah, I've been thinking of joining the Sopranos." I'd hoped for a smile, but didn't get one.

I slid the ring off my finger and put it back in the jewelry box, pausing to pocket the Rolex before closing the box. I figured my dad might like the watch, which I could never see myself wearing.

"This doesn't seem like you," Rebecca said, her face turning more serious.

"What, the ring?"

"Not just that. All of this." She swept the room with a wave. "Thousand-dollar suits, the Rolex, the pinky ring. A car that cost as much as my house. I mean, there's nothing wrong with any of it. It just doesn't seem like . . . well, like *you*."

Mrs. Margolis spoke up. "What *do* you think he seems like, dear?"

"I don't know. Nice. Good. Caring. Not . . . *cold*, like all this stuff."

"It's as strange to me as it is to you," I said. "And I've told you before, I'm not sure that I'd like the person I used to be."

"Nonsense," Mrs. Margolis said. "You're a perfectly nice person. You've just had some bad things happen to you."

I wasn't so sure about that evaluation, but chose not to argue.

"Oh my," said Rebecca, fishing something from the drawer, "these are . . . *special*."

She held up an impossibly small pair of men's underwear, barely more than a pouch and some straps, all in a garish tiger-stripe print.

I grabbed the offending garment from her and stuffed it back into the drawer, saying, "Don't you need to leave soon, if you're going to make it to your show on time?"

"He's right, dear," Mrs. Margolis said, looking at her watch. "It's going to be at least a twenty-minute cab ride to the theatre district."

Rebecca frowned. "Are you sure you want to do this all by yourself? I wasn't envisioning you having so much stuff. We could stay around and help you."

"No, I'll be fine," I said. "Besides, you've already bought your tickets. You go on, and have a great time. We'll reconnect after the show; by then I'll have had time to go through all this stuff."

"You're sure?" Rebecca looked dubious.

"Absolutely," I said. "Now, go. You don't want to be late."

I stopped, thinking about what good people these friends were. "And thank you," I said. "Seriously. Thank you very much.

I couldn't have made this trip without you."

This got a gracious smile from Rebecca. The smile I loved, from a woman I'd never be allowed to love.

"Now, go," I repeated, returning the smile as best I could. "I'll see you after the show."

With the women gone I felt less self-conscious rooting through my old belongings. I tried to be methodical, devising a plan to explore every drawer, every box. Closer examination of my desk revealed some file folders, including one containing paperwork for my car. Although the numbers didn't make sense to me, it appeared that the vehicle was paid in full.

Also in the desk was a framed photo of Victoria, stunning as always, but noticeably less buxom than the new-and-improved Victoria who had visited me in the hospital. The photo was one of the few personal touches I encountered; nearly everything else I unearthed only offered further reinforcement of my priorities, which could be summed up as "expensive is better." Even the boxed and stacked books I found conveyed the same message, with titles that all dwelled on generating wealth and more wealth.

The dresser did reveal one item of personal significance: while rummaging through my embarrassingly lurid underwear collection, my hand closed on a hard, smooth object that felt instantly familiar. Retracting my hand from a melee of leopard spots, tiger stripes, and black silk, I felt a rush of recognition upon seeing the small red statue in my hand.

"Buddha belly," I said aloud.

"Nice car," somebody replied.

I spun around to face the open doorway, where a huge figure loomed, silhouetted by the sunlight. It wasn't until he stepped inside that I could make out his features.

"Hello, Jon-Jon," Brandon Cox said. "Welcome home."

CHAPTER 23

I stuffed the Buddha in my pocket and stammered, "What the hell are you doing here?"

"I could ask you the same," Brandon said, flexing his thick neck first to one side, then the other. "I thought we had an agreement that you'd call me when you came to check out your stuff."

"I guess I forgot," I said. "You know, what with my memory not being very good and all."

"Bullshit."

It was, so I didn't argue the point. "How did you know I'd be here? For that matter, how did you know where my storage space was?"

Brandon smiled. "I had your little brother ask your parents about that. Then I came here and gave the staff a little, you know, *incentive* to call me if you ever showed up here. It seems to have been a fortuitous investment on my part, given your *memory problems.*"

Ignoring his sarcasm, I tried to sound stern and impatient. "What do you want?"

"Three words," Brandon said, his smile dissolving. "My fucking money."

"I haven't found any money," I protested.

"Then let's look together," Brandon said, peeling off his suit jacket. "Based on that car right there, I'd say we're in the right place."

"What do you mean?" I said. "That's not my usual car?"

This prompted a bitter laugh. "Jon-Jon, the last time I saw you, you were driving a two-year-old Lexus. Nice car and all, but not exactly a Lambo."

"Oh."

"And trust me, Old Fistfuckers wasn't paying you enough to put you in a ride like *that.*"

Brandon had made his way over to the desk, where without asking, he began riffling through my drawers. He pulled out the photo of Victoria and waved it at me.

"You do know your brother is nailing her now, don't you?"

"Yes," I said, "I know that."

Brandon winced, shaking his head. "Man, that's got to sting. I mean, that is one major piece of ass we're talking about. Especially since she got the rack job." A smile spread across his face. "Hell, I'd have gone for some of that myself, but your little brother beat me to it."

"The files are in the left drawer," I said, eager to change the subject. "That's the only paperwork I found, and I went through everything."

"You don't mind if I look for myself." It wasn't really a question, so I didn't answer.

Brandon gave Victoria's photo one last leer, then tucked it back inside the desk. He pulled out a handful of files and laid them on the desk. Then he began a methodical search of the entire storage bay, looking in places that hadn't occurred to me, even checking compartments in the car. Initially I followed him, but I eventually got bored and went and sat on the couch.

Finally Brandon emerged from the back of the bay and lumbered over to the desk. Sweat now darkened the armpits and back of his pale blue shirt, with additional dark patches growing under his "man breasts," as I've heard them called in some sitcom.

"Well, you were right," he said. "There's nothing else here."

Picking up the files, he maneuvered his way to the leather chair, where he plopped down with a grunt. "Let's see what we've got here," he said, and began to read.

Not sure what else to do, I sat silently and watched. Brandon ignored me, skimming the various papers he held, skipping back and forth from one file to another.

"You don't have shit in the bank," he said finally. "And it looks like you paid cash for the car. Hell, you must have just got the thing, right before your little brain-fart happened. I know *I* sure as hell never saw you in it."

"I don't remember it," I said. "But I don't remember my old car, either."

Looking up from the files, Brandon stared at me with a combination of contempt and revulsion.

"What the fuck *do* you remember?"

For some reason I felt like leveling with him. "Hardly anything," I said. "Not you."

"Yeah, you already said that."

"Not Teddy," I continued. "Not my parents." Nodding towards the desk, I said, "Not Victoria."

"Jesus Christ," he said, staring at me even more intently. "They weren't kidding about that vegetable stuff. You're like a fucking vegetable that can talk. What good are you?"

I said nothing, having asked myself that same question repeatedly.

After a long moment, Brandon spoke again, his voice softer. "Look, Jon-Jon—we used to be friends. I mean, I was really sorry when you had your coma and all. Not just because of the money, but because I liked you. You were my kind of people."

I controlled a shudder, made worse by the fact that I likely *was* his kind of people.

"But you've got me in a bind," Brandon continued. "You and

I were making some serious money, and it's clear that you were getting your part." He gestured towards the car.

"I just want my part, that's all. I don't just want it—I need it. But it looks like you either lost it, or pissed it all away on yourself."

Brandon's voice dropped, a mannerism I'd learned to dread. "Either that, or you're playing me."

"I'm not playing you!"

"I'd like to believe that."

I wanted this to be over. Suddenly I wanted that more than anything.

"Take the car," I said.

"What?"

"Take the car," I repeated. "Hell, take anything in here."

Brandon was squinting at me. "You're offering me the Lamborghini."

"Yes," I said, "but with a condition. You take the car, and anything else in here you want, and then we're done."

"Done?"

"Yes, done. Meaning that you don't come asking me for anything else. Meaning you're out of my life, and I'm out of yours."

"And I get the Lambo."

"It's all paid for, right?"

"Yeah, that's what the paperwork said."

"So legally I can just give it to you, can't I?"

"We'd have to transfer the title and all, but yeah, you could do that."

"Well, do we have a deal?" I asked, surprised by how easily I'd fallen into all this wheeling and dealing.

Brandon looked at the Lamborghini, his hand idly stroking his chin as he performed some quick mental calculations. Then he sighed heavily.

"Yeah," he said, turning to face me. "We have a deal. I'll have to have it towed to a mechanic, to get it all flushed and recharged and whatnot."

I hadn't thought of that. I'll confess that I was hoping he'd just get in the car and drive away, but I suppose that wouldn't be realistic after years in storage.

"Whatever," I said. "I'll arrange for Teddy to handle that with you—I probably won't be coming back here."

Brandon smirked. "Teddy's going to be pissed that you gave the car to me, and not him."

I matched his smirk, but without the mirth. "I think Teddy already got quite enough from me, don't you?"

This got a harsh laugh out of the big man, who now rose with effort from the chair and stepped towards me, extending his hand.

I worked my way to my feet and grudgingly shook his hand.

"A pleasure doing business with you," Brandon said.

"And once we're done, we're done, right?"

"Yeah, yeah," he said. "I already agreed. Once I've got the car, we're done." Brandon ran a hand through his sweat-soaked hair, then wiped his hand on a pant leg. "I guess there's not a lot of point in trying to rekindle our friendship."

"I guess not."

Brandon reached for his jacket and began working his bulk into the garment. "What are you going to do with the rest of your stuff?" he asked.

"I don't know," I said. "Give it away. Sell it, maybe. Did you want anything? That TV back there is pretty big, and it looks like I've got lots of stereo stuff."

"No, thanks. Electronics came a long way while you were out of it. That stuff you've got is a joke by today's standards. I'll stick with the car."

"Pinky ring?" I said, joking.

"Nope. Got that covered, too." Brandon held up his hand, his ring even larger than the monstrosity I'd found in my jewelry box. "You do have some nice cufflinks, but they're all mono-grammed with the wrong initials for me."

"Sorry."

Brandon shrugged, immune to my sarcasm.

"Oh, and no offense, but you won't have much luck selling that leather chair," Brandon said, nodding towards the seat he had just vacated. "It may look nice, but it's uncomfortable as hell."

He walked to the doorway, squinting in the light shining in from outside. "So Teddy will get ahold of me about picking up the car, right?"

"I'll set it up," I said, thinking about what promised to be an interesting conversation with my brother.

"Don't screw me, Jon-Jon."

"Goodbye, Brandon."

After Brandon left, I wandered around the storage bay for a little while longer, seeing if there was anything I wanted to bring home with me. I had brought a small suitcase with me for that purpose, but nothing was really calling to me. How strange, I thought, that from all the possessions I'd acquired over a lifetime, there was nothing here that appealed to me. Maybe the leather couch, although I imagined the logistics of trying to get it home to Springfield would be a nightmare.

Home to Springfield—I thought about that phrase. It really was my home now; Chicago seemed a nice enough city to be sure, but I no longer had any reason to live up here. No, Springfield was my home now, for better or for worse. In sick-ness and in health.

I thought about calling Teddy, but decided I'd take care of that when I got home. We still hadn't spoken since I found out about Victoria, and today I wasn't really up for a big discussion about it.

I opened my suitcase and withdrew the new cell phone that Rebecca had insisted I purchase. I made sure it was turned on, then I went looking for something to read while I waited for Rebecca and Mrs. Margolis to contact me. In a nearby box I found a stack of magazines, and retrieved a glossy men's magazine from which I gathered I could learn about how to succeed in life, love, and business, all while building "killer abs." Wondering if the advice offered would still be up to date six years later, I sat down in the big leather chair to read.

Soon I was back on my feet. The chair really *was* uncomfortable—I felt like I was sitting on bricks. I started to move to the couch, then curiosity made me go back to examine the chair more closely. I poked the seat cushion, finding it hard and lumpy in places, soft and resilient in others.

I lifted the cushion up from the chair, feeling it from both sides. I felt distinct hard shapes under the leather, with straight, regular features. I fumbled with the cushion, finding a long zipper along one side. The zipper resisted, catching occasionally on the stuffing it contained, but I finally managed to get it open wide enough to reach a hand tentatively inside.

Groping, my fingers closed on something that felt like a small paperback book. Digging it from the soft foam stuffing that surrounded it, I managed to extract it from the leather seat cover.

In my hand I had a thick stack of dollar bills, banded tightly together. The bills all looked alike, and had the numbers *one zero zero* in each corner. Even with my minimal math skills, I knew I was looking at a lot of money.

And the seat cushion was still very, very lumpy.

CHAPTER 24

I needed time to think. That's why I didn't tell Rebecca and Mrs. Margolis what I found. Instead I made small talk with them when they returned, not mentioning my meeting with Brandon or my subsequent discovery. We closed up my storage bay and went out for an early dinner before heading back to Union Station. Through it all, I tried to disguise how much heavier my little suitcase had become.

I know, I could have simply called Brandon, and given the money to him. But I had already given him a car that Rebecca said was worth as much as a house, and I had no idea how much money this was. It might be far more than the value of the car. But it might be much less, and I didn't trust Brandon to do the counting for me. So I kept my guilty knowledge to myself during dinner and the train ride home.

When we got to the train station in Springfield, we walked Rebecca to her car, then I climbed into Mrs. Margolis's car, accepting her offer of a ride home. We were scarcely underway when she said, "So, when are you going to tell me what's in the bag?"

Trying not to sputter, I said, "Pardon?"

"You've had a death grip on that thing for the last four hours. What did you find?"

"Find?" I said. Yes, I was truly a great conversationalist under pressure.

"Jonny, you've been acting strange since we came back from

the matinee. I know you don't want to make a bad impression on Rebecca, but give an old broad some credit. You found something while we were gone, and whatever it is has got you scared to death."

So much for the Hooper poker face.

"It's complicated," I said lamely.

"Life usually is," Mrs. Margolis replied, pausing to flick her turn signal on.

"It's just that what I found, well, it proves that I wasn't a good person. And I don't know what to do about that."

Pulling up at a red light, Mrs. Margolis turned to face me. "Is it drugs?"

"No! Nothing like that. It's . . . well, it's money." I swallowed. "A lot of money, I think."

Mrs. Margolis nodded, her expression unreadable. Then the light changed, and she turned her attention back to the road, coaxing the car forward.

"Well, then," she said, "we'll count it when we get home."

"I don't want to drag you into this."

"Why are you so sure you're dragging me into anything? Maybe you just didn't like to keep your money in banks. You wouldn't be the first person to hide your money in your mattress, you know."

"It was in the leather chair, actually."

She shot me a sidelong look. "Same difference."

"Okay, but I don't think that's it. That car, all this money—it's more than I should have, based on the kind of job I had."

"Maybe you got lucky at the track," she said. In the glow of a passing street light, I saw her smile.

I laughed. "Somehow I don't think—"

"Jonathan," she said, "not to put too fine a point on it, but isn't it safe to say you don't remember how you came to own *anything* in that storage bay?"

I thought about this for a moment. "Well, yes," I said. "I mean, I assume I bought it using money I earned at my job."

"Which you don't remember, correct?"

"Um, correct."

"So how can you be so sure that you came about this money by illicit means?"

I sank a little lower in my seat. "Because my old business partner told me so."

Mrs. Margolis cocked an eyebrow. "Really? When was this?"

I let out a long sigh, then filled her in on my encounters with Brandon.

"Oh, my," she said when I'd finished. "No wonder you seemed so shaken up when we got back from the show."

"Yeah, he really caught me off guard when he showed up today."

"Well, it sounds like you handled it well. He should be out of your life now."

"I hope so. But he pretty much confirmed that I was, well, a criminal."

"Innocent until proven guilty," she said. "Let's count this money and see exactly what we're dealing with."

"*We* don't need to deal with anything," I protested. "This is my problem, and I don't want to get you involved in something, you know, shady."

For the first time her voice went stern. "Jonny, at some point you're going to figure out that the people who care about you don't mind helping you with your problems. Now, shall we head to my house, or would you rather count the money on your parents' kitchen table?" At this she cracked a smile.

"I hadn't thought about that," I said. "Your house is probably a better idea. But isn't it awfully late? Would you rather do this some other time?"

Mrs. Margolis tilted her head. "Jonathan, I'm an old woman.

This is the most interesting thing that's happened to me in years. You think I could go to sleep without knowing what's in the bag?" She turned to give me a mischievous smile, and I felt an instinctive reminder of why I had loved this woman.

"Okay, I surrender," I said. "Let's go to your house."

Mrs. Margolis's eyes flicked to her rear-view mirror. In a hushed voice she said, "I just hope nobody's tailing us."

"What?" I whipped around in my seat, my eyes frantically scanning the street behind us. It was entirely empty.

Mrs. Margolis laughed. "I'm joking, Jonny. You need to learn to see the humor in things—it makes life much more enjoyable."

I shook my head. I had a lot to learn from this woman; that much was clear.

When we arrived at her house, Mrs. Margolis made quick work of opening up the suitcase and spreading the bundles of bills on her dining room table.

"Oh, my," she said again.

"Yeah," I replied insightfully, while she began counting.

"Well, this is just an estimate," Mrs. Margolis finally said. "Based on the number of bundles and assuming each bundle has the same number of bills, I think we're looking at a little more than three hundred thousand dollars."

Feeling simultaneously guilty and stupid, I said, "That's a lot, isn't it?"

Mrs. Margolis nodded. "Let's just say I should have let *you* pay for dinner tonight."

I smiled, but felt panic creeping up on me. "What am I going to do with this?"

Now Mrs. Margolis sighed. "Jonathan, if you're so sure that this money doesn't belong to you . . ."

She paused, then shrugged.

"You could always give it back."

This turned out to be harder than it sounded. The next day, after making my way through a phalanx of receptionists, my call finally got put through to Aaron Fisk, founder of my old firm, Fisk and Tucker. He seemed very surprised—and not at all happy—to hear from me.

When I got to the part I'd rehearsed, about "returning something I had to its rightful owners," he shushed me immediately.

"What is your number?" Fisk demanded. "I need to call you back. But not from here."

I recited my phone number, to which his only reply was, "Ten minutes." Then the phone line went dead.

With nothing else to do, I sat and waited, hoping that ten minutes was not a long time.

It wasn't. The phone rang just a short while later, and when I picked it up he hissed, "I cannot believe you called me at the office!"

Determined not to be intimidated by this man, I said, "I'm fine—thanks for asking."

Unfazed, Fisk tore into me. "Listen, Hooper. I realize that you are brain-damaged, but you simply cannot call our office to discuss such . . . delicate matters. The firm has been under intense scrutiny lately."

"I'm not surprised," I said. Once again I found myself a blithe conversationalist around a man I didn't trust. For once I didn't feel bad about this unexplained ability.

Fisk said, "What exactly do you want?"

"It's like I said," I replied. "I've become aware that I have in my possession some . . . *things* that don't belong to me. So I wanted to talk to you about returning them to their rightful owners."

There was a long pause. Then Fisk said, "We simply can *not* do this over the phone."

"Face to face is fine with me," I said. "I could try to come up there, but it's hard for me to travel."

"No!" Fisk said, nearly shouting. "Do *not* come to Chicago. I cannot afford to be seen with you here in town. I will come to you. You now live in Springfield, correct?"

"That's right."

"This week is entirely shot for me. But I will be down in Springfield meeting with a client on . . ." Fisk paused, presumably checking his schedule. ". . . next Tuesday," he finally said. "I could meet with you that evening to discuss this . . . this *matter* of yours. Will that work?"

My own social calendar was relatively uncluttered, so I was able to immediately respond. "Tuesday would be fine, I guess."

"Done. Tuesday night. Meet me at that new place on Sixth Street. *Sonata*. Eight o'clock. Do *not* bring anybody with you, or I will not sit down with you." He paused. "Do you know where *Sonata* is?"

My parents had driven me by it, and I knew it was considered one of the nicer restaurants in town. "I know where it is," I said.

"Eight o'clock."

"Eight is fine," I replied, wondering how I'd get to the restaurant.

"The reservation will be under the name of Smith," Fisk said, and hung up.

CHAPTER 25

Sonata was one of the trendy new restaurants in Springfield's recently renovated downtown area. Everything about its décor screamed "modern," which I've learned is often the opposite of "practical" or "comfortable." My hostess seated me in a chair that looked more like a piece of abstract sculpture, a contraption of swooping black metal bars and red leather panels into which I had difficulty situating myself, and from which I feared the process of extracting myself might prove even more challenging. I was glad I had brought my cane, and looked for a place nearby to prop it.

Then I reached in my pocket and pulled out the photo of Fisk that I had printed off the Internet. I didn't remember him at all, but I hoped the craggy face and massive glasses he wore would be easy to spot. I folded the photo and tucked it back in my pocket and began to examine the menu. I'm not sure how to label the cuisine, but it seemed to favor unusual combinations of flavors. Kumquat chutney was featured in one dish, and the lobster and fennel spring roll with mango chili dipping sauce piqued my curiosity.

"God, you lost a lot of weight," a voice boomed.

I looked up to see the stern face of a tall, solidly built man with thinning white hair and heavy black-rimmed glasses. He stood across the table from me. I rose with difficulty, but managed to do so without resorting to my cane.

"Mr. Fisk," I said, offering my hand.

"Hooper," he replied, reluctantly shaking my hand. His grip was firm, though. This was not a weak old man.

We maneuvered ourselves into our chairs while Fisk barked, "Chivas; rocks," at a passing waiter. Fisk nodded to me.

"Me too," I said. I had recently acquired a fondness for Scotch, sharing an occasional late-night cocktail with my father, who referred to the heavy bottle of Chivas in the liquor cabinet as "the good stuff."

At a table nearby somebody's cell phone began playing a noisy pop tune.

"That reminds me," I said, reaching into my pocket. I pulled out my phone, hit some buttons, and laid it on the table, along with my house keys.

"I always forget to mute the thing," I said. "Drives me nuts when it goes off in a restaurant."

Fisk said, "I put mine on vibrate when my driver dropped me off."

A busboy came by, filling our water glasses. Then our drinks arrived. I picked mine up, wondering stupidly whether I should toast him before drinking. I discarded the notion and took a sip. It was good stuff.

Fisk did the same, then set his drink down. "So what is this all about? And be quick about it—I have a flight chartered back to Chicago tonight, so I only have time for one drink."

Apparently tonight would not be my first kumquat chutney experience after all. I took another sip, then set the heavy tumbler down.

"I've got money—a little more than three hundred thousand dollars—that I don't think belongs to me." I had memorized that statement, testing it on Mrs. Margolis to make sure my numerical references were correct.

"And why is this my problem?" Fisk said. A waitress came by, but he waved her away.

I decided to be blunt. "I believe that this is money that Brandon Cox and I bilked out of one of our Fisk and Tucker clients. And I want to give it back."

Fisk stroked his chin, his eyes scanning me like a dog-show judge evaluating a cocker spaniel. Finally he spoke.

"You . . . *believe* this is how you came into this money."

"Yes."

"And that it belongs to one of our clients."

"Yes."

"Which one?"

"Which what?" I said, puzzled.

"Which client?"

"I . . . I don't remember."

"And do you remember how you . . . *bilked* them?"

"Er, no."

"And do you know the total amount for which you allegedly bilked them?"

I noticed he was slipping legal terminology into his conversation. Now my actions were *alleged* actions. But that was the least of my problems. Suddenly my masterful plan to clear my conscience was faltering badly.

"Let me see if I can sum this up," Fisk said, "You *believe* that you bilked an unknown amount of money from an unknown client, by means you do not remember. Am I getting that right?"

"Yes," I mumbled.

"And again, I find myself asking, why is this my problem?"

"What I did—what we did—wasn't right."

Fisk had been sipping his Scotch, but now he slammed the glass down.

"Hold it right there," he said. "What *we* did? Now you are saying *I* was a part of . . . of whatever the hell you are talking about?"

"Yes . . . no . . . I don't know," I said brilliantly. "I assumed you would know what was going on—I mean, it's your firm."

Fisk's voice was an icy whisper. "You do *not* want to try to bring me into any mess you created. That would be a mistake the size of which you cannot begin to fathom."

Then his voice mellowed slightly. "You said yourself, you have no recollection of these alleged actions, correct?"

"Yes."

"But you do recall working with Cox on this."

"It's not that I actually recall it. But he's told me about it."

This gave him pause. "You spoke to Cox," he said.

"Yes."

"Have you considered simply giving the money back to him?"

I'd been flailing, but here he was bringing up a topic about which I had a strong stance. "No," I said, "I don't trust him."

To my surprise, Fisk laughed, a harsh sound more like a cough than an expression of levity. "You may be less brain-damaged than you think," he said. "Cox is a snake."

I stared at him, trying to choose my words. "So, why don't you get rid of him?"

Fisk sighed. "Hooper, with everything that has happened in the past few years, the last thing Fisk and Tucker needs is any negative publicity—so much as a hint of any wrongdoing. If I try to fire Cox, he might raise a stink, and I cannot have that. So I keep him assigned to accounts where he has little or no opportunity to cause any problem. And we watch him like a hawk, and he knows it. So Cox has been neutralized." Fisk spread his hands in an odd shrug. "It is an imperfect solution, but such is life in our line of work."

Your line of work, I thought, but said nothing.

"As far as your little problem," Fisk said, "I fail to see how I can help you."

"So you acknowledge the possibility that what I said is true?"

Fisk nodded. "Cox is a snake. Frankly, I always thought you

were, too. So it would not surprise me to learn that you two were playing it fast and loose back then."

He sighed. "It was a different time," he concluded. The look on Fisk's face suggested that he missed how things were "back then."

"So you're okay with just . . . just sweeping this under the rug?"

Fisk's voice grew more cold. "Hooper, you are an intelligent man. Or at least you were. Even now, you do not come across as a dummy."

I shifted awkwardly in my seat, damned by faint praise.

"You need to be realistic," Fisk said. "Yes, it looks like you . . . *acquired* some money that was not rightfully yours. But you cannot say how, when, or from whom. The person you *acquired* it with will not help you. And I will not allow myself to be dragged anywhere near this grenade. So I honestly do not know what you hope to accomplish."

I had no response to offer, so Fisk went on.

"I am aware that some . . . questionable activities may have taken place at my firm—none of them with my direct knowledge or involvement, I hasten to add—but I have straightened things out now, and everything is under control."

Fisk leaned forward. "Everything is under control," he repeated, "and I cannot let you jeopardize that."

The look in his eyes chilled me, making wonder just how far he would go to protect his firm. I suspected *very* far, and for the first time felt a little afraid of the man.

Helpless, I asked, "So what should I do with this money?"

Now Fisk was becoming exasperated. "For God's sake, Hooper, *spend it*. Look at you—you lost everything. You will never work again, at least not in accounting. I have heard about your brain damage in that respect, you know. Your brother is not the most tight-lipped person in the firm."

Teddy. I gritted my teeth.

"Spend it," Fisk repeated. "Buy yourself a house. Hell, buy your parents a house. Whatever—just spend it. Think of it as compensation for all you lost."

"But it's somebody else's money."

"So give it away if you feel so strongly about it." Fisk drained his glass and rose from the table with a grunt. "But not to me."

He laid some money on the table, and walked away.

I stayed a little longer, finishing my Chivas. Then I wrestled myself out of my chair, tucked my phone and keys in my pocket, and grabbed my cane.

"Thank you *very* much, Mr. Smith," a waiter called after me as I walked out. Apparently Fisk was a good tipper.

I stood at the curb in front of the restaurant, taking in my surroundings. Sixth Street was bustling with activity, mostly people my age or younger roaming around the shops, clubs, and restaurants that lined the street. Music from several different establishments mingled and clashed in the air, and car horns honked as drivers battled for parking places.

Finally I felt a tap on my shoulder and turned around.

Mrs. Margolis beamed up at me. "So, did you get it?" she asked eagerly.

"I don't know," I said. "Let's find out." I pulled out my cell phone, and pressed the combinations of buttons she had shown me. Then I held the phone up to my ear. In a moment I smiled.

"Got it," I said. "It's faint, but you can hear our voices."

"Wonderful!" Mrs. Margolis said, reaching into her purse. She pulled out her cell phone and flipped it open. "I managed to get a couple of decent shots of the two of you from where I was sitting. It was tough because of the lighting, but I think this one came out particularly well."

She held her phone in front of me, and I could make out the

image of Fisk and me leaning over the table in intent conversation.

"Wow," I said. "I had no idea a phone could do all this."

She smiled, snapping the phone shut. "Technology is a wonderful thing. Now, come along—I'm parked this way."

As we walked to her car, I briefed her on the conversation I'd just had with Fisk.

"So you got him to admit they were cooking the books?" she asked.

I shook my head. "He was being pretty careful about what he said. And he made sure *never* to admit that *he* was involved in any way. But he did make it clear that he was aware of some of the problems inside the firm." I paused, remembering his words. "He says it's all under control now."

"Well, *now* the law makes him responsible for that sort of thing, whether he's directly involved or not. I'm not surprised he's being careful."

"I doubt we can use anything we recorded tonight in court," I said. "He was *very* careful."

"Still, it's good insurance. I doubt he'd want anybody seeing these photos of the two of you together, or reading transcripts of your conversation, no matter how cagey he was with his words."

Mrs. Margolis beeped her car open, and we climbed into our seats. She started the car, but left it in idle. I became aware that she was staring at me. Then I saw how broadly she was smiling.

"This was more fun than I've had in years," she said. "I feel like Mata Hari. And you'd make a good James Bond."

I laughed. It had been a little fun, I had to admit. Then my spirits crashed again.

"But I still don't know what to do with this money."

She smiled, putting the car in gear. "You're smart. You'll think of something."

CHAPTER 26

Traffic lightened up once we got out of the downtown area, and Mrs. Margolis's car picked up speed.

"That went a lot quicker than I thought it would," I said. "Can I take you to dinner somewhere? It's still early, and you've done so much for me."

Mrs. Margolis shook her head. "I ate earlier, because I wasn't sure how long you two would take. But I still have some of that homemade lasagna in the fridge—I could heat it up for you in a jiffy."

I really wanted to take her someplace nice. But I'd had her lasagna before, when I was over at her house planning our little cellphone espionage mission. It was wonderful.

"That's awfully tempting," I said, "but I don't want to impose. And I wouldn't want to deprive you of any of that amazing lasagna."

She smiled. "Don't be silly. I made plenty—enough for several meals. I had an inkling I'd be seeing a fair amount of you this week, after our little Chicago adventure."

She was beaming as she drove—it was clear she was really enjoying this, nerve-racking as I found it all. I smiled in spite of myself.

"Well, okay," I said, "but only a small helping."

"That would be a first for you," she said, still smiling.

She had me there, so I shut up and let my thoughts shift

from kumquat chutney to homemade lasagna.

"That was incredible," I said, wiping my mouth with a napkin. "I can't believe you're not Italian."

"Oh, but I am," she said. "My maiden name was Spinelli. My parents came over from Sicily."

"Ah, no wonder."

"Oh, I caught plenty of grief from my family when I started getting serious about Howard," she said, as she rinsed some dishes in the sink. "My parents wanted me to marry a nice Italian boy, and here was Howard, with his red hair and his freckles . . ."

Her voice trailed off, and she absently wiped a dish with a towel, her eyes welling up.

"Listen, I'm sorry I brought it up," I said.

"Don't be sorry," she said, surprising me with her stern tone. "I wish people wouldn't react like that. I *like* thinking about Howard. I *like* remembering him." She nodded to herself, a wistful smile on her face.

Then she turned her attention to me again. "People don't need to try to avoid everything that might make them feel bad. If you do that, you'll also miss out on the things that can make you feel good."

"I'm not sure I understand," I said. "Do I do that?"

"My God, your whole family does that!"

Mrs. Margolis clapped a hand over her mouth, eyes wide. Then she sat down heavily across from me and reached out to touch my hand.

"Jonny, I am so sorry. I had no business saying something like that."

She seemed unduly upset, so I tried to appease her.

"Don't worry about it," I said. "I think I know what you mean. I mean, even with my, uh, reduced capacity, I can tell my mother is in total denial about how much I'll recover from my stroke."

"Denial?" Mrs. Margolis said, starting to smile. "You've had time to study psychology in the short time you've been awake?"

I shrugged. "I remember some concepts from before—that's why I woke up with a decent vocabulary. Plus, I watched a lot of soap operas in the hospital, and they all seem to have a character who's in therapy."

This got a chuckle out of her. She let go of my hand and sat back in her chair.

"And actually, I have read some psychology, now that I know how to look up stuff on the Internet. There's a lot of information about stroke victims, and I've been trying to see which of it I can apply to myself."

I paused, struggling for words. "It's hard—I've got to basically figure out who I am as a man, without the benefit of growing up."

She was looking at me appraisingly. "I think you've done a lot of growing up," she said. "And I think it's pretty clear who you are."

"Not to me it isn't. I mean, I have feelings about what I like, and who I like, and what's good and what's bad. But it doesn't seem to connect to anything I've learned about my past."

I sighed, trying to put a finger on it. "It's like I'm not me anymore. And I don't even think I'd want to be me, based on what I keep learning."

"Oh, honey," Mrs. Margolis said, reaching for my hand again. "You stopped being you many, many years ago. And it had nothing to do with any stroke."

There was such an odd look on her face. Sadness, but there was something else. Pity? Love?

"What . . . what are you saying?"

Mrs. Margolis stood up. "Let's go to the living room," she

said. "I have something to show you."

I followed her out to the living room and sat down on a loveseat next to her curio cabinet. Mrs. Margolis busied herself going through the drawers of a dark wooden hutch, then approached me holding out a small photo album.

I took it from her but didn't open it, still waiting for an explanation.

"You were over here a lot as a little boy," she said, gently smiling. "I accumulated quite a few photos of you before your family moved away,"

She nodded towards the photo album. "Go ahead. Take a look." Then she sat down in a small chair across from me, never taking her eyes off my face.

I began to leaf through the album. Some of the photos were familiar—she must have exchanged copies with my parents. But others were new to me, showing me in her backyard, climbing that wonderful tree, or sitting at her kitchen table, stuffing my face.

I noticed that most of the photos were of me alone, with Teddy only making rare appearances. Some showed me and Mrs. Margolis together, working in her garden or mixing batter in the kitchen. Her hair was much darker, and she was a lot thinner, but it seemed that her face never changed.

I looked up at her, seeing the same smile on the woman sitting across from me as in the photo taken so many years ago.

Then I turned the page.

This photo showed me sitting in an old-fashioned red wagon. But I was not alone; sitting next to me was a little girl with brown hair, and eyes that looked . . . like mine.

"Maggie."

The word came out of my mouth involuntarily, foreign yet familiar.

"Mag—" I started to say again, but I stopped myself, springing out of the loveseat and nearly tripping as I ran to the bathroom. I lunged towards the toilet, landing painfully on my knees and grasping the bowl with my hands as the contents of my stomach spewed from my mouth. Spasm after spasm wrenched my body, leaving me crumpled and prone on the bathroom floor, my head hanging over the toilet, arms and chin resting on its porcelain rim.

After a long moment mercifully free from heaving, I heard Mrs. Margolis's voice.

"Is there anything I can do?"

I realized I hadn't even managed to close the door. "Give me a minute," I gasped. "And close the door. Please."

There was a long pause, then I heard the door click shut.

Pulling my head back, I flushed the toilet. Then I flushed it again and sat back tentatively on my haunches, afraid of getting too far away from the bowl. But my stomach seemed to have stabilized, so I eventually clambered to my feet and cleaned up after myself.

Finally I opened the door, to find Mrs. Margolis still standing there.

"Please," I said, "sit down."

On shaky legs I navigated back to the loveseat. The photo album had fallen to the floor. Gingerly I picked it up, mentally plotting the optimal path back to the bathroom, just in case.

I found my way back to the photo that had so badly rocked me, and forced myself to remain calm as I examined it.

"Maggie," I said again, trying the name out on my tongue.

"Maggie." It felt more natural this time.

Mrs. Margolis's voice was barely more than a whisper.

"Do you remember?"

I looked at the photo, awash in feelings more powerful than I had ever experienced.

"She was . . . my sister," I said, again barely conscious of

216

forming the words.

"Yes."

"My sister. Maggie."

"Yes."

I turned the page. Maggie and I were playing in Mrs. Margolis's back yard, me in a ridiculous cowboy hat, Maggie in a patched set of overalls.

"She was such a tomboy," Mrs. Margolis said, sitting down next to me on the loveseat. She was smiling, that smile she had that showed happiness and pain at the same time. It was a feeling I was beginning to understand.

"My . . . little sister," I said.

"Yes, she was a year younger than you," Mrs. Margolis said. "Between you and Teddy."

"She . . . *was* younger?" I said, noting the past tense.

"Yes, Jonny."

"She's . . . not here now." It wasn't a question, but Mrs. Margolis answered me anyway.

"No, Jonny. She's gone. She died, Jonny. When you were just a little boy."

On top of everything else I was feeling, my eyes hurt. And my face was wet. Then I realized I was crying. To my knowledge, I had not cried since I woke up from my coma, so essentially this was my first time crying. I didn't like it. But I couldn't control it. In retrospect I guess that's what crying is—a physical result of surrendering to feelings you can't control.

Mrs. Margolis bustled to her feet and brought me a box of tissues. Reaching underneath my glasses I dabbed absently at my cheeks, not wanting to take my eyes off the photos I was staring at. The little girl was so pretty. So happy. And in every photo that showed us together, so was I, grinning stupidly in the midst of whatever activity the camera had captured.

"You two loved each other so much," Mrs. Margolis said.

217

"She called you the best big brother in the whole world."

I began to bawl, a wordless keening that hurt my throat and tore at my chest. My heart hurt, and I gave voice to its pain, calling to powers unknown in an awful full-body lament.

At some point my breathing returned to normal, and I was once again capable of speech. A mountain of crumpled tissues cluttered the coffee table in front of me, and Mrs. Margolis had returned to her chair across from me, letting me find my breath, my voice.

"How?" I said.

"Pardon me?"

"How did she . . . how did it happen?"

Mrs. Margolis sighed. "She was hit by a car. A hit-and-run driver. They never caught him."

I felt my eyes welling up again but willed the tears back, at least for now. "Did she . . ."

"They say she died instantly."

"Oh," I said.

"She was only eight years old."

"I don't know what that means," I said.

"It means she was only a little girl."

"Oh."

"That picture of you two in the wagon? That was taken right before she . . ."

"Oh."

We sat for a long time in silence. I leafed back and forth through the photos; thinking, remembering, loving. Hurting.

"My parents," I said finally. "They never said anything."

"I know."

"There are no photos of her at home."

"I know. I saw that when I visited. But it's what I had expected."

"Not on the walls. Not even in any photo albums."

Mrs. Margolis sighed. "I had wondered about that. That's why I held off on showing you this album."

"I'm . . . I'm glad you showed it to me."

"Are you?"

I thought about this. I felt awful—truly awful. Maybe *glad* wasn't the right word. But I had needed to know the truth.

"Yes, I am," I finally said. "It's like you were talking about. We shouldn't be so afraid of upsetting somebody that we hide the truth from them."

"Unless of course a woman is asking you if a pair of slacks makes her rear end look fat," Mrs. Margolis said, immediately looking sheepish for having made a joke.

But it was just what I needed, and I found myself laughing out loud, the sensation curiously intensified after my lengthy crying jag. I've since figured out that crying leaves you emotionally raw, magnifying the impact of every subsequent feeling. At least it does for me.

I caught myself. "God, it must be late. I can call for a cab or something."

"Don't be silly. I can take you home." Mrs. Margolis stood up. "Now, where did I put my purse?"

"Actually," I said, "I don't know if I'm ready to face my parents. I don't know what to say to them. I don't even know what to think about them."

"Why don't you stay here tonight?" Mrs. Margolis said. "I've got two guest rooms—you can have your pick."

"I don't know. I'd have to call my parents. I've never not come home before." Yes, I was a grown man, and yes, I was pretty upset with my parents. But they had been taking care of me, and I didn't want them to worry.

"I'll call them," she said. "I'll tell them you're not feeling well, and that I'll bring you home in the morning."

"I feel weird asking you to do that."

Mrs. Margolis shot me a look that reminded me about how she felt about friends asking for help.

"Okay," I said. "Thanks."

Moments later I was listening to Mrs. Margolis's side of the conversation.

"Oh, it's no trouble. I've got this huge house, and frankly I enjoy having some company."

"No, no, you don't need to come pick him up tonight. I don't think he's feeling well enough to ride in a car right now, are you Jonny?"

She looked at me for my response. Gratefully I shook my head, and she resumed her conversation.

"That's fine, Ellen. I'll either call you in the morning, or I'll simply drop him off if I'm in the neighborhood. No, it's no trouble. You take care now."

Mrs. Margolis put down the receiver. "There. Now you've got all night to collect your thoughts."

"Thank you," I said. "You've been so—"

"Don't mention it," Mrs. Margolis said, cutting me off with a gentle smile. "Now let's pick out a room for you. Are you up to tackling the stairs?"

"Absolutely. I'm getting pretty good at them these days."

But as we headed upstairs, my legs still wobbled, and I clutched the banister tightly until completing my ascent.

"Good night, Jonny," Mrs. Margolis said after making sure I had everything I needed in terms of towels and bedding. "Sweet dreams."

It took me a long time to get to sleep. At one point I got up and made my way as quietly as I could down Mrs. Margolis's creaking staircase, rooting around until I retrieved the photo album that had shaken me up so badly. I took it back upstairs with me and pored over it by the light of a lone bedside lamp, alternately crying and smiling as new memories bobbed to the surface, each prompted by a faded image on a plastic-covered page. My stomach growled occasionally, but never forced me to make any more sprints to the bathroom, likely due to the absence of any remaining food.

After catching myself nodding off several times, I switched off the light and lay back in the soft but unfamiliar bed. And then Mrs. Margolis got her wish: when dreams finally came, they *were* sweet.

I dreamed of Maggie. My little sister.

CHAPTER 27

I woke up to the smell of bacon. It took a moment to realize where I was, and then I remembered how the evening had ended. My cheeks were wet—apparently I had been crying in my sleep. Yet I felt oddly happy, as if I'd spent the night catching up with an old friend.

My dreams of Maggie were still clear in my mind, and in those dreams I was a little boy, not a grown man recovering from a stroke. In those dreams I was happy, and I guess I brought some of that happiness back with me when I awoke.

After rinsing my face in the upstairs bathroom, I put on my shirt and pants from the night before and padded barefoot down the stairs, following that wonderful smell.

"Look who's up," said Mrs. Margolis as I entered her kitchen. The smile she greeted me with was a great way to start the day. "Are you hungry?"

"Extremely," I said. "For some reason I'm utterly famished." Then I remembered why and added, "I guess I wasted some great lasagna last night. I'm sorry about that."

"Don't be silly. You had quite a night last night—that couldn't have been easy for you."

Her expression grew more concerned. "How are you doing after all that? Did you sleep all right?"

"I didn't really sleep much," I admitted, gratefully accepting a cup of coffee. "But thanks for letting me stay here."

She waved a hand. "You're welcome here any time. Now,

eat." She gestured sternly at the plate she had placed in front of me, heaped with bacon and eggs.

I obeyed, eating in silence while she bustled about the kitchen.

When I finished, she cleared my plate before I could get up and refilled my coffee. Finally she sat down across from me, a cup of coffee in her hand.

"Thank you for . . . well, for everything," I said.

She nodded, smiling.

A sudden bang on the window to my left startled me. I turned to see a squirrel clinging to the outside of the window screen. He must have launched himself from the branch of a nearby tree. From the sound of the impact, I was surprised he hadn't cracked the glass.

"Oh, my," said Mrs. Margolis. "Looks like Stanley is rather impatient today."

"Stanley?"

"Stanley the squirrel, of course," she said. "I'm late in bringing him his breakfast, and he's making his displeasure known."

Sure enough, the look on the squirrel's face as he stared through the window at us did seem to register a certain indignation. He moved his head in sudden jerks, like a badly animated cartoon, always keeping an eye trained on us.

"You feed him every day?"

"Oh, just breakfast," she said, standing up and opening a cupboard. "I wouldn't want to spoil him with lunch and dinner, too."

"Of course not," I said. I was smiling now, feeling a vague recollection of having helped Mrs. Margolis feed some backyard wildlife when I was a small boy. "And just what does a squirrel eat for breakfast?"

"Whatever I damn well feel like feeding him," she said, trying to sound stern but failing. "Although he's shown a preference for walnuts. Oh, and he loves Cheerios." She withdrew a bright yellow box from her cupboard and poured some cereal into a bowl.

"Come along now," she said. "We can't keep Stanley waiting, now can we?"

"Perish the thought," I said, following her as she stepped out onto her back porch.

We sat down in a pair of weathered patio chairs that overlooked her back yard. Watching us warily, Stanley made his way down from the window screen and scampered across the porch, choosing a location on its outer edge to perch, just above the steps that led down into the yard. He turned himself to face us, sitting on his hind legs, his front paws twitching eagerly.

Mrs. Margolis tossed a Cheerio in his direction. Stanley snatched it off the floor in a blur of motion and returned to his position, eyeing us as he chewed, his cheeks bulging with his prize. This transaction was repeated several times, and I noticed that each time the squirrel chose a spot on the porch a little closer to Mrs. Margolis for the consumption of his circular treats.

"Here," Mrs. Margolis said, handing me the bowl. "You give him one."

I plucked a Cheerio from the bowl and threw it towards Stanley. At least that was my intent; the oaten projectile flew far left of its target and skittered off the porch, lost in the grass somewhere. Stanley glared at me with contempt.

I handed the bowl back to a smiling Mrs. Margolis. "I guess we can add *throwing* to the list of things I can't do anymore."

"Well, you're new at this," she said, throwing another Cheerio to the ravenous rodent.

"True," I said. "And I'm sure there were some complex aerodynamics at play."

"No doubt."

After a few more throws, Stanley's cheeks were swelling to

comical proportions, and he sat back on his haunches, chewing contentedly. I decided to launch what might become an uncomfortable conversation.

"I have some questions," I said.

She turned to face me. "I thought you might." Again, that sad, caring smile.

"You said that I . . . that I stopped being me a long time ago."

Mrs. Margolis inclined her head but said nothing. She turned and aimed another Cheerio at Stanley.

"So," I said, "what did you mean by that?"

She stirred uncomfortably in her chair. "Jonathan," she began, "how much do you remember about Maggie?"

"I don't know. I remember playing with her. I remember . . ."

I paused, thinking out loud now, essentially commenting on snippets of memory as they passed through my mind. "She was ticklish," I continued. "And she called me . . . she always called me *Jonathan*. Never Jonny or Jon or anything else. And . . . and it took her forever to learn to ride a bike, even though I tried to help her."

I was smiling, but my cheeks were wet again. Damn, these newly awakened emotions could get complicated.

Mrs. Margolis was smiling, too. "Well, despite your good intentions, you may not have been the best teacher in that regard. I seem to remember an awful lot of skinned knees when you finally took the training wheels off *your* bike."

"I don't remember that," I said. "Just the part where I was trying to help her."

"Do you remember when she died?"

The question hung there in the air. Mrs. Margolis sat perfectly still, waiting. Even Stanley stopped chewing and seemed to stare at me expectantly.

I thought for a moment. "No," I said finally. "I don't."

"Do you remember anything else after that?" she asked. "Do you remember moving away? Or the couple of times I came to visit you at your new house?"

I thought some more. "No. None of that."

"I didn't think so."

I looked at her, unable to read her expression. "Why do you say that?"

She sighed. "Well, you changed. Goodness, your whole family changed." Her voice grew soft, but she kept going. "Everything changed after Maggie died."

She sat across from me, maintaining a level gaze. Seeing if I wanted to go on.

I did. "What kind of changes do you mean?"

Stanley advanced a few steps, growing tired of being ignored. To buy us a moment's peace, Mrs. Margolis grabbed a handful of Cheerios and sent them scattering across the porch, leaving the squirrel twitching in confusion as to which one to eat first.

Turning her attention to me, Mrs. Margolis said, "Well, your parents just couldn't seem to accept it. They seemed to want to, I don't know, wipe the slate clean. Act as if it had never happened. But the house kept reminding them. The house, the street—everything."

"Did she . . . did she die on this street?" I steeled myself for the answer.

Mrs. Margolis nodded. "Right in front of your house. I don't think your parents could ever get past that."

Thinking how awful I had felt the first time I had seen my old house, I gathered that I never got past it either. Sitting on Mrs. Margolis's porch I was aware of the house, looming just to my left, but I consciously chose not to look in its direction. I'd already lost my dinner, and didn't want to lose my breakfast as well.

"So we moved away right after that?" I asked.

"Yes, later that year. To where your parents live now."

She sighed. "I missed you—both of you—so much." With a slight smile she added, "Although I can't say I really missed young Teddy."

I chuckled, then continued my inquisition. "You said you came to visit us at our new house?"

She nodded. "Months went by, then your family finally invited me over for a visit. I think I guilted your mother into doing that."

She dipped into the bowl and let loose another spray of cereal, to Stanley's combined delight and consternation. Then she picked up her coffee cup and stared into it, forming her words.

"Everything was so . . . different. Your mother was so cheerful, but in this strange, forced way. And downright hyperactive—she must have gotten up to refill my iced tea twenty times, even though I had barely touched it. Your father—well, he didn't seem to hear a word I said. He just nodded a lot, and tried to smile, but you could see he was still in pain. He looked like he hadn't slept in days.

"As for Teddy," she said with smirk, "his personality was probably the one thing that hadn't changed: he was still a snotty little brat!" Abruptly her smile faded, and her voice went soft.

"And you," she said, shaking her head. "You were like a zombie. You barely spoke to your parents, or to Teddy. You lit up when you first saw me, but then it faded away, and after a while, so did you. You were in the room with us, and then you weren't, but I never saw you leave."

"Was I sad?" I asked, realizing how stupid the question sounded when spoken aloud.

But Mrs. Margolis surprised me by shaking her head. "No, you didn't seem particularly sad. You didn't seem particularly *anything*. It was like you had just switched yourself off."

A sudden noise from the street startled Stanley, and he swiveled, frozen in profile in front of us so that he could keep one eye on us and the other on the back yard. Looking at the squirrel I wondered idly what the view was like when you had eyes on either side of your head. Certainly not as narrow as our own. But how do you see what's directly in front of you?

Mrs. Margolis sipped her coffee, then continued.

"I went back for one more visit, and it was even worse. Your mother was so bouncy and chipper I just wanted to shake her. Your father just sat there like a lump, looking even more haggard. And you seemed so ill at ease around me, like you were glad to see me, but wanted to get away from me at the same time."

She grimaced. "It all made me very uncomfortable. And so sad. And then when I noticed the pictures, it only made things more awkward for me."

"The pictures?"

"You've already mentioned it, Jonny. There are no pictures of your sister in that house. None. It's as if they want to pretend she never existed, like that's the only way to . . . to escape the pain."

We sat in silence while I processed what she had said. Stanley turned to face us and was soon rewarded with more airborne oats.

Finally I said, "Rebecca and I talked about it once. About you being the only person I remember. Well, you and Maggie, as of last night."

Mrs. Margolis looked at me but did not reply.

"Rebecca wondered if I only remembered the people I loved, and forgot everybody else."

At this Mrs. Margolis's eyes began to well up. I started to apologize, then stopped myself, thinking about my previous conversations with her.

I went on. "That would explain why I remember you and Maggie. I loved Maggie." I paused. "And I love you, too."

"Oh, Jonny," she said, a tear breaking free and working its way down her cheek, soon followed by another. But through her tears she smiled.

"It kind of makes sense to me," I said, "but what about my parents? Didn't I love them?"

"Not after you decided not to," she said, again with that hard, level gaze.

"What?" I said, trying to grasp this bizarre statement. "I . . . *decided* not to love my parents?"

Mrs. Margolis's eyes stayed locked on mine. "At least that's what I think," she said. "You loved Maggie. And you loved that dog of yours—what was his name?"

"Rufus," I said, unable to suppress a smile at his memory.

"That's right," she said, also smiling. "Rufus. He was a sweet dog—you definitely loved him. And you loved your parents, too—I don't want to think you didn't. But . . ." Her voice trailed off.

"But what?"

She sighed. "Jonny, I'm no psychologist. But it seemed to me that after you lost Rufus and then Maggie—and this was all in the space of one year, if I remember correctly—I think you just decided to take . . . preventative measures."

I started to speak, but she held up a hand. The movement startled the squirrel, who froze in mid-chew.

"You were always such a bright boy," she continued. "Very logical. I think you looked at your situation, and decided that the things you loved most were being taken away from you. So you decided—and again, this is just my take on this—you decided that the way not to lose somebody you love was . . . to simply stop loving anybody."

She leaned forward in her chair. "I've thought about this a

lot, and that's what I kept coming up with."

I tried to piece this together in my mind. "So I shut myself down, to keep from getting hurt?"

"That's part of it," she said, "but I think it goes beyond self-protection. You were always so caring, so sensitive. Always watching out for your little sister, and so considerate to everybody around you. It really was your defining quality."

Again she sighed. "I don't know, Jonny—it's probably really out of line for me to say any of this."

"No, please—keep going."

"Well, the more I thought about it, the more it didn't seem like just a case of you shutting down to protect yourself. Instead, I think you were following your own sense of logic. From experience you had determined that when you loved something or somebody, something bad would happen to them. So the way I see it, you decided to stop loving anybody, so nothing bad would happen to them. You stopped loving your parents . . ."

I finished her sentence. "To protect them."

She nodded. "To protect them. At least that's my theory."

"What about you?" I protested. "I didn't stop loving you."

"You didn't need to. I was out of the picture after your family moved away. Those two times I visited, I saw a little spark when you talked to me, but you had already completely shut down with the rest of your family. And that probably took a conscious effort, since you saw them every day."

Mrs. Margolis sent the last few Cheerios to the insatiable Stanley with an underhand toss.

"With me," she said, "I think it was out of sight, out of mind. I wasn't around, so you didn't need to consciously shut down your feelings for me. In the long run, I think that was just as well. I can't bear the thought of you completely shutting me out."

I shook my head, trying to take all this in. "God, that must have been awful for my parents."

She shrugged. "Jonny, it sounds horrible to say this, but at that point your whole family was damaged goods. Each of you just found a different way to deal with it."

Her expression changed, and she got up abruptly. Startled, Stanley scrambled off the porch, vaulting the steps to land on the concrete walkway below, where he turned to look at us.

"Oh, what do I know, anyway?" she said, as she stooped to gather up her coffee cup and cereal bowl. "I'm just an old woman—not a psychologist."

I stood up and gently laid a hand on her shoulder.

"No," I said. "You're a wonderful friend."

She turned to face me, and I continued.

"And what you said makes sense. It . . . it rings true. Thank you."

She said nothing, but her eyes showed her relief.

"Thank you," I said again, wishing the words could more accurately convey my gratitude for the woman's candor with me.

Bored with the conversation, Stanley turned and darted up the massive maple tree, disappearing into its foliage.

I stepped aside as Mrs. Margolis bustled past me, and followed her inside the house. She busied herself around the kitchen while I stood and absorbed our recent conversation. I think we'd both run out of things to say.

After a moment Mrs. Margolis put down a dishtowel and faced me, with just the hint of a smile.

"You go put your shoes on," she said. "I'll drive you home."

CHAPTER 28

When Mrs. Margolis dropped me off, I braced myself for greeting my parents, but found the house was empty. Both surprised and relieved, I took the opportunity to freshen up with a much-needed shower and shave. That helped, but I was still tired from my fitful night in Mrs. Margolis's guest room. I decided to brave the intricacies of the coffeemaker in the kitchen, and was filling its water reservoir when my father walked in.

"There you are," he said, smiling. "I hope I didn't miss your call."

He laid the car keys on the kitchen counter. "Your mother is playing bridge, and I went out to run a quick errand, and it ended up taking longer than I thought. Sorry."

I shook my head. "It wasn't a problem," I said. "Mrs. Margolis dropped me off. She said it was on her way, anyway."

"So, how are you feeling?" he asked, his smile fading. "Your mother said you got sick last night. Was it from that restaurant you went to? What's it called, Sinatra?"

I had forgotten I told him about my plans for the previous night. Now it seemed a lifetime ago, both in time and importance.

"Sonata," I said. "And no, I only met somebody for a drink there, as it turned out. I ended up eating at Mrs. Margolis's, and her cooking is excellent."

"Tell me about it," Dad said wistfully. "The thing I miss most about living next door to her was her leftovers. That woman could *cook!*"

Feeling somewhat vindicated that my father had been the first to bring up the past, I decided to take the plunge.

"Dad, if you're not doing anything, I wondered if you could maybe give me a ride." I fiddled with the coffeemaker, not meeting his gaze.

"Sure, no problem," he said. "Where did you want to go?"

I turned to face him. "I was thinking maybe the cemetery."

Dad's eyebrows furrowed, more an expression of confusion than concern.

"What cemetery? Oak Ridge? Did you want to go to Lincoln's Tomb or something?"

Meeting his gaze I quietly said, "Wherever Maggie is."

The only sound was the hiss of the coffeemaker, which I absently hoped was an indication that I'd loaded it correctly.

Dad's mouth opened, but he didn't make a sound. Finally he swallowed, then stammered, "You . . . you mean . . ."

"Wherever Maggie is buried," I said. The words felt strange on my lips—I found it difficult to use the name of somebody I loved in the same sentence with a word associated with death. Whether this was grief or some post-stroke neural hypersensitivity, I was keenly aware of how much I didn't like hearing those words together.

My father was still groping for words. "How . . . how did you . . ."

"I found a picture of her."

"But when?"

"It doesn't matter." I didn't want him angry at Mrs. Margolis, although I'll admit I had a hard time picturing this man angry about anything. He was, as Mrs. Margolis had observed, perpetually distant and unengaged, though not in a cold way.

My father's next question surprised me.

"Do you remember her?"

"Yes." I decided he deserved more than that, so I added, "I didn't. But now I do. Not everything, but some of it is coming back."

Dad was looking down now, so I was unable to read his expression. Finally he said, "Do you remember when she died?"

"No. And nothing after that, either."

Dad nodded. "That's kind of what I thought."

I guess Mrs. Margolis wasn't the only one who had noticed me shutting down. While I was digesting this, Dad dealt me one more blow.

"You don't remember me, either. Or your mother."

He said it calmly, with no note of accusation. And I felt I owed him an honest answer.

"No," I said. I wanted to add something to that, but I was at a loss.

Dad nodded again, the two of us staring at each other in silence. Then the coffeemaker beeped.

"Well," Dad said, "let's not tell your mother about that, if it's all the same to you."

"Okay," I said, still thrown by this conversational turn, but somehow touched by my father's immediate show of concern for my mother's well-being.

"You make enough coffee for both of us?" He nodded towards the coffeemaker.

"I think so."

"I'll get us a couple of travel mugs. We can take it with us out to Oak Ridge. Are you ready to go?"

Dad had gone from airy and unengaged to direct and no-nonsense. But there was no anger or impatience. No sternness. Just a pragmatic acceptance that the cat was out of the bag. And yes, that is the phrase I conjured as I evaluated his behavior, further evidence of my stroke having left my mental dictionary of clichés completely intact while cleaning out all my mathematically-oriented grey matter. I guess that's the way the cookie crumbles.

It wasn't far to Oak Ridge, which was Springfield's main cemetery. We drove for a time in uncomfortable silence, but then I decided to quit skirting the matter.

"How could you not tell me?" I demanded. "I thought you promised there'd be no more surprises."

Dad kept his eyes on the road as he spoke. "To be fair, Jon, you were talking about surprises that happened while you were in a coma. Maggie's been gone for . . . twenty-something years." Catching himself in a math reference, he said, "It happened back when you were all little kids."

"I know," I said, "but you never brought her up. My god, there's no evidence that she ever even existed. No photos or anything."

"Oh, there are photos," he said. "They're just all put away."

"Hidden, you mean." My anger was creeping out now.

"Jonny, they're in the same drawer with all the other photo albums. We just don't bring those albums out anymore."

"But why?"

We came to a stoplight, and Dad took the moment to turn to face me. "Do you have any idea how painful it is to look at the face of a child you lost? A child that's supposed to *outlive* you, for Christ's sake?"

I had never heard this normally taciturn man raise his voice before, and the effect was unnerving.

The light turned green, and he shifted his focus back to his driving, his voice more calm. "It's not like we made a conscious decision to hide her, or wipe out her memory or anything. It's just something that gradually happened. Little adjustments we made, like taking her photos off the wall. Not hanging her stocking at Christmas. Not because we don't want to remember her, but because we don't want to be reminded that she's gone."

Dad ran a hand through his hair as he drove. "Christ, it wasn't like we knew what we were doing. We were in shock, or something like it. Hell, nothing felt normal, not for a year or so. And even then, it wasn't normal. It was just what we had left. The way we found to get by." He stole a glance at me. "And we had to find *some* way to get by, because we still had you two kids to raise. And we still had a marriage—what was left of it—to try to keep together."

Now I was feeling a little sheepish. "I guess I hadn't thought about how hard it must have been for you."

"It's not the sort of thing people think about. Because it's too terrible to think about. But as a result, when it happens to you, you're completely unequipped."

Dad shook his head. "Christ, Jonny. We were groping. Both of us. It got easier over the years, but it's still there. This stuff doesn't ever go away. It's always there. And then your stroke happened. I mean, what the hell was *that* about?"

His last question baffled me until he went on.

"First I lose my daughter. My little girl. And then—then I lose you." There was a catch in Dad's voice, something I'd never heard before.

"But I'm back now," I said, eager to ease this man's pain.

Dad looked over at me, his voice soft and defeated. "And you don't even remember me."

I had no reply for that. We drove on, each sipping our coffee. Finally Dad broke the silence.

"Your mother . . . well, the way she handles all this is to talk herself into seeing the bright side of things. You know, like believing that Teddy's worth a shit." Dad smiled grimly, and I felt myself responding in kind.

He continued. "Me, I take kind of the opposite approach. I lost my little girl. Then I lost you. After that, I quit kidding myself that I could hang on to anything I cared about. God was going to do whatever the hell he wanted, no matter what I did or how I prayed. And it seemed like he only went after the people I cared about. Your sister. You. Your mother."

Dad paused to sip his coffee, then sighed. "Jesus—you don't know how it hurt me to see your mother suffer, first over Maggie, then over you. So I just decided to start playing my cards closer to my vest. I figure maybe if I don't let on that I care about somebody, God won't—hell, I don't know—smite them or whatever." He took another sip of coffee, then he turned to face me.

"Because I honestly don't know if I can take any more smiting."

It was the single longest speech I ever heard the man make. And it made me realize that the way he coped with loss was not unlike my own method—we both shut ourselves down to pain. I just pushed it a little more, apparently: I also shut myself down to love. I guess Father really does know best.

The entrance to Oak Ridge Cemetery opened on to a narrow but well-maintained blacktop road that snaked its way around grassy hills adorned with a variety of tombstones and statues, some old and ornate, others sleek and modern. Dad drove slowly, staring intently from side to side, I presume watching for familiar landmarks.

"How do you find anything around here?" I asked, as we rounded yet another identical turn, surrounded on both sides by the stately trees that shaded the graves.

"The sections are all numbered," he said, "but I know the way, even without them."

I looked at him. "Have you been back here since . . . well, since she was buried?"

"Many times," Dad said, his eyes focused on the road. "I

come here every year. On the anniversary of the day that it happened."

"Oh."

"Your mother came once. It was more than she could handle, so now every year I come out here on my own. And she stays home and . . . well, I don't know what she does. We don't really talk about it. It's just what we do. But I take my time coming home, and I usually find the photo albums on the bed, and a wine glass in the sink."

"Oh," I said again, feeling even more guilty for having assumed my parents had forgotten about my sister.

Some large structure—are they called mausoleums?—caught my eye as we passed, triggering a memory.

"Did I ever come here with you?"

Dad nodded, slowing the car and pulling to the side of the road at the foot of a hill.

"Once," he said. "I brought you and Teddy out here. Big mistake." He shook his head, remembering.

"Teddy started running around the tombstones, yelling about ghosts and skeletons and vampires. It was all I could do not to smack him."

He looked at me.

"And you—you fell on top of her grave and started clawing at the dirt. I was too busy trying to round up Teddy to notice before you'd made a complete mess of yourself. Your hands were covered with dirt, and you were crying in a way that was just . . ." He shuddered at the memory. "Jesus, it was an awful thing to see."

"Sorry," I said instinctively.

"Ah, hell. So am I," Dad said, again with that break in his voice that was excruciating to hear. "Anyway, we're here."

With that he killed the engine and unbuckled his seatbelt. I sat stupidly frozen in my seat.

Dad looked at me expectantly. "You still want to see her grave?"

At that point I wasn't sure I did. But I felt I had put him through too much to not demonstrate the proper level of respect.

"Yeah," I said. "Okay."

"Okay then," Dad said, and opened his door.

On foot, we made our way uphill, stepping gingerly around gravestones that rose like buildings on some miniature green-paved street. Many of the graves were meticulously maintained and decorated with fresh flowers. Others stood stark and unadorned, looking lonely and neglected by comparison.

"It's over there," Dad said, "by that tree."

A lone grey marble stone stood in the shade of a large, misshapen tree. On it was engraved "Margaret Elizabeth Hooper— Beloved Daughter," along with numbers that I assumed were the years of her birth and death.

"I bought this whole section," Dad said. "There's room for all of us here, in addition to wives and children for you and Teddy."

He looked away, his voice cracking. "I just didn't want her to be surrounded by strangers, you know?"

Regaining his composure, he said, "Some people go ahead and put their own gravestones up in advance, marking where they'll eventually be buried, you know, so that people know it's a family plot. The salesman tried to talk me into that, but I just couldn't put my wife's name on a tombstone, not at the same time I'm putting my daughter's name on one. Jesus."

With that he stopped and turned away, wiping his eyes.

I drew closer to the stone. It stood about knee-high, and without thinking I stooped to touch it. The marble was smooth and cold under my fingertips.

From behind me I heard my father's voice.

"I'm going to, uh, take a little walk or something . . ." His voice sounded shaky and small.

"Okay," I said. I was on my knees in front of the stone, but I didn't remember kneeling. "I'll be here."

"Okay," came my father's voice, already farther away.

"Maggie," I said, perhaps to the stone, or to the ground, or to the small coffin it concealed. Or maybe to myself.

I looked at the ground between my knees, and realized I recognized the sight. I had knelt in front of this stone before.

Without thinking I reached my hand down, probing the grass just in front of the stone. Then I was probing deeper, thrusting my fingers into the soil, trying to break the surface, feeling for . . . feeling for what? My fingers struck something round and smooth, and I knew.

I dug both hands in now, and in a moment I had excavated the small hard object I'd been drawn to like a dowsing rod to water.

I brushed the dirt off it, and the red smooth surface glinted in a ray of sunlight that had managed to penetrate the shade of the gnarled tree.

"Buddha belly," I said, regarding the small smiling figure that sat cross-legged in my palm. The last one. The one Mrs. Margolis said had been lost.

"Jesus, Jonny—what the hell are you doing?" My father's voice broke my reverie, signaling his unexpected return.

But I was neither startled nor upset. Without looking up I said, "I just found something I left for Maggie. Something I knew she always liked." I was smiling. Kneeling and dirty atop my sister's grave, I was smiling.

I turned to face my father, holding the ceramic figure out for him to see.

If he recognized the object, he didn't show it. He regarded me intently, as if reevaluating some assessment he had made of me.

"You buried that thing the time I brought you here? *That's* what you were doing?"

"I think so. But I never remembered it until now."

Dad looked pretty uncomfortable, but I had to acknowledge he'd been having an unexpectedly rough morning. "So," he said, "you want to keep that thing to remember her by?"

I looked at the Buddha, considering. "No," I finally said. "I want to leave it here. For her to remember *me* by."

Now it was my father's turn to say "Oh."

I turned and dug my fingers back into the soil, creating a small opening for my parting gift to my sister. Just as it had seemed important so many years ago, it seemed important now to return this gift to its proper place.

Dad stood over me, watching in silence as I re-buried the small statue, then straightened and smoothed the surrounding turf.

Finally I stood up, working the dirt off my hands as best I could.

"You ready to go home?" my father asked.

"Yeah," I said, "I'm ready." I started to walk towards the car, but then my father surprised me by striding past me and stooping over the stone. He put his left hand on the stone and crossed himself with his right. Then he said something I couldn't quite hear, and turned to join me on the path back to the car.

"Thank you for bringing me out here," I said. "And I'm sorry for the way I sprung this on you."

Dad cleared his throat. "We've all had a lot sprung on us this year. I'm just glad this is out in the open."

Hastily he turned to me, his voice concerned. "I'm not sure how much this will change things at home. You know, as far as Maggie's, uh, situation. I mean, we've kind of fallen into a routine."

"That's okay," I said. "I think we all have to find our own

way to deal with things." I realized as I spoke that I had just paraphrased Mrs. Margolis.

"Yeah," my dad said. "I think you're right."

"And Dad?" I reached out and touched his arm, startling him. We stopped, standing among the graves of people unknown to us, looking at each other.

"Even though I don't remember you," I said, frightened about what I was about to say but convinced of it being what I needed most to say, "I love you. Here and now. I love you."

Dad nodded awkwardly, his voice a choked whisper. "Yeah," he said. "You too."

We walked in silence back to the car, where an electronic chirping noise came faintly from within.

"Is that your phone?" Dad asked.

Patting my pant leg, I said, "Maybe so. It must have fallen out of my pocket while we were driving."

Dad clicked his remote at the car, which unlocked itself with a thunking noise.

"There," Dad said, "see if you can grab it before they hang up."

"Hello?"

"Jonathan, is that you?"

"Yeah, who's—"

"It's Leon, man. From the hospital?"

"Oh no," I groaned. "Was I supposed to show up for PT today?"

"No, no—that's not it, man. Listen—you know that chick Rebecca what's-her-name? That fine-looking chick had the stroke, and then cut off all her hair?"

I smiled. "Yes, I know Rebecca."

"Well, she's here in the hospital, man. I thought you might want to get down here."

My smile got bigger. "Why, is she asking for me?"

"No, man—don't you understand? She is *in* the hospital. In the ICU. Crazy bitch tried to kill herself."

CHAPTER 29

While Dad drove me to the hospital, Leon filled me in on what he knew, his voice tinny and punctuated by static.

"Looks like she swallowed a bunch of pills. Her husband went for a run, and when he came back, she's lyin' on the floor, out cold. They pumped her stomach in the ER and sent her up to Intensive Care. I sometimes hang with one of the chicks that works up there, and she told me about it when we were getting some coffee. I guess she remembered Rebecca from when they brought her in after the stroke or—"

"Is she okay?" I managed to say, interrupting Leon's narrative.

"I don't know. On one hand, it ain't exactly a good thing to be in intensive care, know what I'm sayin'? On the other hand, that's the best place to be when you sick—they watch you like a hawk when you in the ICU."

"I guess that's true," I said lamely. "Leon, thank you for calling me."

"It's all right. I seen you two together. I know you was tight."

"She's my best friend," I blurted.

"Yeah, well, like I said. I know you was tight. Listen, man, I gotta go. But I'll be around most of the day—you come down to PT if you need me, all right?"

Dad was pulling into the drop-off lane in front of the hospital. I unbuckled my seatbelt and said, "Thanks, Leon. I just got here. I'll try to catch up with you later, okay?"

Leon said, "You got it," and hung up.

I turned to my father, who gave me a worried look.

"You want me to stay?"

"No," I said. "Let me find out what's going on, and then I'll call you later. I can take the bus home if I need to."

Dad looked dubious, then he nodded. "Okay, but don't be afraid to call. Your mother or I will be happy to help."

"Thanks, Dad. I better go."

I got out of the car and hurried to the bank of elevators. Although I'd never been inside the ICU, I knew its location well from the many laps I'd done around all the hospital's hallways, first in a wheelchair, and then pushing my walker. I was thankful to be able to move much more quickly than I had back in those days.

"She's in Bay Six, but I can't let you in to see her," said a stern-looking woman dressed in hospital scrubs made of a fabric printed with images of a popular cartoon character. "Immediate family only. No exceptions."

"But I just want to see her for a minute," I said. "I'm a good friend of hers."

"No exceptions." The woman possessed none of the warmth of the cuddly yellow bear that festooned her clothing, an irony I doubted she would appreciate if pointed out to her.

"Hey, aren't you that coma guy?" A younger man had walked up behind my current adversary and was eying me intently.

"Yes," I said, my hopes rising. "I was in a coma for six years. Then when I woke up they brought me from St. Louis to the stroke unit here. That's where I met Rebecca—the woman in Bay Six."

"I knew I recognized you. And I've seen you and her down in the cafeteria."

I nodded. "That was us. She was a big help during my

recovery. Is there any way I could see her, just for a minute? I just want her to know I'm here."

The man and the woman stared at each other at length, engaged in a dialog that seemed to require no words. Finally the woman let out a sigh and said, "Fine. But if I catch any flak about it, I'm throwing *you* under the bus—you got that?"

"I got it," the man said, allowing himself a smile. "One bus. My name on it."

"And not *my* name," the woman insisted.

"Of course not," he said. "We never even had this conversation."

"Fine."

"Fine."

Their business concluded, the woman went back to her paperwork, ignoring me entirely. The man turned to face me, jerked his head to the left, and said, "This way. And if anybody asks, you're her brother, got it?"

"Got it," I said. "And thanks."

The man said, "Hey, the way I figure, you're one of our best customers. Just be discreet, okay?"

"Discretion is my middle name," I assured him.

"Better than mine," the man said. "Who the hell names a guy Beverly anymore?"

Before I could proffer a response, he held up a hand, stopping me outside an area obscured by a sliding curtain.

"Let me check to see if she's alone," he said. I finally caught a glimpse of his nametag, which showed my host to be named Jason B. Drake. I could see why he preferred his first name. Jason stuck his head behind the curtain, then re-emerged and whispered, "Come on back here."

I followed him behind the curtain, where my breath caught in my throat. There she was, propped in a hospital bed with tubes hanging down all around her. Rebecca's skin was a pasty white, and her lips were unnaturally dark—almost black. Her eyes were closed, with dark, hollow rings underneath them. I'd never seen her look so bad, and I felt the impact of this dreadful sight at a physical level.

"My God," I said. "How is she? I mean, is she going to be okay?"

"Sorry," Jason said, "I should have braced you for how she looks." Walking closer to her bed, he read some of the gauges and digital displays on the machines that clicked and whirred next to her, then consulted a chart clipped to the foot of her bed.

"I think she's going to be all right, because we got her stomach pumped pretty quickly after she ingested the pills. But we still need to monitor her, to see how much got absorbed into her system. We use charcoal to help absorb the toxins—that's why her lips are black. But it makes her look even sicker than she is."

"Thank God," I said.

"I'm not making any promises here," Jason said, apparently concerned by my relief. "She's not out of the woods yet. But based on how quickly she was treated, I think her chances are good. She's strong, and she's in really good shape. That helps a lot."

I vowed to find Lucinda in PT and thank her for working Rebecca so hard, even if the act of expressing my gratitude to the daunting woman might prove fatal to me.

Frightened of the answer I might get, I dared to ask, "Do you have any idea when she might regain consciousness?"

Jason surprised me by saying, "Oh, she's not unconscious—she's just sleeping. The stomach pumping woke her up, I can assure you, but it also wore her out. That's a lot to put a body through, on top of the overdose. She's going to be sleeping a lot while she's healing."

"Was she . . . lucid?"

Jason shrugged. "Fairly, I guess. I mean, she was groggy. And likely pretty upset. Most of all I think she was scared."

"Scared?"

Jason's face grew more serious. "Most people who try this sort of thing—they don't really want to die. So then when they realize they might actually die anyway, even after they've decided they don't want to . . . well, it's pretty scary to contemplate. You wake up with all these tubes stuck in you, puking up black liquid charcoal—that'll pretty much scare the shit out of anybody, no pun intended."

Part of me was thrilled to learn that Rebecca had regained consciousness. But the idea of her so sick, so frightened—it was painful to contemplate.

Eyeing a chair next to Rebecca's bed, I asked, "Is it okay if I sit here for a while?"

Jason considered this for a moment, then said, "Yeah, I guess. But we'll have to kick you out at some point. And when her husband gets back, you'll have to work it out with him—we don't want too many people in here at a time."

I then realized how strange it seemed that Big Bob wasn't here. "Where is her husband?" I asked. "Isn't he the one who brought her in?"

Jason frowned. "Yeah, he came with her in the ambulance. He might be down in the cafeteria getting coffee. Or maybe in the chapel."

Based on what Rebecca had told me about Bob's religious fervor, I suspected it was the latter.

"Jason, I really appreciate this. Really."

He shrugged. "Hey, it's no problem. Just remember . . ."

"I know," I said. "Discretion."

"Beats the hell out of Beverly," Jason muttered as he walked away.

I sat for a long time watching Rebecca. I felt terrible, my stomach and chest clenching at the sight of her looking like this. Looking like she was dead.

I tried to calm myself by calling on the medical insights I'd picked up through my own not inconsiderable time spent in a hospital bed. The fact that she was not on a respirator was a good sign: she was breathing on her own. And the fact that she was not surrounded by a frantic bevy of medical personnel indicated—I hoped—that things were under control. Still, it was awful to see her like this, just awful. My entire torso hurt, and I suspected that some world-class indigestion was on the way.

In my helplessness, I found myself talking to her, my voice cracking as I said, "You're going to be okay."

I cleared my throat and tried again, saying, "I'm right here, Rebecca. It's me—Jonathan. You're going to be fine—they're taking good care of you."

My voice was taking on the singsong quality some people use when talking to their babies or their pets, and I suddenly felt silly. Embarrassed, I sank back in my chair, closing with one last "I'm right here, Rebecca."

"Jonathan?"

I jerked forward.

Rebecca was stirring, blinking her eyes and looking confused. Her parched, blackened lips moved, and she said it again.

"Jonathan?" It was barely more than a croak.

"I'm here, Rebecca!" I leaned in close. "Right here!"

She turned her head, tracking the sound of my voice. Then she looked at me, her eyes bloodshot and ringed with dark folds of skin.

"You're here," she said, her lips forming the beginning of a smile.

"I'm here," I said, stupidly. "Right here."

Her mouth was still working on trying to form a smile. "I

thought I heard your voice," she whispered. "But I thought that was a dream."

"I'm right here," I said, growing aware that my remarks were becoming redundant. "That was me talking to you. I was hoping you could hear me."

"I thought it was you," she said hoarsely. "You always call me Rebecca. Not Becky. I like that." She succeeded in giving me a weak smile, one which I returned unabashedly, forgetting how misshapen some of my facial expressions can be.

Then her smile dissolved, replaced by a grimace.

"I did a really stupid thing." Her voice was a little stronger, but still raspy and choked. I didn't know what was involved in pumping somebody's stomach, but I suspected it was not easy on a person's throat.

Treading carefully, I said, "I heard you took a bunch of pills."

Rebecca nodded, closing her eyes briefly as if the movement of her head had been quite painful.

"I pretty much swallowed our whole medicine cabinet," she said. "But it didn't stay down very long."

"Thank God for that."

Rebecca's response chilled me. "Yeah, I guess."

"Do you really want to die?" Instantly I regretted the question, which in retrospect was probably a very stupid thing for me to ask. I knew nothing about talking to suicidal people, and perhaps a question like that opened the door to a train of thought I did *not* want to encourage. But there it was—I had asked.

"No," she said, to my immeasurable relief. "I don't. But I don't want to live like this, either."

Unsure of how to proceed, I said, "Live like what?"

"Like what I am," Rebecca said. "Damaged goods."

"Don't say that."

"But I am. And so are you."

I had nothing to say to this. She was right. At least about me. But I couldn't accept that assessment of herself. Focusing on that, I tried to counter her argument.

"You're not damaged goods. You're just . . . changed. You're different. But not in a bad way. I like the way you are." I stopped myself from saying *I love the way you are*—a small victory on my part.

"But it's not like I used to be," she protested.

"So what?" Conscious that I had raised my voice, I took a breath, then said, "There's nothing . . . *bad* about the way you are. You're still nice. You're still smart. Hey, at least you can count past two."

This won me a slight upturn in those blackened lips, but it didn't last. Instead, her eyes began to well up.

"You don't understand," Rebecca said. "You don't know how I was."

"Bubbly," I said. "You've told me. What's so great about bubbly?"

"You never saw me," Rebecca said. "Not before."

"I didn't need to. I like you right now."

"You never saw me," she repeated. Her voice grew soft. "But I did."

"I don't understand."

Rebecca looked at me with eyes unblinking. "I saw myself. Before."

Seeing the puzzled look on my face, she went on.

"There was a video. I think Big Bob left it out for me to see. You know, part of his whole *let's get Becky back to normal* training program. Just another way to remind me of who I once was."

The bitterness in her voice was hard to listen to.

"It was from a friend's wedding. Down in Key West. The reception was in a nice hotel, and we were all drinking and dancing and having fun."

She looked away, remembering. Then she returned her gaze to me, her voice growing even harder.

"You should have seen me. My hair is all blonde and big. My boobs are nearly hanging out of my dress. I'm joking. Laughing. Dancing. Singing." Rebecca sighed. "Let me tell you, you haven't lived until you've heard me do *Sweet Caroline.*"

She closed her eyes for a moment, then reopened them, her stare even more intense.

"I was the life of the party. The person everybody wanted to hang around with. Saying all the right things. Smiling my Hollywood smile. Flaunting my body. Laughing like crazy at jokes that weren't funny. I was fun. Sexy. Perky."

She paused.

"Bubbly."

A tear began to trail down her left cheek.

"That's not me anymore. I can't do it. I can never be like that again. Looking at that video this morning, I don't know—it just had never been so clear to me before how much I had lost."

I said, "So that's when . . ."

"That's when I took the pills," she answered.

She wiped absently at the tear on her face, just as another one began its descent.

"I couldn't take it. I was looking at a woman I could never be. At a standard I could never live up to. So I gave up. Or at least I tried to give up."

"I'm glad you failed."

Rebecca gave a slight nod. "I guess I am, too. Right now I'm mostly just tired."

Taking my cue, I began to scramble to my feet. "I'm sorry, Rebecca. I'll get out of here."

"No," she said. "Stay. I mean, if you don't have something you need to be doing right now." Again her lips tried to smile.

"It's nice knowing that you're here."

Easing back into my chair, I said, "I'll stay as long as you want. Now, get some rest."

I sat back in my chair and watched her as she slept. Slowly the exhaustion I'd been staving off began to envelop me. I blinked it away as best I could, trying to focus any positive energy I could on Rebecca's pale, sleeping face, but ultimately my eyes closed and I surrendered to a dreamless sleep.

Chapter 30

"Who the hell are you?"

The deep, angry voice tried to penetrate my slumber, but I resisted.

Then I heard a thump, one that shook my bed. Only I wasn't in a bed; I was in a chair. A chair that somebody had just kicked.

"I said, who the hell are you?"

I opened my eyes to see a huge man looming over me, dressed in a dark blue warm-up suit. One hand clutched a large paper coffee cup; the other was clenched in a fist.

Fighting through the fog of sleep, I adjusted my glasses and stammered, "Jonathan. I'm . . . Jonathan. Friend of . . . Rebecca's." Not, apparently, a friend of complete sentences.

The man's face, already scowling, squeezed itself into a look of even greater consternation.

"The guy with the coma?"

"Yes," I answered more succinctly.

The man pulled back a little, surveying me slouching beneath him.

"Wow, Beck was right," he said. "You really are skinny."

I scrambled out of the chair and stood to face him. He was taller than me, but not by as much as I'd expected. I recalled Rebecca's suspicion that the man lied about his height.

"I'm Jonathan Hooper," I said, extending my hand. I had decided to ignore the remark about my physique.

The man considered my hand for a moment, then reached

out and shook it, exerting far more pressure than necessary.

"Big Bob Chase," he said. "Becky's husband."

"Nice to finally meet you," I said, immediately cringing at calling a meeting in front of an attempted suicide victim "nice." My embarrassment was diminished by concerns as to whether I would need to get my hand x-rayed after Big Bob released it.

"I thought only family was allowed back here," Big Bob said, his scowl returning.

I didn't want to throw Jason under any buses his cantankerous coworker might deploy in his direction, so I said, "I might have made them think I was her brother. I'm sorry—I was just really worried about her."

The scowl deepened. "How did you hear about this?"

To my surprise, a lie presented itself readily. "I was here for physical therapy when they brought her in," I said. "You know, from my stroke."

This response seemed to satisfy him. His expression relaxed a bit, and he nodded.

"Yeah, Beck told me about that. Said you had a lot of brain damage, too." Big Bob grunted. "I guess I figured you'd talk like a retard or something."

I felt less than inclined to share my cerebrocortical woes with the man, so I just said, "I got pretty lucky as far as my speech being affected." Trying to shift the focus of this unexpected encounter, I said, "So, what are the doctors telling you?"

Rebecca stirred in her bed, halting our conversation. We stood and watched her attentively, but she remained asleep.

Finally Big Bob whispered, "We should probably move this conversation out to the hallway, okay?"

I filed out of the ICU behind him, ignoring the angry glare of the colorfully clad woman so reluctant to let me see Rebecca. Out in the hallway, we stepped aside to let a young man in blue scrubs wheel a cadaverous old man past us in a rolling bed.

"Man, hospitals give me the creeps," Big Bob said once the pair was out of earshot.

"You get used to them," I said, drawing on my years of expertise.

Big Bob began to walk aimlessly down the hallway, and I followed along.

"Anyway," he said, "the doctors think she's going to be okay. They're pretty sure she only had the pills in her stomach for a few minutes. I was out running, and I usually knock out my morning two-miler in about twelve minutes, so I found her pretty quickly, thank God. Plus, the combination of stuff she took made her nauseous, so we think she threw up a lot of what she'd swallowed."

"What kind of pills did she take?" I asked, hoping I wasn't crossing some line. The etiquette of discussing spousal suicide attempts was uncharted territory for me.

"You name it, she took it. There were empty bottles all over the counter—aspirin, sleeping pills, some prescription painkillers from when I tore my rotator cuff, even some antibiotics. Like I said, it made her sick—I found her in a pool of vomit on the bathroom floor. Between that and how fast I got back from my run, God was really looking out for her."

We had come to a bench placed against a wall under a large painting of a kindly looking old woman. The hallways were decorated with many such portraits, commemorating people whose families had presumably given money to the hospital.

Big Bob sat down on the bench and sipped his coffee. He gestured to me, and I joined him.

"Man, what a mess," he said. "First the stroke, and now this. Sometimes I really wonder what the Lord is trying to teach me."

"You think this is all some kind of lesson?"

Big Bob turned to face me. "It's got to be, doesn't it? I mean,

God doesn't do things by accident. There's something I'm supposed to learn from being put through all this."

"*You're* being put through all this? What about Rebecca?" The words spilled out of me before I could stop them.

If I expected my words to anger him, I was mistaken. Instead he furrowed his brow and said, "Well, yeah. This has been rough on her, too. That's why she really needs me to take care of her, now that she's, you know, not right in the head."

He sighed. "Man, you should have seen her before the stroke. You wouldn't understand what it's like to lose somebody like this."

"But you haven't lost her!" This came out louder than I'd meant it to, causing Big Bob to pull back in surprise. I watched as his face registered surprise, then anger, then resignation. When he spoke, his voice was calm.

"It's like I said. You wouldn't know what it's like."

He nodded his head in the direction of the ICU. "That's not Beck. I mean, it is, but . . . but it isn't."

He sank back in his chair. "You should have seen her before."

I'd had just about enough of this. "So why don't you divorce her?" I'll admit, I was pushing things, but hey, if he hit me, I was in a hospital, right? At least medical care would be close at hand.

Anger returned to Big Bob's face. To his credit, he took a deep breath before addressing me in a carefully measured tone.

"First of all, where do you get off asking me something like that? That's way out of line, pal. Secondly, you're not Catholic, are you? We don't do divorce in the Catholic Church. It's all or nothing. Death do us part and all that. That's the deal. It's what I signed up for, for better or worse. I just got stuck with worse. But that's my problem, not yours."

"Rebecca is not a *problem*. She's a—"

"She's none of your fucking business, is what she is." Looming in close, suddenly Bob looked very big indeed. He must have seen the fear in my eyes, because he then softened his tone.

"Look, I'm all stressed out. And frankly, you're not helping, not when you say things like that."

He let out another heavy sigh. "You've got to understand, it's been a *really* rough day. And I just can't stop thinking about what would have happened if I hadn't found her. I mean, I can't even imagine how I'd deal with that. And this may not mean anything to you, but suicide is a mortal sin in the Catholic Church." He shook his head. "Man, there's no way to live something like that down."

Okay, *now* I'd had enough.

"Well, thank God for small favors," I said, standing up. "I need to go."

Oblivious to how angry he'd made me, Big Bob offered me his hand. "Listen, Jon—thanks for checking in on Beck like that. I know she likes you, and that you helped her a lot during rehab."

Reluctantly I shook his hand. To my relief he refrained from crushing any metacarpal bones this time.

"What are friends for?" I said bitterly.

Then feeling a little sheepish for growing so angry, I tried to shift my focus back to Rebecca's plight. "Have they said how long she'll be here?"

Bob nodded. "They'll probably keep her in the ICU for the rest of the day, unless she has any problems. Then late tonight they'll put her in a regular room overnight, you know, for observation. If all goes well, I should be able to take her home tomorrow afternoon, God willing."

"I see," I said. "Do you, uh, have any problem with me maybe visiting her, once she gets set up in her regular room?"

His scowl came back, then softened. "I guess not. Actually,

that could give me a chance to get into the office and take care of a few things. I had to move a lot of stuff around because of this."

"I'll bet," I said, with what I hoped was a sympathetic expression.

"Just don't say anything that would upset her, okay?"

I wish I had heard more concern in Big Bob's voice, but instead the remark came across as a threat. "Of course not," I said, swallowing my anger. "I just want her to see a friendly face."

Bob looked hard at me, and I almost expected him to make some crack about my twisted face, but if he felt that temptation, he resisted it. Maybe he didn't like to make fun of *retards*, sensitive sort that he was. And okay, maybe I needed to dial back on the defensiveness. Fair enough.

"Anyway," I said, "I'll see you around, I guess." On impulse, I added, "I could give you my cell number, you know, in case you need any help or anything."

Big Bob looked at me as if I'd just offered to shampoo his hair. Finally he said, "Nah, that's okay. I've got it from here."

"All right," I said, "I'll be around." Then I walked away, doing my best not to limp.

I dawdled uselessly around the hospital for maybe an hour, then I remembered to call my father. He was first shocked, then relieved as I relayed what had happened.

"Listen, Jonny, why don't I come pick you up? Rebecca's husband is there if she needs him—there's really nothing more you can do."

"I know," I said. "But I'm going to hang around just a little longer and see if I can arrange for somebody here to call me if there's any change."

"You could ask her husband to . . ." Dad's voice dwindled off as he realized what he was proposing was probably not an optimal tactic.

"Anyway," I said, "I'll just be a little longer, then I think I'll just catch the bus home."

"It's really no trouble for me to—"

"No, that's okay. I need to do some thinking." Remembering how our day together had begun, I added, "I've already put you through a lot today."

"That's okay, Jonny. I'm glad it happened."

This surprised me. "Are you?" I asked. "Really?"

There was a pause. Then Dad said, "Yeah, I guess I am. Oh, and Jonny?"

"Yes?"

"I put something in your room, for when you get back. It's a . . . it's a photo album."

"Maggie?" A lump formed in my throat.

"Yeah, it's all photos of Maggie. And when you get home, I'll be . . . I'll be happy to go through it with you. You know, if you have any questions or anything. I . . . well, I remember where and when pretty much all of those photos were taken."

"Wow, Dad, I—"

"Just one thing, Jonny. I don't think your mother is ready to look at those. Or talk about them, either."

"I understand."

"But I want you to know that I am. Just say the word, and we can talk about, well, whatever you want to talk about."

After processing this for a moment, I started to say *thank you.*

But what came out was "I love you."

A long pause ensued, then Dad said, "Okay, then. I'll see you when you get home."

CHAPTER 31

Be nice to your physical therapist. I advocate this not just because it's a good practice in general, but because it can also pay off when you need to find out the status of an ICU patient who is not a blood relative.

Leon came through for me, activating a complex network of nurses and administrative personnel—all of whom just happened to be female and attractive, if I know Leon—to ensure that I was updated on Rebecca's condition. I received several phone calls that evening: true to Big Bob's prediction, she was moved out of the ICU late that night, and in short order I had her new room number and telephone extension.

I was at the hospital first thing in the morning, wearing what I considered to be my nicest jeans and a black golf shirt adorned with either an alligator or a crocodile—the distinction between those reptiles had not been made clear to me when I was relearning animal names back in speech therapy. I had it on the highest authority that this clothing combination looked particularly good on me. Okay, the highest authority in this instance was my mother, but I had limited resources in this area.

Even armed with her room number, finding Rebecca was a little tricky. Despite all the time I had spent in this facility, the system behind its numbered floors and rooms still eluded my math-free logic. But I had long ago devised some rudimentary techniques to navigate the hospital's many levels and corridors.

Keith Cronin

For instance, I had learned that the first digit in a patient's room number was the number I needed to locate and press on the bank of buttons inside each elevator. From there I'll admit my system became far less elegant, and I had to simply wander that entire floor, looking for a number that matched the one I had scrawled on the piece of notepaper I clutched in my hand.

Finally I saw the number I had been looking for—406—and checked it against the number on the crumpled page. Yes, this should be it. Elated, I approached the room, eager to see Rebecca, and hoping to find her awake. The door was open, so I tentatively stuck my head in.

But if I had hoped to beat Big Bob to the hospital, I was out of luck. To my surprise I found him asleep in the chair next to Rebecca's bed, an open Bible tented over one of his legs.

Rebecca was asleep as well, but she looked much better now. She was still very pale, but her lips were no longer stained black. And she had considerably fewer tubes and wires plugged into her, which I took as a positive sign.

Not wanting to wake either of them, I quietly took my leave. I took the elevator down to the ground floor, where I decided to brave some of the hospital cafeteria's coffee, which Rebecca and I were pretty sure was made by straining hot tar through dirty socks. I found an empty table at which to sip the toxic brew, and watched as men and women wearing a pastel rainbow of different-colored scrubs hurried in and out of the cafeteria, some with food, but most simply clutching their own cups of the same vile black fluid I was attempting to coax past my taste buds. This hospital definitely ran on caffeine.

I sat there for a while, spending the time daydreaming, people-watching, and occasionally thinking up clever things to say to Rebecca. Wincing after each sip, I worked my way through as much of my coffee as I could. Then I dumped the remainder in the trash and headed back to the elevator, where I hunted for

262

a button with the number four on it.

Just as the elevator doors were starting to close, somebody called out, "Yo, hold the 'vator!"

I caught the edge of one door with my left hand, and the doors reopened to reveal Mr. Samuels, this time being pushed by a good-natured young orderly we all called "Spike," in reference to his porcupine-like hairstyle, which I assume required liberal applications of hair care products that were likely strong enough to glue space-shuttle tiles. I stepped back as Spike wheeled Mr. Samuels inside.

"Thanks, dude—could you hit three?" Spike said, as he swiveled the wheelchair around to facilitate their exit.

"No problem," I said, although I'm sure I took longer to locate the three button than Spike would have. "Hi, Mr. Samuels," I added, nodding to the old man.

Mr. Samuels nodded back, replying with a perfunctory "Lampshade."

Spike gave me a knowing look, and I smiled at both of them. The elevator doors closed, and we rode upward in silence. When the number 3 lit up above the elevator doors, Spike caught my eye and said, "Later." The doors slid open, and as the prickly-haired orderly slowly pushed the wheelchair out into the lobby, Mr. Samuels mumbled something over his shoulder.

It sounded like "Tell the girl."

"What was that?" I said.

Apparently Spike had heard it, too—he stopped in his tracks and turned the chair to allow Mr. Samuels to face me through the open doors.

The old man's face, uncooperative though it was, somehow managed to look intensely serious as his eyes found mine. He opened his mouth to speak, then paused. Finally, he said, "Bazooka phonebook. Lemonade."

Spike chuckled, and said, "Oh, well. We better get a move on, Mr. S."

With that he began to steer the wheelchair to the left, but Mr. Samuels held my gaze as long as he could. As the doors closed I heard his voice faintly repeat, "Lemonade." Then the elevator continued its ascent.

Back on Rebecca's floor, my memory of her room's position relative to the nurses' station made it much easier to find this time. I walked in quietly to find Big Bob still asleep, snoring softly in his chair on the opposite side of the bed. But Rebecca was awake, and lifted her head off her pillow when she saw me.

"Hi, Jonathan." Her voice was still a parched whisper, but she seemed much more alert. I hurried over to her.

"Hi, Rebecca," I said, forgetting the far more clever opening line I had rehearsed downstairs. "How are you feeling?"

I leaned forward, placing one hand on the rail beside her bed. Rebecca reached out with her one tube-free hand and touched my wrist.

"I just woke up, but I feel a lot better than I did yesterday," she said. "I'm really glad to see you."

"You too." Suddenly self-conscious, I stood upright, and gestured towards her sleeping husband. "Big Bob is here," I said, stating the obvious.

"I know. He spent the night last night. He was worried about me."

"So was I."

Rebecca closed her eyes and nodded. "I know."

"Anyway, I met him yesterday. While you were sleeping." I felt obligated to comment, so I added, "He seems nice."

As if on cue, Bob stirred briefly, then his eyes opened abruptly and locked on mine. I was suddenly very glad Rebecca was no longer touching my arm.

Bob scrunched his face up, trying to blink away the sleep. I decided to try to launch this conversation, with hopes of preempting any negative reaction on his part to finding me once again at his wife's bedside.

"Hi Bob," I said. "I just came by to see how Rebecca was doing. Wow, did you spend all night in that chair?"

Bob grunted, and then set about the task of unfolding his large frame from the battered Naugahyde chair. He stretched himself this way and that with an alarming series of pops and groans. Then rearing to his full height, he reached a hand over the bed and said, "How you doin', Jon."

Resigned to another crippling handshake, I gritted my teeth and extended my hand, relieved to feel it enveloped in a grip powered by slightly less testosterone than our initial encounter.

"I'm fine, thanks," I said. "I just—"

But Bob had already let go of my hand and was bending down to greet Rebecca.

"Beck, honey—you're up! How are you feeling? Can I get you anything?"

I'll admit, the intensity—and apparent sincerity—of Big Bob's solicitousness towards Rebecca made me feel a bit loutish for having held him in such low regard. But only a bit. My loathing for him was quickly rekindled when Rebecca smiled at him, making me aware that my capacity for jealousy had apparently not been impaired in any way by my brain damage.

Bob and Rebecca fell into a dialog covering how she felt, how she had slept, *where* he had slept, and how sweet he was for having slept there.

I felt simultaneously superfluous and invisible. Stretching my mathematical capabilities to their utmost, I found myself finally comprehending the adage maintaining that while two may be company, three was definitely a crowd.

"Um, I can come back later," I said, turning to leave.

"No, wait."

Sadly, it was Big Bob's voice, not Rebecca's. I turned to face him.

"Listen, Jon," he said, "I could really stand to get into the office for a couple of hours. If you could stick around and keep an eye on things here, I'm sure Becky would like that. And you'd be doing me a major solid."

"Well, I—"

"Please." This time it was Rebecca who spoke. She looked up at me with the beginnings of a shy smile. "I'd really appreciate it if you stayed," she said hoarsely. "It's really nice that you came to check on me."

"No problem," I said. "I'll be happy to stay."

"Outstanding," Big Bob said. He began rounding up his keys, cell phone, and other personal effects, then leaned forward and kissed his wife on the cheek.

"I'll be back by lunchtime, babe. Just call me on my cell if you need anything, okay?"

Rebecca nodded, and Bob lumbered towards the door. He clamped a heavy hand on my shoulder as he passed me. "Thanks, man," he said. Then he was out the door, punching buttons on his cell phone as he walked.

I turned to find Rebecca smiling at me.

"Hey, you," she said.

"Hey yourself."

She nodded towards the now vacant chair. "Why don't you sit down?"

"Thanks." I made my way around the bed and eased into the chair, still warm from having served as Big Bob's bed the night before. "Can I get you anything?"

"No, thanks," she said. "I'm definitely not ready to eat or drink anything. But this IV is giving me so much fluid that I keep having to pee."

"Oh," I observed insightfully. "Um, do you need me to get you a . . . a bedpan?"

Rebecca made a choking noise that I then realized was actually a laugh, and said, "No, that will *not* be necessary. I can get up and go to the bathroom all by myself, thank you."

"Glad to hear it," I said.

"Anyway," she said, "sorry about kind of excluding you just now. You know, when Bob and I were talking. He's still pretty freaked out, and frankly I think he's watching for any signs that I might still be a suicide risk."

Suicide risk were two very unpleasant words to hear coming from her lips, but they jolted me back to reality.

"Um, are you?"

"A suicide risk?" She shook her head. "No. But I still had to answer a lot of questions last night, before they moved me here."

"Questions?"

"A psychiatric evaluation. I had to convince some social worker that I wasn't suicidal. Otherwise they'd have me on what they call 'suicide watch,' or maybe even move me to some psych facility or something. It was pretty humiliating. And kind of scary, like if I said the wrong thing, they might take me away and put me in a padded cell."

"I guess you didn't say the wrong thing."

"Well, they were looking for signs of problems that I'm not really having. Stuff like drugs, spousal abuse—they interviewed Bob, too, which was even more humiliating. But the lady was nice, and the way she summed it up was that after my brain damage, I was *having problems fitting in.*"

I couldn't help but chuckle quietly. "Now that's a problem I'm familiar with."

"I know," she said, with just the faintest trace of a smile. "I figured you could relate to that."

Looking around the room I said, "Well, I don't see any padding. Looks like you convinced her."

Rebecca smirked at me. "Yeah, apparently I did."

Then her face grew more serious. "But I wasn't lying. For one thing, I don't want to die, and I don't think I ever really did."

She grimaced. "And I *never* want to feel as sick as I did after the stomach pump. God, that charcoal stuff was nasty—I can still taste it."

"It wasn't the best color on you, either," I said. "I prefer you in lighter shades of lipstick."

This got a smile, but then it faded.

"This is really embarrassing," she said. "You keep seeing me at my absolute worst. Saying stupid things. Doing stupid things."

"That doesn't matter to me. What I care about is that you're okay. I'm just so glad Bob found you in time. If he hadn't . . ."

My voice trailed off. Not liking this conversational tangent, I said, "Besides, you've certainly seen *me* at my worst. I couldn't even stand up when you first met me. And when I talked, it was like slow motion back then."

"Plus you were unbelievably skinny," Rebecca added helpfully.

"Yes, let's not forget that," I said. "Perish the thought."

I was hoping my attempt at banter would cheer her up, but she scowled and said, "But you didn't do anything stupid. You didn't try to kill yourself."

Instinctively I put my hand on her arm. "I'm just thankful you didn't do a very good job of that." Maybe touching her had emboldened me, because without thinking I went on. "And you're not the only person who does stupid things. I did some unbelievably stupid things."

Rebecca adjusted her head on her pillow to look more directly at me. "What things are you talking about? I don't remember any. You're always so smart when we talk or when you send me email."

"It was before," I said.

"Before what? Before I met you?"

I cleared my throat. "I mean before. You know, before my stroke."

"But I thought you said you didn't remember anything before then."

"Let's just say some memories came back to haunt me."

Rebecca pulled her arm out from under my hand, and I was suddenly horrified, sure that I had unintentionally crossed some line by touching her. But then I saw that she was fumbling with a remote control device of some sort, and then her bed began to tilt upwards, bringing her into more of a seated position.

In a measured voice she said, "Jonathan, would you mind telling me what the hell you're talking about?"

So I did.

At great length.

What started out as a halting admission of my apparent malfeasance with my former accounting coworker then cascaded into a description of my discovery at the storage warehouse, my subsequent effort to return the money, which in turn led me to recount how Mrs. Margolis revealed the existence of my long-lost sister. Soon I was replaying my graveyard conversation with my dad.

By the end I was crying. So was Rebecca. I know, some suicide-prevention counselor I would be.

"I'm sorry," I said between sniffles. "I shouldn't have . . . I mean . . . I don't know why I unloaded all that on you. I just meant to tell you about the bad things I've done. The rest just sort of spilled out."

Now Rebecca reached out to touch my hand. "Jonathan, you needed to say those things. And you promised you wouldn't lie to me, so you were doing what you promised." She patted my hand absently as she spoke. "I'm glad you told me. And I'm really sorry your sister died."

This got a not-terribly-manly sob out of me before I reeled my emotions back under some semblance of control. "I'm sorry, too," I said. "I miss her."

"I know you do. But I'm glad you can remember her now."

"Yeah," I said, removing my glasses and wiping my eyes. "So am I. But it hurts."

"I know."

I dug into a packet of tissues I found sitting on the tray next to her bed. As I dried my cheeks, I thought back to the confession that had launched this emotional torrent. "So now you know I'm not as nice a guy as you thought."

"Yes you are," she said, her hand landing firmly on mine again. "Maybe *before* you weren't. But now you are. I've seen how you are, and you're nice."

She paused, thinking. "Maybe when you lost your memory, you forgot how to *not* be nice."

I smiled. Then I thought about some of my less than charitable sentiments towards people like Brandon. And Big Bob. "I don't know about that," I said, "but thanks."

"Well, whatever you did to get all that money, you wouldn't do it now, would you?"

"No. No way."

"See? I know that about you. And you'll figure out what to do with that money. I know you will. You're smart."

"Thanks." I was both surprised and flattered to hear her echo Mrs. Margolis's positive assessment of me.

Rebecca sniffed. "Now pass me the Kleenex."

Before doing so, I took a few more for myself.

CHAPTER 32

After some unceremonious nose-blowing and eye-dabbing, our conversation resumed.

"Look," I said, "I'm really sorry for venting like that. I mean, here you are in the hospital, and I'm talking your ear off about *my* problems. Real sensitive of me."

Rebecca's expression grew stern. "Would you please stop apologizing? You needed to talk about that stuff. And I bet you don't have many people you can talk to."

"It's a short list," I admitted.

"You and me both."

"And you're my favorite person to talk to."

I hoped I wasn't out of line saying this, but I was feeling that maybe I needed to quit worrying so much about what I did or didn't say to her. She was showing herself to be a true friend, accepting me for what I was, good or bad. Still, her reply caught me off guard.

"You are, too."

My surprise must have shown on my face.

Looking down, Rebecca said, "That's probably not something a married woman is supposed to say to a man who's not her husband." Then she leveled her gaze at me and said, "But it's true."

We looked at each other for a long moment, while I mentally tried out and discarded possible replies to this disclosure.

A nurse saved me, bustling in to check on Rebecca. After

examining and adjusting some of the medical apparatus to which Rebecca was attached, she turned to me.

"Sir, I'm going to need you to step outside for just a minute."

Well acquainted with the indignities that can accompany a stay in the hospital, I stood up, smiling at Rebecca. "No problem. I'll be in the hallway—just let me know when you're all finished."

Rebecca gave me a small smile as I was whisked out of the room.

While I loitered in the hallway outside Rebecca's room, I noticed a man and woman in street clothes coming slowly down the corridor towards me, pushing a small child in a wheelchair. As they drew closer, I saw that they were about my age. Neither one was speaking; instead each of them simply stared straight ahead, as if at something a great distance away. The child—a little girl with hair a color I believe they call strawberry blonde—slumped in her chair, sound asleep under a pale blue blanket.

As my eyes drifted downward, I became aware of the unusual way the girl's blanket fell, which made it apparent that she had no legs.

The couple passed by me without a glance, the only sound the squeaking of the wheelchair's axles. The dark rings under their harrowed eyes suggested that their daughter was the only one of them who had slept in the last day or so.

Not wanting to stare, I looked down, and saw my own legs, skinny but intact. I resolved to be more thankful for the gifts I still had, reminded that we do not control how long those gifts may be in our possession.

This may seem uncharacteristically introspective of me, but I was finding the experience of being in a hospital due to health problems that were for a change not my own was causing a powerful shift in my perspective. I thought back to my parents' first sight of me after I awoke from my coma: their horror and pain at seeing me incapacitated. And the nearly physical blow of seeing Rebecca looking like death yesterday. Emotions can definitely run high in these facilities. Spend a little time in a hospital fretting about somebody you care about, and you may find yourself waxing equally philosophical.

Eventually Rebecca's nurse emerged from the room and gave me the all-clear. I walked back in to find Rebecca looking fresh and alert, her short, once sleep-tousled hair now more neatly arranged. She was sitting up, with a blue plastic covered dish on the tray in front of her.

"You look like you're feeling better," I said hopefully.

"A little," she said, a trace of a smile emerging. Then she shot a dubious look at her tray, which appeared to be untouched. "They want me to try eating something, but I'm still not wild about the idea."

"Well, you're going to need to eat something eventually . . ."

"I know. And I will. Just maybe not right now."

"Fair enough," I said. "I'm not going to pressure you."

"I know you won't," Rebecca said. "That's one of the things I like about you. Everybody else is always trying to get me to . . . to do stuff. To change. To improve. To . . ."

"To be like you were before," I said.

"Exactly."

"Same here," I said. "To be fair, I think they mean well. They know we each got sick, and they want us to get better."

Rebecca nodded. "That's what Bob is always saying. He wants me to *help me get better.*"

"Better is a funny word," I mused.

Rebecca wrinkled her face. "How is it funny?"

I spoke slowly, forming my words deliberately as my thoughts crystallized. "Well, when you're dealing with things you can cure, like an infection, or things you can accomplish, like learning to walk again, *better* is a positive thing. It's a goal—something

273

to aim for. So wanting to get better is good, at least in that situation."

Rebecca looked at me expectantly, so I went on.

"But when you're dealing with stuff you can't necessarily fix, like me being able to count or remember certain things, or you being, you know . . ."

"Bubbly?" Rebecca said.

"Ah, yes—the dreaded B-word," I said, trying without success to elicit a smile. "In situations like that, the idea of always trying to get better . . . well, it sort of implies that right now you're not good enough."

I shook my head. "That didn't come out very well. What I mean is—"

"No, no—I understand," Rebecca said. "And that's exactly how it feels—like you're not good enough, so you need to get better. You need to *be* better." She sighed. "And that's a lot of pressure to be under."

I shrugged. "I don't think they mean to make us feel that way. I mean, here in the hospital, that's everybody's job. To try to help people get better."

"I know."

"And our families," I went on. "I guess it's only natural for them to want us to be as healthy as possible."

"But I do feel healthy," Rebecca said. Looking at the IV in her hand, she added, "Well, I did, before yesterday. But you know what I mean."

I nodded. "I do. And I feel pretty healthy, too."

"But it's like that's still not good enough," Rebecca said, shaking her head. "We're still not the people we used to be. Neither of us. And I don't think we ever can be, do you?"

I couldn't lie to her. "Frankly, no."

We sat together in silence, considering this. My thoughts drifted to the little girl I'd seen in the hallway.

"I think maybe it's different when it's not physical."

"Maybe *what's* different?" Rebecca said, confused by my sudden and seemingly disjointed remark.

"People's expectations."

Judging by Rebecca's expression, I had not succeeded in clarifying my observation. I tried again.

"Suppose you were in an accident, and you lost a leg," I said. Rebecca looked even more confused, but I plowed ahead. "Nobody's going to tell you to *cheer up, think positive, and just stay focused on growing that leg back.*"

"But that's because everybody knows legs don't grow back," Rebecca said, beginning to look a little exasperated with me. "They don't, what's the word—regenerate. People know that."

"Exactly," I said. "People know that. They . . . *accept* that. They don't try to change that fact or pretend it didn't happen. Instead, they take it as a given, and then look into what they can do *next*, now that the leg is gone. Maybe try a wheelchair. Or crutches. Or an artificial leg."

"So what are you saying?"

I wrestled with my idea, trying to pin it down. "Maybe when it's clearly a physical thing, it's easier to accept. It's somehow more . . . absolute. It's certainly more obvious—if you're missing a leg, nobody can deny it. But people can't see the things that have changed in us. I mean, we're not missing any arms or legs or anything."

I paused, honing in on my target.

"But what they have seen is you and me making a lot of progress. We both had to learn to walk again—hell, I had to learn to do pretty much everything again—so it's probably natural for them to expect us to eventually get back to the way we were. Back to being the people they remember when they look at you and me."

I leaned forward, gripping the arms of my chair as I flailed away at the idea. "What I'm getting at is that maybe it's hard for the people who care about us to accept that some of these changes in us are permanent. But you and I know that they are. We didn't choose for this to happen, but there's some stuff we simply can't fix, any more than somebody could grow a new leg."

I stood up, finally getting a grip on the point I was trying to make.

"I just think life has got to be about more than *fixing* ourselves. I mean, that's really all we've been focusing on, but at some point I think we need to draw a line in the sand and say *this is who we are—take it or leave it.* And quit trying to rebuild ourselves into what we once were, because we both know that's just not going to happen."

I sat down, suddenly aware I had been raising my voice.

"At some point," I said, "we've got to stop trying to restore our lives, and start actually living them. That means we have to quit focusing on being broken."

I looked at her. "Rebecca, you are not damaged goods. Yes, you are a changed woman. I'm changed, too. But I think it's time we start to look at that change as . . . well, as an opportunity, not a handicap. I mean, look at it this way—with no memory, I've basically got a clean slate to work with. And you—well, it's sort of like you got a do-over, with a different personality this time. Like a . . . a new, revised version of you. And of me, too. So why don't we explore that? Focus on who we *can* be, not who we used to be."

I was on my feet again, but I didn't recall standing up. Caught up in my own rhetoric, I began to pace the tiny patch of floor next to Rebecca's bed, words flowing more quickly and urgently from me than they ever had before. I couldn't stop them. So I didn't try.

"I just think it's time to start truly accepting who we are—

just like you'd have to do if you lost a leg—and then say *okay, given that, what's next?*"

At the foot of the bed, I turned to face Rebecca.

"But if I'm going to find out what's next, I've got to start by being okay with the fact that no, I will never be the same as I used to be. And neither will you. But you're smart, you're a good person, and you're beautiful, goddamn it. With your short hair and your little smile and your hoarse little voice and your incredible honesty. And any man who doesn't see all that—who doesn't *love* all that—well, he's an idiot." With that, I sat down heavily in the chair next to her bed.

I believe the term *a stunned silence* adequately describes the effect my tirade generated.

My mind and my heart were racing, trying to think of what to say next, while also trying to come to terms with what I was feeling.

Reflexively, I started to apologize for my outburst, but then I stopped myself. Because I realized that whatever else I might be, I wasn't sorry. Embarrassed? Somewhat. Out of line? No doubt. A delusional fool? Quite possibly.

But I wasn't sorry.

Rebecca's eyes never left mine, and the prolonged silence was making me very uneasy. But I was bound and determined not to be the first to break this impromptu staredown.

Finally she spoke, in a voice so low as to be almost inaudible. "You're right."

My heart leapt, but then my mind caught up with it. Right about what? I'd just unleashed a jumbled torrent of ideas and emotions in her direction. Which part was she agreeing with?

As if reading my mind, she said, "About everything."

This time it was my turn to be stunned.

Her eyes unwavering, she went on.

"Instead of trying to change ourselves, we need to . . . to

change how we think of ourselves."

I nodded stupidly.

"And we need to get our families to understand that. To change how they think of us, too. I mean, so far it's like you and I are only ones who've tried to get to know each other for who we are now, instead of who we used to be."

Apparently still bereft of speech, I nodded again.

"But I don't think . . ."

Rebecca stopped, the pause pulling me unconsciously forward in my chair like some unseen magnet.

"I don't think," she said again, her voice slightly stronger, "that I can be married to Bob anymore."

CHAPTER 33

"Wow, Jonny—this *is* a surprise."

From the sound of Teddy's voice, it was clear this was an understatement.

We had still never spoken since I'd learned that he and Victoria were what my mother would call "an item." But to be honest, I wasn't really mad at him. It was hard to begrudge him a relationship with a woman of whom I had absolutely no memory. Still, as the weeks had passed, I'll admit to having harbored a certain perverse pleasure in knowing that the longer this inevitable conversation was postponed, the more uncomfortable it was likely to be for Teddy. Whether this sentiment was a holdover of my days as a mean-spirited big brother, or simply some not entirely unjustifiable indignation over how voraciously Teddy seemed to have absorbed all that had been mine the moment I was out of his way, I couldn't say.

At any rate, I was attempting to rise above all that now. When I arrived home from the hospital, my mind and my heart were still racing (though I couldn't say which one was winning), and I'd decided it was finally time to make this phone call. Partly to clear the air, but also to find out whether I was as smart as both Rebecca and Mrs. Margolis seemed to think I was.

God, I hoped they were right. The shame I had felt after confessing my sins to Rebecca was still fresh in my mind, an open sore that threatened to fester if not treated quickly. I needed this money out of my life if I were ever going to feel good about the kind of man I was becoming. And I thought Teddy might be able to help.

But first things first. "Well," I said, "I thought we should probably talk."

"Absolutely, bro. And look, I'm really sorry that I haven't called you before this. I've been meaning to. Really."

"It's okay."

"It's just that things have been really crazy at work, and—"

"Really, Teddy—it's okay." Trying to let him off the hook, I added, "Besides, it's not like there was anything keeping me from calling you."

"It's just . . . God, bro, this is awkward."

"Don't worry about it," I said. "Seriously. I don't have any problem with you and Victoria being together."

I was getting good at causing stunned silences, it appeared. It was a long time before Teddy spoke.

"Seriously?"

"Seriously. Six years is a long time. Nobody expected me to wake up."

"I swear to God we never thought you'd wake up," Teddy said, the words pouring out in a rush. "You gotta believe me, bro. I would never try to snake her from you if I thought you were going to wake up."

"I know."

"I mean, the doctors all said . . ."

"I know."

"Swear to God, bro. Seriously. No way I would have—"

"Teddy, I know. It's okay," I said again. "*We're* okay."

"We are?" Teddy's voice was nearly a whimper.

I was actually starting to feel bad hearing Teddy squirm like this, particularly given my indifference towards Victoria. I couldn't even take satisfaction from making the man who stole my girlfriend uncomfortable. The old Jonathan would likely shake his head in disgust at what I had become.

"Yes, Teddy. We are. We're fine. Really."

Teddy let out a sigh. "Man, I'm so glad to hear you say that. Seriously, bro. I've been totally dreading this conversation."

"That's sort of what I figured," I said, smiling.

Finally gathering his wits, Teddy made some polite inquiries about my health, and fervently promised to find time to come down to Springfield for a visit. To his credit, he was making an effort. I couldn't have been an easy person for him to talk to.

I decided it was time to get around to the other reason I'd called. The main reason.

"Teddy, I was wondering if you could give me some accounting advice."

He laughed. "Wow, bro—now that's a switch. You asking me for advice, I mean. Particularly about accounting. Who'd have thunk it?"

"The irony is not lost on me," I said, noting that Teddy seemed to be enjoying this reversal perhaps a bit too much, given how contrite he'd been just moments before.

"Anyway," I said, "now that you've been an accountant for a while, I'm curious. Are you any good?"

Another laugh. "What can I say, bro? Brandon taught me everything he knows."

I smiled grimly. "Then you're probably just the right person to ask this.

"There's this . . . person," I began, "and he asked me for advice, knowing I used to be an accountant. Seems he has a sizable amount of money—around three hundred thousand dollars, I believe—that he'd like to donate to charity."

"Oh, that's no prob. I bet I can get him a killer write-off."

"But here's the thing. He's not really interested in the write-off. Instead, he's looking for a way to give this money away anonymously."

"Really? Like, totally anonymously—so that even the charity doesn't know who he is? Or just not publicly announcing what he did?"

This was a distinction I hadn't considered. "The first of those, I think. He really doesn't want to call any attention to himself."

"Well, he can do that, but if it's going to be totally anonymous, he's not going to get a receipt or anything. He could do that, but frankly I wouldn't recommend it."

"I think the no-receipt thing is probably okay," I said. "But there's another thing, and I don't know if this makes a difference or not. It's all in cash."

There was silence on the line while Teddy processed this. "Well, that's a little more tricky. I mean, if he converts the money to, I don't know, money orders or something, the banks still have to report any large cash transactions. And frankly, converting a bunch of cash in a bank these days is sort of the opposite of not calling any attention to yourself."

"Why is that?"

"Money laundering, bro," Teddy said. "Banks are looking out for that kind of thing, bigtime. They've got all kinds of new regulations, ever since September Eleven. You know, so that terrorists can't move too much money around without people noticing."

Teddy's voice grew concerned. "Seriously, bro—how well do you know this guy?"

"Oh, he and I go way back," I said, trying to sound self-assured but growing increasingly uneasy about my great idea. Steeling myself, I went on. "I mean, I can personally vouch for him, and tell you with absolute confidence that he is not a terrorist."

"Drug dealer, maybe?"

"Definitely not," I said. "I'm sure of it."

Teddy wasn't letting go. "I got it—I bet the dude's getting

divorced and would rather give his money away than let his wife get any of his stash."

That was pretty good thinking, I had to admit. "You know, I never asked, but it probably is something like that."

"Man, that's some serious vengefulness there! Talk about cutting off your nose to spite your face, am I right?"

"Yeah, it's pretty crazy," I said, my words summing up my plan with alarming accuracy.

"But about all this bank stuff," I went on, "is there any way the guy can just give away the cash, without converting it to checks or money orders?"

"Well, yeah—I guess so. I mean, nothing's stopping him from just handing a bag of cash to some bum on the street, am I right? But whoever gets the money is obligated to report it. Like if he gave it all to some non-profit, they'd have to file a Form Nine-Ninety, I think it is. I'd have to check."

Teddy paused again, then said, "Thing is, you give that much cash to somebody—even a charity—you're still talking about some human being handling all that money. That's an awful lot of temptation. So he'd probably want to break it up into a lot of small chunks and deal with only the most reputable charities."

This was sounding increasingly complicated. With everybody so endlessly eager to have more money, I was amazed at how hard it seemed to give the stuff away.

"Tell you what," Teddy said, "let me think about this. I'll need to check some of the regulations—this kind of crap changes every year." He laughed. "Man, I thought I'd be done studying once I passed the CPA, but you've got to stay on top of this stuff, bigtime."

"Teddy, I'd really appreciate it if you could help make this happen. And I can probably see to it that there's some commission money in it for you. In cash, of course."

Long silence.

"Actually, I think I'll have to pass on that, bro. I'm doing really well here at the firm, and I really don't want to get into anything that's even slightly iffy. Let me just do this for you as a favor."

Teddy had just moved himself up significantly in my esteem, surprising me with his ethics. Maybe Brandon hadn't taught him everything he knew after all. Which reminded me . . .

"Speaking of favors," I said, "could you maybe *not* tell Brandon about this?"

"Way ahead of you, bro. He taught me a lot about the biz and all, but between you and me, I don't trust him any farther than I could throw him."

"Smart man," I said.

Teddy didn't reply for a long time—I started to wonder if our call had been dropped. Finally he spoke.

"Did you just say I was . . . smart?" The word came out slowly, as from a man trying his luck at pronouncing some newly learned term in a foreign tongue.

"Well, yeah," I said. "You're considering every angle of this situation. Including some I never would have thought of. It sounds like you're really good at this."

"Okay, now you're just fucking with me, right?" Teddy said, laughing uneasily. If his earlier discomfort had been awkward for me to endure, this was downright painful. I realized it was a safe bet I'd never said a nice thing to Teddy in his entire life.

"No, Teddy. I'm not. I do think you're smart, and it sounds like you're a terrific accountant."

Another long pause, then Teddy said, "Seriously, did they crank up your meds or something?"

"No, I'm drug-free," I assured him. "I'm . . . well, I'm different than I used to be."

"That's putting it mildly. I mean, seriously, bro. I've never heard you talk like this."

I tried to lighten the mood. "Well, don't get any ideas. I can still kick your ass."

This succeeded in getting a laugh. Teddy said, "Well, unless you've been working out an awful lot since I last saw you, I kinda doubt that. But I'll watch my step."

"You do that."

We seemed to have run out of things to say, so I decided to wrap up the call. "Listen, thanks for your help on this."

"No prob, like I said. I'll call you in a day or two with some ideas, okay?"

"That would be great. You'd be doing me a . . . a major solid." Don't ask me why I'd pulled that phrase out of the air.

Teddy cleared his throat. "Not for nothing, bro, but nobody says *major solid* anymore."

"Darn comas," I said. "They'll mess you up every time."

Teddy laughed. "I'll give you a call in a day or so. Oh, and bro?"

"Yes?"

"Thanks for . . . well, for calling. I'm really glad we're cool."

"Me too," I said, and meant it.

Rebecca emailed me later that night, letting me know she was home from the hospital and feeling "a lot better."

The next day I kept my cell phone with me at all times, hoping she might call. Even though we were just friends, I'd still never worked up the nerve to call her. I somehow sensed it was more appropriate to let her be the one to decide if and when she wanted to speak to me.

I know, real friends don't fret about this sort of thing—if they want to talk to each other, they pick up the phone and call. But I was finally admitting to myself that my feelings for Rebecca extended far beyond friendship. That I might actually be completing my transformation into somebody capable of love, if not of being able to count to five. But given our circumstances, that realization only made me proceed with more caution.

I think even someone skilled in mathematics would have had difficulty keeping track of how many times I checked my email during the course of the day. Late in the afternoon there was a new arrival in my inbox, but it was from Teddy, not Rebecca. He had assembled a surprisingly thorough summary of how banks treated large cash transactions, how charitable organizations recorded and reported donations they received, along with some recommendations on ways to make sure the money went into the right hands.

I was impressed—Teddy's email showed a competence and logic I wouldn't have attributed to him, as well as a concern for my well-being that really touched me. Several times he cautioned me to make sure I knew who I was dealing with, that money laundering was a serious crime I should steer well clear of. It seemed there was more to Teddy than a pinky ring and an opportunistically acquired (and notably busty) girlfriend after all. I resolved to make a real effort to rebuild our relationship, even if it meant getting used to being called "bro."

Then I realized I'd never told Teddy that I'd soon be needing his help to sign over that expensive sports car to Brandon. I thought about this for a while, evaluating and discarding possible ways to broach this awkward subject. Then, in true Hooper fashion, I decided to put off this discussion. Until when, I knew not. But if Hooper tradition held, the right moment would make itself apparent to me.

As was my custom, I ended the evening by reading until I was sleepy. Tonight's fare was a detective novel with a protagonist whose endless smart-aleck remarks were beginning to wear on me; I wasn't sure I was going to stick with this one. After finally putting the book down, I logged in to check my email one last time before going to bed and found a new incoming message. And this time it was from Rebecca.

It was just a short note, focused mostly on her having successfully eaten solid food for the first time since she was hospitalized. But her closing line addressed a different topic.

as for the thing we talked about, im working on it. but its not easy and its weird.

I was wide awake now. I wrote back immediately:

So glad to hear you're feeling better!
I'm online now, if you want to talk—er, write—about anything.
- Jonathan

I waited for quite a while, but she didn't reply, which I suppose was not surprising, given the late hour. Finally I went to bed, but I laid awake for a long time, remembering the sound of her voice back in the hospital, tired and scratchy and weak.

I don't think that I can be married to Bob anymore.

CHAPTER 34

I had just finished my morning workout and was helping myself to some orange juice from the refrigerator when the doorbell rang.

"Jonathan, honey, could you get that?" My mother was sitting at the kitchen table with a newspaper open in front of her, caught up in completing the crossword puzzles that typically consumed this portion of her mornings.

"Sure," I said. I took another swallow, then headed out to the foyer, glass of orange juice in hand.

I opened the front door to reveal Rebecca, looking at me through the screen door with a shy smile on her face.

"You're all sweaty," she said, her smile disappearing.

"Rebecca! Er, um, hi," I managed with typical James Bond-like smoothness.

"Are you okay?" she asked, seeing the dark stains on my shirt.

"Me? Oh, yeah—I'm fine," I said. "I was just working out. Dad found an old set of weights Teddy used to have, so we set up a place to exercise down in the basement."

Rebecca took a step backward. "Oh. Do you need to get back to that?"

"No, no. I just finished."

"Oh."

At this point some of the blood I'd just pumped into my muscles managed to find its way back to my brain, and I said,

"I'm sorry—would you like to come in?"

Rebecca shook her head. "Actually, I wondered if you wanted to go for a drive."

"A drive?"

"Yeah. Sometimes I just go for a drive. I don't know why, but it seems to help me think. So that's what I was doing, and then I realized I was in your neighborhood. So then I thought maybe you'd like to come with me."

We were still talking through the screen, I realized. "Okay," I said. "Can I maybe change clothes first?"

"Yeah, you probably should," she said, again eyeing my shirt.

I suddenly became very worried about what I smelled like. "Why don't you come in for a second while I take a quick shower?"

"Okay," she said, and stepped back, allowing me to open the door for her.

"Rebecca!" My mother's hostess radar had apparently drawn her into the living room. "Isn't this a nice surprise!" Mom quickly set about making Rebecca comfortable while I scurried off for some hasty hygienics.

I took possibly the world's fastest shower, wary of leaving Rebecca stranded with my mother for too long. A few minutes later, sporting what might have been an overly enthusiastic application of my dad's cologne, I was strapping myself into the passenger seat of Rebecca's SUV.

"So, where are we going?" I asked.

"Nowhere," said Rebecca. "Anywhere. I just realized a while back that I seem to do some of my clearest thinking when I'm driving, so now sometimes I just get in my car and drive. Without paying attention to where I'm going."

Rebecca backed her car out of the driveway as she spoke. Soon we were headed up the street, to parts unknown.

I said, "You do pay attention to things like red lights, I hope."

"Well, yeah. I'm not talking about not paying attention to *how* I drive. Just *where* I drive. Don't you ever just get in the car and drive?"

"Unfortunately, no," I said.

"God, I forgot," Rebecca said, turning to look at me. "You can't drive."

"Don't worry about it," I said, eager to change the subject. "So, what were you thinking about?"

Her eyes back on the road, Rebecca said, "You know, the stuff we were talking about in the hospital. I asked Bob for a divorce."

It was a good thing I wasn't driving—I'd have probably wrecked the car upon hearing this offhand remark.

"You . . . you did?" I stammered.

"Last night," she said. "Just before I emailed you."

I was still struggling for words. "You did?" I repeated stupidly. "I mean, I had no idea . . . you just . . . what did he say?"

"He kind of freaked out a little."

"Yeah, I could see how he might," I said. As I regained my composure, I added, "I thought Catholics couldn't divorce each other."

"They've got a kind of weird way to handle it. They won't grant you a divorce, but they will annul a marriage."

"What's the difference?"

Rebecca wrinkled her nose. "It gets pretty confusing. I've been researching it on the Internet, and it turns out there's legal annulment and church annulment, but they're two different things. The rules for a legal annulment are really strict— you've got to meet some really specific conditions, like marrying somebody who turns out to be using a phony identity. Bob and I wouldn't qualify for that. So we'd have to get a divorce."

"But I thought you couldn't—"

"The way it works is, the church can annul your marriage,

but only after you get a legal divorce."

"Even though they don't recognize divorce."

Rebecca nodded. "I guess in their eyes, the annulment erases the divorce. Like I said, it's weird. I mean, they supposedly don't recognize divorce, but you can't get an annulment without one."

Trying to process all this, I said, "So you'd need to get a divorce *and* an annulment?"

"Yep. Start out with a legal divorce, you know, in court and everything. And then once the divorce is final, you apply for a church annulment."

I frowned, absorbing this. "I didn't know that."

"Neither did Bob, it turns out. I think most Catholics don't, unless their marriage ends up failing. I found out stuff over the last couple days that I knew nothing about, and I've been Catholic my whole life. Same for him—I had to explain it all to him a couple of times."

"Well, I'm glad there's at least some way to work it," I said, "so that people don't have to be stuck together forever if they're not happy."

"Yeah, but the trick is getting both people to agree to it," she said, frowning as she drove. "You know, to going through with the divorce and then with the annulment."

My stomach lurched. "So what did Bob say?"

We had come to a red light. Rebecca slowed the car, pulling up to the intersection and stopping the car before turning to look at me.

"He said no."

I think my response was something insightful, like "Oh."

The light turned green, and we resumed our journey in silence.

Finally Rebecca said, "But I think he was still kind of in shock. I mean, first of all he didn't really know anything about how Catholics can, you now, end their marriages. And I think he was also shocked that I'd taken the time to find out all this stuff."

She sighed. "This is hard to say—I don't know if I'm getting this across well. Up until last night, I think he's just looked at me as a problem that he's stuck having to deal with. First I have my stroke, and I can't walk, and my personality is all different. Then I have to go through all this rehab and PT. Then, like an idiot, I try to kill myself. It's like I'm this series of problems, of stuff that's broken, that he needs to try to fix."

We came to a T intersection, and Rebecca chose to turn left.

"But this is the first time that I was the one who tried to come up with the solution. I mean, we're not happy. Our marriage isn't good—it's broken. We both know it. But this time I'm the one trying to come up with a way to try to fix things, and I think that kind of threw him."

I said, "So is he opposing the divorce just because it wasn't his idea?"

Rebecca shook her head, checking her rear-view mirror before changing lanes.

"No, I don't think that's it. I mean, he can be stubborn and all, but I think this is more a combination of him being caught by surprise by this new information. I mean, first, that there is a way to get a divorce, and second, that I want one." She scowled. "But there's something else, too."

We were entering Washington Park, a hilly expanse of land wooded with massive trees. The road wound around the landscape in leisurely curves, revealing a deep green lagoon, a picnic area, and a large brightly colored rose garden overlooked by a massive bell tower I'd learned was called a *carillon,* whose bells could be heard all the way over in my neighborhood.

"Any idea what that something else is?" I asked.

Rebecca was silent for a moment, framing her response. "I

think it comes down to him being worried about appearances."

I turned to look at her. "Is there really that much of a . . . a stigma about divorce anymore?"

"I don't think so," Rebecca said. "I mean, it's not as common in the Catholic Church, but when I stopped to think about it, I realized I know a few people at our church who have remarried. I mean, that's really the whole point of an annulment. It erases your previous marriage, which in turn allows you to marry within the church and have it treated like it's your one and only marriage."

She frowned. "But that's not so much what I mean. Sure, there's some stigma to getting a divorce, but to be honest, I think he's really into how our current situation makes him look."

"Your current situation?"

"Him taking care of me. People in our church make a big deal about what a saint he is for dealing with the burden of taking care of me."

Again she turned to look at me, her face tightened in anger. "I actually heard somebody use those exact words. We were at church, and I stopped to use the ladies room. When I came back, Bob was talking to some woman, and she was making this huge fuss over him. *Oh, you're such a saint, the way you're taking care of that poor girl.*" Rebecca had gone into that unnerving, edgy voice she used when she would mimic Big Bob.

"That poor girl," she repeated. "I'm twenty-nine years old and have a goddamn college degree. And she's talking about me like I'm some helpless invalid. But the worst was seeing the way Bob was lapping up all that attention, nodding his head, looking all serious, and saying stuff in this super-sincere tone of voice about how this was apparently *what the Lord had called him to do.*"

Rebecca turned to look at me again. "I think there's a part of him that doesn't want to give that up. I mean, he draws so much of his . . . his sense of who he is from how other people perceive him. That's why it's important to him to be Big Bob, not just regular old Bob. Only now he wants to aim higher. He wants to be . . ."

"Saint Bob," I said, finishing her sentence.

"Exactly."

We drove on, not speaking, eventually ending up on a busy divided street lined with restaurants, strip malls and automotive service centers. In front of one building, a giant painted statue of a lumberjack in a stocking cap loomed over the parking lot, inexplicably holding what appeared to be an old tractor tire in his outstretched hand. As we drove past, some long-inactive neurons helpfully retrieved the name *Paul Bunyan,* but they didn't offer me any other useful information.

Finally Rebecca spoke.

"Anyway, I think he's worried that all the red tape we'd have to go through with the church would make him look like less of a saint. You know, like he's a quitter or something, that he's giving up on me. Even though it's really what I want."

She sighed. "I swear, if there was a way for him to divorce me that made him look *good,* he'd do it in a heartbeat."

She let out a bitter laugh.

"Maybe if I became an axe murderer or something."

Making a show of shifting uneasily in my seat, I said, "Listen, I'm not sure where you're taking me, but you don't by any chance have any axes in the car, do you?"

"Just the one," Rebecca said, not looking at me. "It's behind your seat—do you mind reaching back there and getting it for me?"

For some reason her deadpan little voice made her rare jokes even more amusing to me, but I'll admit I might be slightly prejudiced.

We hit a bump, interrupting the conversation and injecting a new thought into my brain.

"Go back to what you said before," I said. "Before the axe murder stuff."

Rebecca glanced my way. "About Bob?"

"Yes."

She frowned, then said, "I was saying how if divorcing me made make him look good, he'd do it."

"In the eyes of the church, you mean?"

"Yes." Another frown. "Why? What are you getting at?"

"Keep driving," I said. "It seems to work. I think I might be getting an idea."

CHAPTER 35

It's like riding a bike. The phrase remained intact within my mental dictionary of clichés, but I'd only recently discovered its truth.

I was pedaling away on the exercise bike at the outpatient PT clinic I now visited several times a week when it struck me that perhaps I could learn to ride a real bicycle.

There was an old bike in our garage, purchased during one of my mother's repeated but unavailing campaigns to get my father into some sort of exercise regimen. Suited to his more "old school" cycling experience, the dusty blue vehicle lacked all the different gears, levers and hand brakes found on more modern bikes, and as such was an excellent fit for my lack of mechanical aptitude. Dad and I spent an afternoon with the bike, cleaning and oiling its moving parts, and pumping air into its tires. Then it was time to try my luck.

Dad said, "I've got to say, this isn't something I thought I'd ever do again."

"What do you mean? I'm the one trying to ride this thing."

"No," he said, shaking his head. "I mean the whole father-son thing, teaching my boy to ride a bike." He laughed. "You and I have already been through this once."

I smiled as gamely as I could while lifting my leg over the bicycle. "Well, let's see how good a teacher you were."

Dad stood next to me, one hand on the handlebars, while I situated myself on the bike seat, my feet tentatively finding their place on the pedals.

"I found it!"

Mom's voice startled us both. We turned to see her walking up the driveway towards us, clutching a red football helmet.

"I knew Teddy left this here when he moved out," she said triumphantly.

She held the helmet out to me, an expectant look on her face.

"Mom, I'm *not* going to wear a football helmet. Or any helmet."

"Damn straight," Dad pitched in. "I never wore a helmet. Sure, I took some falls, but look at me—I turned out fine."

Mom rolled her eyes. "Jonathan, if *that's* your role model, you're in worse trouble than I thought." Again she waved the helmet in front of me.

"I'm just going down the driveway, Mom. I really think I can manage."

I tried to make a joke. "Besides, I've already had my share of brain damage. It's somebody else's turn."

Note to aspiring comedians: people don't seem to find brain-damage jokes funny.

Dad spoke up. "You ready to do this thing?"

"I guess," I said, not pleased with how unconvincing my voice sounded.

"You be careful," Mom said.

Dad stepped behind me, put a hand on the back of the bike seat, and started to push. "Oh, relax," he said. "He's going to be fine."

And I was.

I wobbled a bit as we made our way down the driveway, me pedaling tentatively while Dad's footsteps and breathing both accelerated. And then I was gone, pedaling out of the driveway, turning gently to the right, and proceeding up the street, a gentle breeze blowing my hair back from my face.

I had never felt so free.

Walking was one thing, but to actually be transported—under my own control, with no assistance from anybody else—was a powerful and utterly new experience. For the first time since I'd awakened, I had a taste of self-sufficiency, and it was delicious.

And the thing that struck me the most was how little thinking was required. Unlike the scant few memories I'd been able to recover, this was purely physical, not mental. It spurred no new images from my childhood, no flashes of beloved bicycles, nor of the paper route that Mom told me I used to have. My mind remembered nothing. But my body remembered everything.

I pedaled with increasing abandon, savoring the speed, the wind, the freedom. And then realized I was probably scaring my parents to death. I checked for traffic, then doubled back to demonstrate my newfound vehicular prowess to my parents.

They were standing in the street in front of our house, and I have to say, I think I was better able at thirty-four to appreciate the joy in their eyes than I could have been the first time they'd experienced this sight. This was another sensation I'd had only the faintest glimpses of, and I made a point of telling myself: *this is it—this is what happy feels like.*

I braked to a stop in front of them and nearly fell over before remembering to take my feet off the pedals. Once stabilized, I graciously accepted their lavish praise and congratulations, and thanked Dad for helping with the rehab work on the bike.

"Now if you'll excuse me," I said, "I think I'll go for a ride."

Politely declining Mom's final attempt at offering me the football helmet, I took off on what would become a daily ritual for me, at least when weather permits. It amazes me to this day how much pleasure can be derived from something so simple, but I'm so grateful to have this morsel of freedom still available to me, when so many other ordinary activities are not.

My bike seemed the logical choice for the journey I was making tonight. I really hadn't wanted to ask my parents for a ride, and the series of buses I would have had to take was too complex to be viable. So with my pant legs tucked into my socks, I pedaled off to Rebecca's house on my hand-me-down bicycle, bracing myself for what promised to be an interesting evening.

I had mapped my route carefully and had explicit directions from Rebecca. Still, given my numerical limitations, navigation was always a challenge. Fortunately the houses on Rebecca's street were painted in a variety of colors, so in the waning daylight I worked my way up the street, looking first for color, then for house number. Eventually I stopped in front of a large two-story structure, the front of the house a combination of rust-colored bricks and dark brown, rustic wood. The color scheme was right; I confirmed the house number against the one printed on my instruction sheet. I had arrived.

I dismounted and looked for a place to lock my bike, ultimately opting for the mailbox that stood at the front edge of the lawn. I fished the key from my pocket and looped my lock through the iron scrollwork on which the mailbox was perched. Then I took a deep breath and proceeded up the walkway to the front door, which was adorned with a large brass knocker in the shape of a dolphin or a porpoise—another pair of animals I could never keep straight. Whatever *Flipper* was, if that helps.

Rebecca opened the door shortly after I knocked, dressed in jeans and a faded grey t-shirt emblazoned with the words *Frank Lloyd Wright* along with some angular geometric designs. She had kept her hair short since her beauty-shop debacle, and I thought it looked wonderful. Much like the rest of her.

"Hi, Jonathan," she said, the nervous beginnings of a smile on her lips. "I kind of can't believe we're doing this, can you?"

"I'm game if you are," I said, a line I'll admit to having rehearsed while on the way to her house. I'd approached this evening like a NASA space launch, ready to abort at any sign of trouble.

"You know I am," Rebecca said. "But are *you* absolutely sure about this?"

I'd been smiling, trying to project confidence, but now I let my face go serious. "I'm sure," I said. "Absolutely."

Rebecca stepped back from the door to allow me in. "Okay, then," she said. "Let's see what happens."

I came in, and she closed the door. Then I noticed she was looking at me intently. But not at my eyes.

"What's with your pants?" she asked, wrinkling her nose.

I looked down and realized my pants were still tucked into my socks.

I hopped from one foot to the other, hastily untucking and readjusting. "Sorry," I said. "Just trying to keep my pants from getting caught in the bicycle chain-thingie."

"I'm just glad it wasn't some kind of new fashion statement," Rebecca said. At a loss for a witty comeback, I shrugged eloquently, and she turned and led me into her house.

I'd describe the décor of the house, but frankly my memory of it is foggy. I was focused on Rebecca, and on what I was going to try to accomplish during this visit.

Rebecca led me to the back of the house, past the dining room and kitchen, into an open area where large leather couches were arranged to face a massive wall-mounted TV screen. On one of the couches sat Big Bob, eyes intent on a basketball game being displayed in incredibly vivid color.

"Bob?" Rebecca said. "Jonathan is here."

Bob turned with a start, then grabbed a remote control and muted the television.

"Hey, Jon. How's it going?" He bounded up from the couch

as if ejected from a fighter jet and reached out to shake my hand. He wore sweatpants and a loose, faded grey t-shirt with the letters SIU arched across the front in burgundy.

"Hi, Bob," I said, bracing myself for the handshake, which felt approximately like slamming my hand in a car door. "Thanks for having me over," I squeaked, retracting my now throbbing hand from his grip as soon as the decrease in pressure allowed it.

"Want something to drink?" Bob said. In his other hand he held a tumbler filled with fluid a rich amber in color.

"Is that Scotch?" I asked, looking around. Rebecca had disappeared.

Bob nodded, then bellowed, "Beck, honey, could you get Jon a Scotch?" Turning his attention back to me he said, "Rocks okay?"

"Perfect," I said.

"With some ice!" Bob shouted. Then he smiled at me and pointed to one of the couches. "Have a seat. Hope you don't have any money on the game—we're getting killed."

I shook my head and sank into the couch, my eyes scanning the screen for a clue as to who "we" might be.

Bob turned the sound back on and resumed his position on the other couch, quickly seeming to forget I was there as the sound of the cheering crowd filled the room, punctuated by whistles and the rhythmic slap of the ball against the arena floor.

CHAPTER 36

"Let me get this straight," Bob said. His glass was empty, but I'd barely touched my own drink. Rebecca sipped nervously from her wineglass as he spoke.

"You want to give me three hundred thousand dollars."

"Well, not *give* it to you," I said. "I'd make it available to you, for *you* to give away."

"But I'd need to give it away anonymously." His voice was without emotion, which I found more frightening than the anger I'd anticipated.

"Well, yes, to avoid a lot of scrutiny as far as taxes are concerned. You couldn't put this money in the bank—then you'd have to declare it as income and pay taxes on it. So you'd need to take what I gave you and disperse it anonymously. My brother's an accountant—I've got a whole list of instructions on how to do this."

This got a cocked eyebrow from Bob. "Didn't Beck tell me you were an accountant, too? Before the . . . you know, the stroke thing?"

I nodded.

"And now you can't even count?"

Rebecca squirmed on the couch across from me, but I tried to give her an *it's okay* look.

"Nope," I said. "It would seem my counting days are behind me now."

"So how do you know you have three hundred grand?"

This was more the type of antagonistic response I'd anticipated. But I felt strangely calm, falling into the easy speech that seemed to bless me when faced with hard-boiled negotiations. It was probably the one remnant of my old personality for which I was thankful.

"Like I said, my brother's an accountant. I've had people tally this up, so I'm well aware of what I'm dealing with." Bob didn't need to know that the concept of three hundred thousand was only slightly clearer to me than the term *lots of money*, nor that my money was managed by a little old lady who used to be my next-door neighbor, not a financial professional.

Bob scowled at me. "So why not have your brother give this money away?"

I cleared my throat. "Because you're in a position to . . . to do more good with it. I know you're active in your church and can probably think of many charitable causes that would benefit from this money. Myself, I don't go to church, and as I think Rebecca has told you, I can't remember anything prior to a few months ago, which gives me somewhat of a limited world view. And my brother—well, charity isn't really in his nature."

I hated the sound of these blithe words as they poured without effort from my mouth. And I worried that they were missing the mark. Bob just stared at me, expressionless. It occurred to me that this man was probably very, very good at poker.

Trying to maintain a cool veneer, I forced myself to take a sip of my Scotch before speaking.

"You've probably guessed that I would have some stipulations," I said.

I might as well have been looking at an alligator, given the absence of emotion in Bob's eyes.

"I only have two," I continued, willing my voice not to wander up into the soprano register.

"First, at least some portion of the money should be given to organizations doing stroke research."

This got a response from both Bob and Rebecca. Bob raised his head slightly, sort of an inverted nod. And Rebecca sat forward in her chair. I hadn't told her about that idea, but it was one I felt strongly about. Although my life might have been improved in some ways by my stroke, I'd seen enough of the catastrophic effects strokes can have to want to help medical science prevent or eliminate them.

Bob's face resumed its blank expression.

"What's the other stipulation?"

It was go time. God knows where I got that phrase—probably some cheesy sports movie, but the term fit.

"Well, I don't know a graceful way to put this," I began. "I—"

"Divorce me." Rebecca had set her wineglass on the coffee table and was looking directly at her husband. Big Bob swiveled to face her, startled by her interruption.

"That's what this is about, Bob. I want a divorce. Jonathan is willing to give you enough money to do . . . amazing things. Things that could help out the church. Or causes that the church supports—whatever."

Rebecca leaned forward, her soft voice packed with an intensity I'd seldom heard.

"You do something like this, nobody in the church would bat an eye over us getting a divorce. They'd be too caught up in your amazing contribution. Doing something like this would make you look . . ."

Her voice tapered off, but I completed her sentence.

". . . like a saint."

There was none of the volatility I'd expected. Bob sat motionless, a stone gargoyle with an empty whisky glass. When he spoke, his voice was chillingly quiet.

"I thought you said these contributions would be anonymous."

"Oh, they would be," I said hastily. "But realistically, *somebody* would have to accept the money from you. And let's face it— people do have a tendency to gossip. So it's not unreasonable to assume that some . . . key people in the church might inadvertently be made aware of your generosity."

At times I really hated my ability to talk like this. This was not one of those times. I did regret that Rebecca had to see this side of me. But I'd sworn to keep no secrets from her, and like it or not, I apparently still had the ability to think and speak in a smooth and calculating way under duress.

Big Bob startled me by standing up. Instinctively I recoiled, but he walked past me, towards the kitchen. In a moment I heard the sounds of ice cubes clinking in a glass, followed by the *glug-glug-glug* of more Scotch being poured.

Bob returned and seated himself in his former position, eyeing me intently. Finally he spoke, his voice dry and edgy.

"I have to say, I'm . . . surprised to have a man I barely know talking to me like this. Here in my own house." He took a sip of his drink. "My own house," he repeated, shaking his head.

"Believe me, I find this very awkward," I said. "It's a . . . a weird situation. And you're right, I don't know you, not well at least."

I leaned forward in my seat, gaining momentum. "But I do know that you're unhappy. Both of you are." I gestured towards Rebecca.

"You've both told me so, face-to-face. Rebecca has confided in me more than once about it." Turning to more directly face Bob, I said, "And you—you told me yourself that she's not the woman you married. You said you lost her, and that I wouldn't understand what it's like to lose somebody like that."

Without meaning to, I stood up, continuing my lecture.

Keith Cronin

"You're both unhappy. You both know it. And I'm offering you a way to . . . to fix that unhappiness, in a way that everybody benefits.

"Everybody benefits," I repeated, gritting my teeth at the Big Bob phrase I was about to use. "It's win-win."

Suddenly self-conscious about my pontificating, I sat back down. We all seemed to have become very thirsty, and there was a long, wordless moment while we sipped our drinks.

Bob broke the silence, setting his glass on the coffee table.

"Becky, do you think you could excuse us for a few minutes?"

Rebecca looked at Bob, then at me, her face registering her uncertainty. Then she stood, picked up her wineglass, and walked away without a word.

Bob waited until he heard the sound of her footsteps on the stairway, then turned his attention to me.

He surprised me by chuckling. "You know," he said, still smiling, "one of the things I did after Becky's stroke was start going to an anger-management class. There's a group that meets once a week at the VFW—I heard about it through somebody at church. I was just so damn frustrated, and felt so helpless."

His smile faded and his face resumed its reptilian stare. "That class is probably why you still have any teeth left in your mouth."

I must have pulled back unconsciously in my seat. Bob said, "Don't worry. I'm not going to hit you."

He paused to sip his Scotch. "But I am going to call you out."

"Call me out?" I was worried that I was having an aphasic moment—his words made no sense to me.

"What's in it for you, Jon?" Bob was leaning in close now, and I felt my calm slipping away.

"I already told you, I—"

"Cut the bullshit. Why are you giving all your money away?"

This was a question I was ready for. "It's not *all* of my

306

money." This was not technically a lie—I did have some money in a long-dormant bank account, although from what Brandon had told me it was a negligible amount.

I went on. "But I'm making some changes in my life. I feel like I've been given a chance at a new life, and I want to start out by doing something good. So I'm giving away *some* of my money. Not all."

Yes, I know, this was clearly Old Jonathan (dare I call him OJ?) holding court. But I'd counted on him to show up, and he hadn't disappointed me with his ability to spontaneously spew and spin information in a manner that best served his purposes.

"You still haven't answered my question," Bob said, apparently immune to some of OJ's tactics.

I stuck to the party line. "I want you to be happy. Both of you. And right now, neither one of you is."

"That's just great," Bob said, in a tone that suggested otherwise. "That takes care of both Becky and me." He leaned in even closer.

"But what are you getting out of this?"

Suddenly my rehearsed line about the joy of helping others seemed inadequate and lame. I'd underestimated Bob: he turned out to be a man who was paying attention.

And now a man who was taking control. "Before you answer," he said, "can I . . . offer a hypothesis?"

Now Bob was standing, and I was the audience. Trying to hide my intimidation with what I hoped was an encouraging smile, I nodded.

"You're in love with my wife."

CHAPTER 37

Shit.

And suddenly OJ was nowhere to be found, leaving me on my own to stammer an unintelligible response. "What? I . . . you mean . . . but I . . ."

"Don't lie to me, Jon."

Bob drew closer, seemed to grow larger.

"Do *not* fucking lie to me, or I will crush you like a grape. That anger management class was good, but not *that* good."

"I probably am," I blurted. "In love. I probably am."

I idly wondered which bay of the ICU I'd be taken to. If I lived long enough to make it to the hospital.

After a long silence, Bob said, "Is she in love with you?"

If I'd been expecting a punch, I instead received a question that hit even harder. And Bob's voice lacked the hardness it had just a moment before. He looked at me, his gaze level, his stance neutral. He was not threatening. He was just asking an honest question.

"No," I said finally.

"Does she know how you feel?"

"I . . . I don't know."

Bob's eyes narrowed. "But the two of you aren't—"

"God, no!" I waved my hands, flailing like a marionette under the control of some drunken puppeteer. "Bob—I swear to you. I would never . . . hell, *Rebecca* would never . . ."

Exasperated, I finally managed a cohesive sentence. "Bob,

you've got to know she would never be unfaithful to you." I shook my head, willing my helplessly gesturing hands to be still. "And I would never ask her to be, out of respect. For both of you."

Bob hadn't moved. He loomed over me, unblinking. "So this whole thing isn't something the two of you cooked up so you can be together?"

"No," I said. "God, no. I've never suggested anything like that to her. She was looking for a way to get divorced that wouldn't damage your reputation at church, and I'm looking to help. But I've never said anything to Rebecca about her and . . . about *us* being together."

"Out of respect," said Bob. I couldn't tell if he was being sarcastic, so I nodded.

"Yes," I said. "Out of respect."

Big Bob seemed to shrink a little, like a balloon several days past its prime. He sat back down on the couch and took a long pull from his drink. I tried to relax, with minimal success.

"So what is this?" he finally said. "Are you trying to . . . to *buy* her love by doing this? I mean, is that the going rate these days? Three hundred K to fall in love?"

"No," I said yet again, sinking back into my own seat. "That's not it. I mean, she's not somebody whose feelings are for sale. I could never think of her like that."

Now I took a turn sipping my Scotch, trying to formulate my words.

"If there's anything I'm trying to buy," I said slowly, "maybe it's . . . freedom. She doesn't want to be married to you."

Bob bristled, but I forged ahead. "She doesn't, Bob. She's told you that before, and I know it. I'm sorry if that upsets you, but she and I are friends and she confided that in me. And she just said it again, in front of both of us, right here in this room."

I sat up, speaking as clearly and deliberately as my smirking lips would let me. "But *your* freedom is at stake, too. Right now you're trapped. You're a good guy—Christ, Bob, you don't know how often Rebecca has told me what a good guy you are. And you're trying to do the right thing—I know that, and so does Rebecca."

I was rebuilding my momentum and prayed that my tongue could keep up with my thoughts. "But you said it yourself—she's not the woman you married. So you're trapped. Trapped in a marriage with a stranger."

For the first time, what I'd been interpreting as anger in Bob's expression now seemed like a profound sadness. He looked at me, saying nothing.

"You're doing your best," I went on. "And people at your church know how hard you're working, and they think the world of you. And maybe for now, that's enough for you to go on. Enough emotional support for you to get by."

I was having difficulty getting my point into focus, and tried a different direction. "I'm thirty-four years old," I said. "You're around the same age, right?"

Bob nodded. "Thirty-one," he said softly. I took the nod to mean I was on the right track and went on.

"Is this how you want the rest of your life to be? Well-respected at church, but sleeping in the guest room in your own house?"

Bob's face darkened, and once again the ICU scenario began to play out in my mind. But I continued. "I've just got to believe that there's more to life. That there's another way. That you should get to be happy, and to be married to the kind of woman . . . well, the kind of woman you fell in love with."

I nodded upwards.

"But like you said, that's not her. Not anymore."

I had run out of things to say. I sat back and finished my Scotch with no idea what response my impassioned oration would elicit.

Bob stared at me for a long time, then nodded towards my drink. "You want another?"

I did, but was conscious of the long bicycle ride awaiting me if I survived this conversation. "I probably shouldn't," I said, attempting a lame smile. "I'm driving."

Bob nodded, playing along. "What's your ride these days? A Schwinn?"

I shook my head. "Too rich for my blood. I'm a Huffy man."

Bob got up and approached me, holding his hand out.

"Oh, what the hell," he said, taking my glass from me. "Those things drive themselves."

He returned momentarily with a healthy dose of single-malt for me and a much smaller amount in his own glass.

"Thanks." I took a tentative sip, flashing on the many drinks I'd seen poisoned in the soap operas I used to watch in the hospital. But the Scotch tasted fine, so I decided to take my chances.

"You're not exactly a catch," Bob said once he'd situated himself on the couch.

"Pardon?"

Bob gestured towards me with his glass. "I mean, no offense, Jon, but let's face it. You're not much of a catch. You talk kind of funny. You can't count. You can't drive. Are you working?"

I shook my head.

"And you're not in the greatest physical shape," he observed.

"What I'm trying to say," he said pausing to sip his drink, "is that you may be kidding yourself. About Becky, I mean."

He set his drink on the table, leveling his gaze at me. "So are you prepared to make a three-hundred-thousand-dollar mistake?"

"Yes," I said without hesitation, "I am. You need to understand: I'm going to give this money away. One way or another.

My offer gives you the opportunity to control where that money goes. To do some real good for causes that matter to you. And, to be blunt, for you to take some of the credit."

"Win-win," Bob said, with absolutely no triumph in his voice.

"It really is," I said. "Because any way you slice it, this money is going to help some people. So no, I can't consider it a mistake, no matter what Rebecca may feel about me."

We sipped our drinks for a moment in silence. Bob finished his, and surprised me by smiling.

"I've got another hypothesis," he said. "Would you consider the possibility that the only reason you're making this offer is that you're too badly brain-damaged to know any better?"

I laughed. "I bet if you asked me that before my stroke, I'd have said you were absolutely right."

We sat for a while, our smiles fading and our ice melting. Then Bob let out a heavy sigh.

"We were happy, you know?" He looked at me with something new in his eyes. Something that suggested that under different circumstances I might have been able to like this man.

"Before all this, I mean. We were really fucking happy. And not just me. I'm talking about the old Becky. The woman you never knew. She was happy, too. She and I . . . well, we just fit together."

He stopped to drain his glass. "And now she's gone."

"I'm sorry," I said, feeling stupid but needing to say something.

"It's not fair," Bob said, looking away as his voice began to break.

"I know," I said quietly, reminded why I wanted to donate money to stroke research. You don't need to have a stroke to be hurt by one.

"Believe me," I said, "I know."

CHAPTER 38

"Know what this is?" Rebecca waved an envelope in front of me, her expression impossible to read. She wore a sleek dark blue dress with a matching jacket, making me wish I'd put more thought into my own ensemble, which consisted of jeans and an open Oxford over an Abe Lincoln T-shirt. Yes, I had finally succumbed to the temptations of the hospital gift shop.

"Fan mail?" I suggested, scooting over to make room for her in the curved booth into which I'd slid myself a few minutes ago. Over the past several months we had fallen into the habit of meeting for coffee in a little sandwich shop that was easily accessible to me by bus and close to Rebecca's new apartment. The décor was retro, but I suspected it was authentic, not the work of some decorator, as the shop had been in business long before I was born, according to my parents. They specialized in a cheese-covered open-faced sandwich inexplicably called a *horseshoe,* whose primary function seemed to be the clogging of all major arteries. That said, they were wonderfully delicious.

Rebecca slid in beside me and said, "No, the fan mail has really dropped off since I canceled the fall concert tour."

I looked at her and then laughed belatedly, caught off guard by her deadpan humor.

"Tragic," I improvised, "what with all those dance moves you've been working on."

But the joke had played itself out, and Rebecca again raised the envelope. "Anyway," she said, "this is something I've been waiting on for a long time. My divorce papers. I just came from the courthouse."

She laid the envelope on the table.

"It's done."

Floored by the news, I stammered, "I didn't realize it was today . . . I mean . . . you didn't tell . . ."

"I didn't tell you about it because I wanted to wait until it was all done. Until it was, I don't know, *real.*"

A waitress with a gravity-defying bun hairstyle brought us coffee while I contemplated this news.

After she left us alone, Rebecca said, "They give you all these last-minute chances to change your mind—I think it's part of why the process takes so long. And I just wanted to make sure Big Bob actually went through with it and signed the papers."

"Did *you* ever think about changing your mind?" There, I'd put it out there. It was awkward, but I needed to know.

Rebecca shook her head. "No, it's like I said. I couldn't live like that anymore."

"So how do you feel now?" I asked, dreading the answer.

She thought for a moment. "Overall, pretty good. I mean, it was weird, doing something that, well, basically ended such a huge part of my life. We were both crying a little when we signed the papers."

"Big Bob was crying?" I couldn't contain my surprise.

"Yeah, and I can understand why. I mean, he really sees it as having lost somebody he loved. And knowing he feels that way, well, it makes me feel bad."

Rebecca selected a yellow envelope from a plastic caddy containing a variety of sweeteners, and tore it open, pouring a fine white powder into her coffee.

"Face it," she went on, "this isn't what either of us expected when we got married. You don't figure somebody's personality is going to radically change, particularly somebody you're in love with. I may be brain-damaged, but I get that. Believe me, I get that."

She paused, a pained expression on her face. "But it's not like I did it on purpose."

"I know, Rebecca. I—"

"No, wait—I'm not finished." She took a moment to frame her thoughts. "I didn't do it on purpose. And Big Bob knows that. Despite what you may think, he's not a bad guy."

Thinking of my last encounter with him, I nodded. "I know."

"And he tried really hard to be patient and supportive."

"I know."

She inhaled, then let out a long breath. "But something you really helped me realize is that I just can't go through the rest of my life focusing on being broken. Focused on what I can't be. I've got to find out what I *can* be. And frankly Big Bob has a right to be with the kind of woman that, well, that is the right kind of woman for him. And that's not me. Not anymore. So this divorce—it needed to happen. And we both knew it."

"Then I'm . . . happy for you," I said carefully.

Rebecca poured some cream into her coffee from a small steel pitcher. "Me too," she said. "But it was still kind of weird."

Our waitress came back, pen at the ready. Judging by the size of Rebecca's order, getting divorced can make you very hungry.

"So what's next?" I asked when we were once again alone.

Rebecca grimaced. "Now we file for the annulment. That could take a while."

"The whole system seems weird to me," I said. "Having to do a divorce *and* an annulment. Seems like overkill."

Rebecca nodded. "I agree, but that's how it works with the church. And normally the annulment can take more than a year after the divorce, and even then it's not a sure thing. But the people at the church have assured us that our petition will be *fast-tracked*"—Rebecca drew finger quotes in the air—"and that they *foresee no obstacles.*" More finger quotes. "To put it in Big Bob's terms, it's a *slam dunk.*"

I reached for the cream pitcher. "At least they're being co-operative about the annulment."

Rebecca smirked. "Well, they have three hundred thousand reasons to be cooperative." She paused, taking a long look at me. "I still can't believe you gave Big Bob that money."

"Well, technically I only made the money available for him to *donate.* I wouldn't have just given it to him to keep."

"I know," she said. "And it made him look like this super-generous guy to donate all that money to all those different causes that the church sponsors."

I tried my hand at arching an eyebrow, but cannot vouch for the results. "So his anonymity has been compromised?"

"Just a little," she said. "But apparently it was enough. I swear, he's like a rock star in our church these days. He can do no wrong."

"So it's win-win," I offered.

Rebecca grimaced. "Please don't start talking that way."

I held up my hands in surrender. "That was my final at-tempt."

The grimace was replaced by a smile. "Thank God."

"And I promise not to call you Becky."

"Even better," she said, her smile growing.

"I'm just glad the money went to good causes."

"Oh, it did," she agreed. "I can give you a list of where it went and how it was divided up. Bob gave me a photocopy of it, in case you wanted proof. It's all accounted for."

I shook my head. "No, thanks. Plus, it's not like the numbers would mean anything to me."

"I still can't believe you didn't keep any for yourself." The look on her face had softened, as had her voice.

I shrugged. "It wasn't mine," I said simply.

Before she could argue, I said, "I'm sure of it. There's no way I'd have kept legitimately earned money hidden in a leather chair. So I needed to give it back, or at least give it to somebody who deserved it. And Big Bob helped me do just that."

"I know, but weren't you tempted to keep just a little bit?"

I chuckled. "Well, with my less-than-stellar grasp of mathematics, *a little bit* is not a concept that's very meaningful to me. Plus, I get my disability insurance, and I live pretty simply. I may even have an income soon."

Rebecca put down her coffee cup. "Really? Doing what?"

"Do you know what blogging is?"

When Rebecca nodded, I said, "I've been asked to write a blog for an online newsletter for stroke victims. They pay a small fee for each article they accept."

"That's wonderful—how did that come about?"

"Mrs. Margolis. She and I have been emailing each other, and she would occasionally compliment my writing style. I'd always shrug it off until she bothered to mention that she used to work at the newspaper here in town, and she actually knows something about writing. She's the one who thought of looking for a publication that my, um, special circumstances might lend themselves to."

I went on to describe how she'd arranged for an editor to help me with any number-related issues that might crop up, and then gradually realized that although Rebecca was looking at me, she wasn't really listening.

And she was looking at me in an odd way. Not unpleasant, but odd nonetheless.

I stopped talking, and she continued to just look at me. Finally I asked, "Is something wrong?"

She shook her head, never taking her eyes off me. Then she softly spoke.

"Do you remember the poem you wrote for me? The haiku?"

I paused, caught off guard by the question. Then I nodded.

Her expression grew more intent. "Does that mean you remember writing it, or that you remember the words?"

This was an easy question. "Both," I said, meeting her gaze.

"Can you say it for me?"

"Out loud?" This was something I'd never done at more than a whisper, even when I was crafting the poem, testing the rhythm of its syllables.

"Yes," Rebecca said. "Out loud. If you remember how it goes, that is."

"I remember," I said, a strange calm coming over me. "I definitely remember."

"How do those work again? Was it five syllables, then seven, then five?"

"That's right."

Rebecca inclined her head, her eyes still locked on mine. "Go ahead."

I ignored the inclination to clear my throat, mindful of the delicacy of the moment. Instead I took a deep breath, then spoke the words of the poem slowly, clearly. Honestly.

Quiet little smiles
on Rebecca's face make me
glad that I woke up

When I was done speaking, her face shone with just such a smile. She held my gaze in silence for a long time. Then she spoke.

"I was thinking . . ."

I smiled encouragingly. "Yes?"

"Now that I'm officially an unmarried woman, I was wondering if I could do something that, well, that frankly I've wanted to do for a long time."

Before I could answer, Rebecca leaned in close.

I first kissed a woman on a Thursday afternoon. The fact that I was thirty-four years old at the time made it a particularly nice kiss.

ABOUT THE AUTHOR

Keith Cronin's fiction has appeared in *Carve Magazine, Amarillo Bay, Zinos,* and a University of Phoenix management course. A professional rock drummer for over two decades, Keith has performed and recorded with artists including Bruce Springsteen, Clarence Clemons, and Pat Travers. In addition he has worked as a librarian, a truck driver, an environmental activist, and a copy writer for Office Depot (go ahead, ask him anything about paperclips). Keith has a bachelor's degree in music from Indiana University, and earned his MBA at Florida Atlantic University. The proud father of one daughter, Keith lives in South Florida, where he divides his time between drumming, writing corporate speeches and newsletters, and serenading local ducks and squirrels with his ukulele. Visit him online at www.keithcronin.com.